DEDICATION

This book is dedicated to the memory of Timothy M. Durkin. Tim was a truly consummate radio sales professional, a successful and strategic Director of Sales and a very kind and compassionate gentleman who positively mentored the lives of his family, friends, sales people and clients.

AKNOWLEGDEMENTS

I'd like to recognize the following people for their help and support in this effort; Dianne Edwards and Maryann Jones who unwittingly flattered me into thinking I could actually write a book, Mary Ann Yonki, the woman I wed for her mountains of patience and understanding, Dana Kashula for her steadfast faith in all my abilities, my sister Sandra Barnett who read the first draft when no one else would, to my mother, Mary Elizabeth Yonki mainly because if you can't recognize your mom then what use to humanity can you be, and to the broadcast industry for attracting such colorful characters that made writing this story so easy.

This is a fictional story. The characters and situations are not real. Any resemblance or similarities to persons living or deceased as well as occurrences are purely coincidental.

ALUBIRP PUBLICATIONS MMV

DECEMBER 2054

The couple looked at the alarm clock and knew they had to get back to normal. Death and the grief that follows are always difficult. But somehow the passing of a mother is more traumatic, no matter what the age.

"Are you okay?" Robin asked as the big man trudged off to the bathroom for his morning shower. "I'm fine" he replied as he went on his way. After a brief interval, he reappeared, toweling himself and saying, "My mom loved baths, I'm more of a shower man myself. Funny. I have to get to work today, get back on track. I have a meeting with the lawyer today. We have to figure out the estate. I think I might want you there. You know how bad I am with finances". Robin replied, "Of course, you tell me the time and place and I'll be there. But you know it can't be that confusing. Your mom pretty much led a straight-arrow life. From what you told me she just banked her money, right? No investments either?"

"Well there was one holding I have to divest myself of, a radio station of all things. An AM station" replied the heir. Robin looking confused said, "what's AM radio?" "It was a form of radio communication popular in the middle of the 20th century. It died a very lingering death and when my mom bought it, the thing was all but extinct, certainly not a good business investment. I think she bought it for sentimental reasons" added Robin's mate.

"Your mom? Sentimental? I can't see how" countered Robin. "Oh yeah, there was a time long ago when AM radio got her attention. And believe it or not, it had to do with a guy!" said the tall man as he tied his shoes. Robin exclaimed, "A guy? This had to be some guy. Your mom was so religious, so straight laced. A guy? You're staying right here and telling me about this guy".

"The story's not worth telling unless I start from the beginning when this man was a boy. We're talking the early 1960s here, you got time?" asked the significant other with a smile. "Oh I have the time, these are your roots, right?" asked Robin. "Oh yeah, the story of one Jake Yanick, my mom and Amplified Modulation - that's AM radio to you, is part of my very being. Remember, you asked for it. Ready?" he asked. "Ready. Tell me about radio. I'm all ears!" joked Robin.

PART ONE

The summer of 1965 was very quiet for 11 year-old Jake Yanick until the phone rang on that hot July day. Jake's mother put the phone down and began to cry. Her oldest brother Drew had died. Jake was informed that he had to attend the wake and funeral. It would be three days out of his summer schedule of ball playing, bike riding, baseball card collecting and acquiring girlie magazines. Other than the assassination of President John Kennedy, this was the young boy's first encounter with death.

Entering the funeral home, Jake followed his parents, paying his respects to his uncle. His mother's side of the family spanned nearly half the century with Uncle Drew being born in 1900 and Uncle Larry arriving in 1932. There were 14 brothers and sisters. Family gatherings were like block parties. Unlike the joyful Christmas season, gatherings with food and football, this was a more subdued occasion. Working class aunts and uncles he was accustomed to seeing in worn work clothes now wore their Sunday best. The women in simple black mourning dresses and the men in starched white shirts received the legion of friends who came to say goodbye. As was the custom, the wake went on for three days.

Jake positioned himself on one of the couches by the door. He missed his sister Toni who was away at school. Jake gazed at the body and the immediate family. Two sons survived uncle Drew. One named

Bobby looked just like the dead man. The other was familiar to Jake only from the 11 by 14 black and white glossy that sat on his aunt's TV set in the family homestead. The photo came to life in the person of Ed Prince. Leaving home at the age of 18, Cousin Ed was a big time radio announcer in Cleveland. Jake wondered what that was like, to be noticed, sought after and admired.

As he sat, his Uncle Jim joined him. After a quick pat on the boy's buzzed head, the man said, "You know who's in that box, don't you? That's my brother in that box. He's not moving. Wednesday they're going to put him in a hole and then that's it. This is life; this is death. This is serious stuff," intoned his uncle.

Jake was momentarily stunned. Looking at his uncle, he said, "What should I do? Should I pray?" His uncle answered him, "Yeah, if you want but more importantly, live everyday like it's the day before you wind up in one of those boxes".

No one had ever spoken to Jake like that in his young life. Jake pondered its meaning until he was interrupted by another uncle. Andy Zack had married into the family. He was a congenial man with a booming voice who had an animated way of expressing his numerous opinions. Since he was one of Jake's favorite relatives, the young boy decided to get Uncle Andy's explanation of what his Uncle Jim had just told him.

When Jake asked the question, Andy roared back in laughter and said, "It means, kid, hit the ground running. There's not much time. Play hard and work hard. But when you work, find something you want to do. Not like me and your dad there, breaking our backs on the railroad. Find a job where your bones won't ache, where you won't work in the cold or the heat. Be like Bobby and Eddie - work inside. And when you get married, marry a girl who has two things, common sense and money. Your chances of finding a job you like are way better than landing that combo!" His Uncle, getting louder with each pronouncement, was hushed by his wife Sue. Jake and his uncle quietly resumed speaking but this time about the sorry state of their team, the Philadelphia Phillies.

After the funeral Jake met briefly with Eddie who gave him the inside dope on what radio broadcasting was all about. His tales of the industry only heightened the young boy's interest. When Ed began to tell Jake of the sports and movies celebrities he met, Jake could not contain his glee. Ed recounted the time he appeared on the Ted Mack Amateur Hour and how he even introduced dancer Gene Kelly at a live show.

Unlike his parents or even his older sister, Jake's entire life centered on the small electronic box in his living room that kept him entertained and informed. He infuriated his first grade nun when he insisted President Eisenhower was his grandfather. The youngster stayed at home with his laid-off father in the 50s, while his mother worked. Every time the President was on TV, Jake's father told him to quiet down so that he could hear the words the important man spoke. When Jake persisted, his father told him the old man was his grandfather and that he should pay attention. Not yet grasping the concept of death, Jake saw one grandfather, his dad's father, every day. He had never seen his mom's father, who died before Jake was born. So in his mind, it made perfect sense that the Supreme Allied Commander of WW II speaking out of the mahogany box in his living room could be his grandpa. When the enraged nun called the house to complain and ask which fool told this little boy that the 34th President of the United States was Jake Yanick's grandfather, his father, nonplussed admitted, "Me!"

When the new, young and handsome President appeared on the TV in his frequent news conferences, Jake insisted his mother allow him to wear his Sunday suit and tie so he could look like the busy reporters querying JFK. By the time Ed Prince told Jake about his radio career, the youngster was primed and ready to be swept way by the electronic media.

The broom that did the final sweeping came in the most unlikely and mundane place, a grocery store. Jake's parents lacked a car in the 50s and 60s. In order to get to the supermarket they relied on friends and relatives. One Thursday night when Jake was in the 6th grade he accompanied his parents to the store along with two kindly neighbors. As they entered the store, they were greeted with a large sign that simply read "LIVE BROADCAST". While the adults went to pick out food staples, Jake headed toward the sign. A small desk was set up with a huge sign that said, "LIVE

TODAY—THE BOYS FROM BAM". Two turntables were at the edge of the desk anchored by a small control unit and a microphone. It fascinated Jake that the front of the unit was clean and shiny. When he looked at the back of the glimmering jewel he was struck by the convoluted mish mash of wire, rust and steel. As he walked around the table mesmerized, a huge hand landed on his shoulder. "Hello there son" the booming voice called out. Jake turned and towering over him was none other than Uncle Red. Born Thaddeus Rose, uncle Red was a favorite children's icon of early local TV. A decorated World War II vet, Rose won the Purple Heart and Medal of Honor for wiping out an entire Japanese platoon. The legend went that the Japanese had interrupted his poker game. Enraged, he stood up to enemy fire until he mowed them all down. Rose had bought WBAM and was known for community involvement, willingness to try something new and exaggerating the number of people who came out for his live events. Jake introduced himself and Rose said, "Say boy, I need a man like you. Want to pass out free records to the people coming through the door?" Jake, looking at the huge sign, the sandy haired man talking into the microphone and Red's beaming face, jumped at the chance. His job was to hand out free 45s to the shopping public. As the masses came through the door, there was Jake handing out a freebie compliments of the Boys from BAM. The grade school boy noticed the change of attitude of the shoppers as they walked by the BAM desk. Looking grim and determined to eke out a few luxuries as they passed through the doors, a smile came to their faces when they saw the broadcast sign. When he handed them something for nothing, even a beat up record by someone they never heard of, their eyes brightened. A girl a grade behind Jake saw him handing out the 45s and squealed to her mother, "Mommy that's Jake Yanick, he's in my school. He works with the radio". The buzz and excitement was something he had not seen in his young life. Just when he thought it couldn't get any better, Red called him over to meet Johnny Ashgash, the Polka king heard mornings on WBAM. As Jake stood in front of them, he heard Ashgash speak into the microphone, "Now ladies and gentlemen, let's welcome one of the youngest boys from 'BAM, Jake Yanick. Jake, say a few words to our audience". The boy was dumbstruck. He started to sweat and panic. He looked at the professional duo and for a split second wondered what to say. After what seemed like an eternity, Jake began, "I'm proud to be here with the boys from 'BAM today. Come on down, do your food shopping and stop by and get a free gift from us, the boys from BAM." When he gave the mike back to the two men, he could see he made a huge impression. After he got off the air, Red told Jake he had done very well and even gave him an extra 45 to take home.

As he rode home in the car, Jake was tingling with excitement. His family and neighbors were happy for him and Jake was more than thrilled that the next day at school people would know all about his radio debut. From the front seat, his father asked how much Red Rose paid him for his efforts. Jake replied, "Nothing. I did it for free". With those words, Jake's father knew the kid was hooked on the media spotlight. How many times had he heard entertainers of his era say they'd perform for free? Now his son was saying the same thing. Steve Yanick thought about that a long while in the car and decided it was way better than his back-breaking job maintaining the railroads. As they rode home in silence, both father and son knew that a career path had begun that night. Neither could ever imagine the winding and changing road that lay ahead.

When John Kennedy was killed in 1963, Jake Yanick was 9 years old. What he remembered most about those four awful days in the nation's history was the reaction of his father. As the family watched events unfold in their living room, Steve Yanick kept on muttering, "television is a wonderful thing". His father explained to Jake that events in his own childhood were stories told in a newspaper only. Jake's entire young life intersected with great events of the time. The killing of JFK, his assassin Lee Harvey Oswald, the subsequent killings of Malcom X, Bobby Kennedy, Martin Luther King, the body count in Vietnam as well as the moon landing shared one common denominator. That of course was TV. But the Yanick family did not limit themselves to just the boob tube, but read newspapers and always had a radio playing in the house.

Jake had the broadcast bug in him. His childhood was pretty normal anchored by two loving parents and a large extended family of doting aunts and uncles. He did well in school but three things captured his interest. Baseball, politics and radio. The three were interlocked by subject matter, message delivery and his passion for each.

Baseball in the 1960s for a young boy was nirvana. Before free agency and the large salaries, players stayed with one team the length of their career. Stars like Sandy Koufax, Mickey Mantle, Willie Mays, and Hank Aaron dominated the game. His friends emulated the superstars while Jake adopted the lesser lights of the game as not only role models but heroes. Gus Triandos, Smokey Burgess, Art Mahaffey, Pat Corrales and Clete Boyer were his favorites.

At night, Jake would listen to the radio he inherited when his sister left home. A 7 by 9 inch portable with tan leather, the radio had 2 large knobs on the side and took 8 batteries. The radio opened up the world of baseball to him. Mostly, he would listen to the east coast games. The Phillies, the Mets, the Yankees. One night Jake nodded off with the radio on his chest and accidentally bumped the tuning knob. When he awakened, Jake was listening to a Cleveland radio station. He was startled to discover that at night, he could pick up signals from distant cities. Every night during the baseball season, Jake listened to the Indians. It would be the start of a life long passion. The young boy studied the style of the announcers and began to pick up the nuances of the game.

He became fluent in public affairs thanks to following the news on the radio. Around the Yanick dinner table at family gatherings, Jake held his own when debating the issues of the day. In addition to current affairs, the boy would recite baseball stats as well as radio line ups from teams and radio stations miles away. There was a virtual media buffet before him, and Jake feasted on every morsel that came his way.

If politics and sports were the main course, then music was dessert. Music took Jake to places in his

soul. No matter how bad things got in the news or how badly his team floundered, there were the songs.
A non musician, Jake heard every nuance of a ballad, could tell you when there would be a pause, a crescendo, and take the words and make them part of his life.

The logical bridge to music was of course women. As early as 1961, Jake's father knew he loved women. Just 7 at the time, he stole the show at his sister Toni's "Sweet 16" party. Much to the chagrin of the teenage boys invited, Jake got all the slow dances with the girls. He wasn't sure what he liked about them or why, but he knew they smelled good, felt soft and reached a part of him he did not yet fully understand. The music and the women were united as one. Every song had a woman attached to it for Jake. "Sleepwalk" was the song for the girls at Toni's party, "Pretty Woman" was for an older lady in church, a New York city matron no less who smelled good. Jake could not hear a song without conjuring up some particular type of woman. He used it as a bridge to meet them, a road to woo them and a link to their past when they moved on.

The sounds of music at night fed the romantic side of him. His concept of what love came from those songs. The amazing thing was that Jake grasped the concept of romantic love at all. The negative aspect was that even as an adult, Jake never got out of the early 60s and a boy's perception of women and love. Naïve to a fault, his Dobie Gillis perception of the world remained intact. Just as on TV, if a woman was beautiful she would never lie, or be a bad person. Mostly, When the pretty woman was in need, that was the cherry on top of the sundae. It was not lost on some of Jake's peers that the women he developed his first crushes on were beautiful but flawed. He was certainly gutsy enough to seek them out, engage the young girls with his charm but he did so with a mission. While his friends took their initial steps into romance with a carefree attitude, Jake plunged the depths of the young girl's psyche. It was also telling that he picked women, even in grade school, who were needed. His first crush was on a girl a year older than he who had lost her father when she was only ten. His next young beautiful friend's house had burned down when Jake arrived on the scene to give comfort and aid. So there was a pattern developing.

As Jake entered high school, from the age of fourteen, his values were pretty much set. The young man would work hard for his grades. He did find employment at a newspaper and a grocery store too. But at the age of sixteen, he had the opportunity to become a radio newsman. He played a little baseball, and became a popular student government leader. It was evident that Jake Yanick was the kid who was going places in the small town. Everything Jake Yanick did was with honor and dignity. But with all of that, Jake if given the chance would trade it away in an instant. All it would take would be a beautiful woman in trouble. Jake knew this, his father knew it admonishing him more than once, " A man can get killed over a woman, remember that". Like many things his father told him as a youth, Jake disregarded. Years later, none would be more prophetic than Steve Yanick's warning to his son.

Throughout Jake's school career he was tabbed as a person going places. It would be the first building of the illusions in his life that he presented to the public. On the outside, he projected an image of confidence, overwhelming personality and energy. His insides were in turmoil. On one hand he internalized all the slights and teasing young people endure. But just as quickly he put on a front of defiance that daunted his critics. Jake planned everything in his young life while conveying the image that his good fortune was happenstance. It was a very strange tug of war, he wanted the recognition, craved it. But publicly, he downplayed it. Part of this was most likely from his parents' admonition "Never get too high-never get too low". They hoped to keep Jake on an even keel.

Jake breezed through high school with no big plan in mind, other than to be in radio. At the age of 15 he began working for both a newspaper and radio station. The pay was low but the compensation for Jake came in the currency of popularity. He pursued the prettiest girl in the class without success, asking her out 20 times. While some would look upon this as a stalking event, Jake's charm and good humor made it into a cute joke and part of the Yanick legend. Much to his surprise, Jake won a Citizenship Award at graduation and to his shock came in third for the Person Most Likely To Succeed. Again, there was that dichotomy of self promotion and self aggrandizement, then the shock that the goal was nearly achieved. It was as if Jake felt he was undeserving of the success. Jake was told by his High School Guidance Counselor that he should forget about college. Stunned but not defeated he knocked around politics and radio in the Washington, D.C. area. He was relatively happy until his cousin, Ed Prince on business in the nation's capitol heard Jake imitating a black announcer on a low power radio station that played soul music. The first thing radio people do when they get to a new town is go up and down the dial to hear familiar voices in the business. When Ed heard his young cousin on the radio doing a horrible imitation, he went to the small, run down outlet and asked for Jake. The senior radio man was appalled at the filth of the studios as well as the awful neighborhood. Ed told the story about a man in a uniform who followed a trail of elephants in a circus picking up after the animals had relieved themselves on the street. When asked why he was doing such a menial job, the man with the broom said, "At least I'm in show business!!" Ed's point was that there were many levels to the business and Jake was at the very tail end of it. His older cousin persuaded Jake that he might do better back home instead of inner city D.C. When Jake told his cousin that there was scholarship money with his name on it at a local university, his cousin nearly pulled him out of the building by the scruff of his neck. After Ed's visit, Jake agreed to enter college.

His college run was a carbon copy of high school. Heavy emphasis on radio and TV, pursuit of the prettiest girls (this time with a little more success) and campus recognition were his forte. When Jake was in college, he worked for a Public Radio and TV station. His major was dual, Government/Politics and Communications, The job in TV was in the public arena. The era was Watergate when politics and the media became merged forever. And Jake was a part of it.

After graduation he stayed on at the Public TV/Radio station hosting three radio shows and one weekly TV show no one saw except his parents. The expectation of his broadcast career proved greater than the actual realization of it. Jake felt empty. After all that hard work, that craving to get known, Jake wanted something more. This pattern would go on through his entire working life.

There was no doubt that Jake was a capable, accommodating hard worker. His learning skills were complimented by his huge personality and his great attention to detail. His friendly, gregarious manner projected an image of caring, trust and comfort. Each job in his career was sales oriented but varied. He did fundraising for Public Broadcasting, managed a Pennsylvania State Senatorial campaign, worked as a Development Officer for Social service agencies, a Communications Director for the United Fund and then as a full time substitute school teacher. Each job lasted about five years. In each position he did well but there was always a reason to move on, whether it be a promotion he was denied or just a downsizing of his particular skill set. There would be some who would argue that Jake's resume had no holes in it but was varied in scope thus giving him a true generalist designation. Later in his career, others would say his work history reflected an erratic pattern that had no final destination mapped out. As the end of the century neared with its age of specialization in all jobs, this wide ranging resume was not really embraced. This negative however never stopped Jake from advancing anywhere in his career. He always had the uncanny knack to make a positive into a negative.

Unlike Jake's scattered career profile, Adrienne Kresge's was consistent, and focused on one area, books. Adrienne grew up in the fifties as an asthmatic child who learned to read at an early age. She was possessed with a quick and curious mind. Always encouraged by her working class mother and father, she craved learning. Shy but not retiring, she discovered the world of books at a small town library down the street from her home. Adrienne projected an air of stability and jovial tranquility. She thought before she spoke and that attribute was sometimes mistaken for meekness. Adrienne set her sights on a college degree and began her career as a regional manager of a chain of book stores. Having access to this world of information continually fed her curiosity.

Adrienne's personal life, like her professional represented a calm line. There were no peaks or valleys, just a flat right to left existence in a polite, well ordered world. That changed dramatically when she met Jake Yanick. Jake was lunching with one of Adrienne's coworkers, a skittish, manic woman from his college days. One day as the two were coming back from lunch, Adrienne walked by them. Jake had nodded hello and Adrienne smiled back. That minor sign sent Jake off to the races. He began to pepper his lunch mate with questions about the tall sturdy blond they had just encountered. Even though she was stingy with her answers, Jake had enough information to do what he loved best with women: pursue. As for Adrienne, she was hit intensely with the feeling that someway, somehow she would wind up marrying the man in the three piece suit she just passed on the street.

Two days later, Jake went into action. He already had three women in his bachelor life, what was another going to cost him. How much trouble could a bookseller be was Jake's reasoning. He stopped in the bookstore looking for a book on baseball star Thurman Munson who had died the summer before. Much to his delight and surprise, he spied the woman who was the object of his chase. Luck was prevailing here, Jake thought. What he didn't know was that Adrienne had seen him coming into the building and positioned herself at the ready so she could just happen to bump into the object of her own pursuit. The conman was being out gunned by the bookworm.

Both formally introduced themselves to each other, made small talk and then excused themselves to get back to work. Adrienne was sure Jake would call. She had thought about giving him her business card but somehow knew she didn't have to. For his part, as he walked out of the building, Jake kept mumbling her last name and phone number to himself, sounding like a well dressed street rummy until he got out of her sight. Then he frantically wrote down her name, title and work phone number.

Jake plotted strategy for women like generals plotted a combat campaign. He waited two days before he called Adrienne. She accepted his invitation for lunch. After that went well, dinner followed. The two spent more and more time together. Jake was attracted to her intellect, her beauty and her personality. But there was something more. Adrienne resonated a calm, a confidence, a stability in a woman that Jake had not found in his various pursuits. The summer before he met Adrienne, Jake's father died suddenly. To him it was a great loss and he retreated into a reflective mode. While coping with the loss of his father, Jake began to see things in a different light. At his father's wake, Jake's family shuttled his various women from room to room. All were divorced and had kids. Jake, who was great with the children and endeared himself to the women saw clearly the baggage involved in that type of relationship. After the death of his father, Jake decided he needed to be selfish in a relationship. His hallmark was "give give give'. It made him feel good but it also indebted the women to him insuring that they would never leave him because he became indispensable. While the family had a great laugh at Jake's juggling act, he needed to focus on himself, his healing and where he was going. As his father lay in repose, Jake looked around the room and saw all the cousins he grew up with. All adults now, they each had a spouse. But their mates were more than a partner, each was a rock. Jake saw clearly that at the darkest time in his life, he had no boulder to lean on but a rather flimsy posse of women who had problems of their own.

No one was more aware of this need than Adrienne. She became Jake's rock. Listening to his hopes and dreams, she let him know that's all they were. She had no expectations for riches or greatness.

Adrienne helped heal his wounds letting him rest from his role as cheer-leader to the world. It was okay to be silent. More importantly, it was all right to sob and cry for the loss of a father. As for his part, Jake uncovered Adrienne's psyche like a boiled onion. Her shy and unassuming personality began to blossom just a bit more. He helped her confront emotional issues from years past and urged her to fight for herself. Jake spent his whole life "being on", with Adrienne all he had to do was just "be". They both complimented each other in the best way possible. Jake jettisoned all of his other relationships (much to the chagrin of the divorcees) and concentrated solely on Adrienne. The next logical step would be marriage. Adrienne advocated for it, Jake avoided the subject.

Both loved each other deeply. There was no doubt about that. But Jake still loved women. He loved to flirt with them, chat with them, schmooze them. He liked the way they made him feel. His commitment to Adrienne was unwavering but he still adored women in general. Adrienne wanted a marriage commitment and finally received one from Jake more than a year after they started to date. She had to throw a tantrum to get Jake to take action on this issue that was very unlike her. For his part, Jake responded immediately, lovingly and generously in spirit. It surprised Jake that Adrienne fought for her position. He remembered her words, "We must do this within a year, if not, this thing between us won't mean anything. You have to make a choice here because I'm not going to wait forever for you to decide if this is what you want". The best way to sway Jake was to give him an ultimatum. Of course Adrienne didn't know this was going to work. She took the chance on Jake's sense of decency and commitment. Jake on the other hand saw Adrienne's promise to him as something he never had before in a relationship: unconditional love. Jake recalled the first night they went to dinner. He was so nervous he started to choke on a glass of water. And at the end of the night, when he asked her if he could kiss her goodnight, the simplicity of her answer thrilled him. All she said in response to his request was "I wish you would". The moment would stay in Jake's heart and mind forever. Adrienne had won the complicated soul of Jake Yanick with her simple response.

Before a crowd of 300, Adrienne and Jake wed, honeymooned in Hawaii then set up house keeping above a Lebanese grocery store in Harvey's Lake. Married life melded beautifully for them. Life was good and they enjoyed each other immensely. Jake's rock was solid, the seas were calm. This should have been a cakewalk for both of them. While they had more in common with each other than most couples, there was one major divide. Adrienne embraced the calm marital waters while Jake was looking to sail their ship into heavy seas.

Jake and Adrienne hardly ever fought. If anything the closest thing they ever came to a full-blown argument was when each got frustrated over some mechanical task. They had the utmost respect for one another and had a decent existence. Adrienne had found the love of her life in Jake. He boosted her spirits, made her feel beautiful. She shared her deepest feelings with him and despite any situation they were in, he made her laugh. Jake regarded Adrienne as a true equal. Therein lay one of the concerns. Adrienne had much to teach Jake and conversely he had much to learn. But his ego stood in the way of even thinking he needed advice and Adrienne never really pushed the issue. No matter what Adrienne or for that matter any woman gave to Jake, it just wasn't enough.

A well-adjusted, intelligent man, Jake was a bottomless pit of need when it came to women. Psychologists traced it back to his rejection by women when he was a teenager. Others said that in reality Jake had a dark side when it came to women, that he really enjoyed manipulating them as sport thereby manifested his hate for them by his actions. Both sides of this argument were extreme in their nature. Perhaps closer to the truth was something in the middle. Jake loved the women who adored him, but could not stand to be ignored by the women who spurned him. He gave them many chances to experience the Yanick magic, but once they made it clear they weren't interested, they were done. Women to Jake were like a buffet to a hungry person. There was much to choose from, but each dish fed a hunger that kept on returning. Unlike other men who were rejected, Jake tried to figure out "why" before he went on to the next conquest. There was much thought about why the attraction wasn't there, why the relationship ended, and Jake made a mental checklist to improve himself when he took the leap to the next woman waiting in the wings.

When Jake was in the 8th grade, a teacher asked him if he was related to his younger cousin Tommy. He answered yes and the teacher unsympathetically said, "You'd never know you were from the same family, Tommy is so handsome and you are so ugly compared to him". Jake was devastated. He was on the honor roll, President of his class, had the lead in the school play, was an honorary member of his town council as a junior citizen but none of that mattered. For the last half of the school year, Jake shunned the advances of his frequent grade school companion, a plain girl by the name of Donna and went all out to win the heart of a 5 foot 9 blond bombshell Susan Iracki who would later go on to be a Flight Attendant. When Jake accompanied her to the last school dance, it was more important than anything he had ever achieved in his final academic year. In a way, with women, it was never about the sex but more about the chase. The more impossible and unattainable the woman seemed, the harder Jake tried. For as much as Adrienne loved and provided for Jake and as much as he cared about her, it was unrealistic to think Jake would not wander off the reservation given his past history, his formative years and his access to women through his career.

The fourth year into the marriage, the shenanigans started. In the course of 6 years, Jake became involved with an alcoholic brunette, an ex weather girl who proved needier than he, a cardiac care nurse he met at a concert he was attending with the ex local TV star, a church receptionist he met at a Sexaholics Anonymous meeting, an attorney he met in a wine tasting class, and a practical nurse who turned out to be the meanest human being God ever allowed on this green earth. In addition to this roster, there were scores of assignations with women Jake could never recognize later on even if a loaded gun was aimed at his head. All the while Jake led a double life, tending to his wife but having several other revolving pursuits too. Jake's peculiar sense of honor mandated that the girl friends have nearly equal parity with Adrienne. It was not uncommon for Jake to go to three Christmas church services and eat three separate turkey dinners. Each holiday was planned with the precision of a lunar landing with seconds to spare. Each woman had a fond memory of a holiday spent with Jake while he added one more woman to his notch of "achievements". All the while he attended weekly church services with Adrienne and was home every night to share their bed.

At one point during this time Jake was thrown out by his distraught wife. Adrienne suspected there were serious issues of commitment when the couple won an all expenses paid vacation to Barbados and Jake recommended she go with a girl friend. If Jake loved anything more than women, it was the sea and sand. During the couple's honeymoon, his wife's main task was trying to get Jake off the beach. So when he refused a trip to the Islands, she suspected infidelity. Thinking she'd shock him into a cold dose of reality, she threw all of his belongings out on the front lawn and changed the locks on the doors. After calming her down, Jake thanked her for her efforts and then obligingly found himself an apartment, having dual residencies. His rationale was that Adrienne let him go. In reality though, Jake had never seriously considered divorcing Adrienne but he never considered stopping his behavior that was piercing her heart and soul.

The relationship between Adrienne and Jake was one that could only be viewed as a series of definitive contradictions. Both were very intelligent, giving and generous with each other, but had their own individual needs, wants and preferences as well.

Jake seemed gregarious and the life of the party but once he was married, he enjoyed the peacefulness and steadiness of the family home. His wife, Adrienne, though a tough business person, retreated to a quiet existence inside her marriage. The couple had few close friends. Jake's circle consisted of a boyhood chum from grade school, a die-hard baseball fan he met on a bus trip and a college buddy who relocated to Denver. Adrienne had no friends from her childhood in her life but had a close friend she met in college and the chef of a local diner she frequented for lunch. There were no social occasions of consequence in the Yanick household. Both believed that friends from work should be kept at there. Home was a sanctuary.

It is against this backdrop that Adrienne and Jake lived their marriage. The two were committed to each other but the equation was hardly equal. Jake's constant need for the affection of beautiful women should have caused a major, breaking strain in the relationship. It did not and had nothing to do with Jake's selection of women or how discreet he was or wasn't. Rather it was the way that Adrienne chose to react to his behavior. Certainly Jake did not throw it up to her but he always gave her hints of a new friend in his life. It was almost a testing of her commitment to the marriage, or how much she could stand before she rejected him as a partner. If Jake had wanted that, his wife never gave it to him. A smart woman like Adrienne would not be so naïve as to believe that her husband acquired female friends to play checkers with. Yet whenever the subject came up, she chose to remain passive in her response, which drove Jake's need for attention off the charts.

Adrienne was a cool customer when it came to knowing what her husband needed and her response to his attention-seeking dalliances was to pay him no mind at all. In the short term, this was good for Jake and enabled him to have an unimpeded playing field. But in the long run, when the flirtation inevitably crashed and burned, Adrienne was standing steady in the batter's box awaiting the next pitch.

There was an amount of arrogance in knowing
and believing she'd be the only one but also a
pragmatic faith in the person she fell in love with. One
time at the urging of a friend, Adrienne saw a priest
for council on her marriage to Jake. It was really more
of an intervention because Adrienne was reluctant to
spill her guts to just anyone, clergy or not. Her
response to the issue of Jake's marital fidelity was
telling. "There are good and bad people in this world,"
she said softly. "I believe I married a good person who
has this flaw. I can blame his up bringing; I can even
tag him as a culprit in the infidelities - if there are any.
The behavior is going to be what it is going to be. I
can't change that at all. However, I can react in a way
that will preserve my dignity, but keep the door open
for when he comes to his senses. It may seem arrogant
but deep down I know he loves me and sooner or later,
he'll know it too," concluded Adrienne as she left the
speech-struck padre alone in his office.

Adrienne's friend Rose maintained that Jake's
wife was attracted to this dangerous side of him. But
the ironic thing about this was that it was Jake flirting
with the danger, not Adrienne. She had made her mind
up that no matter what the facts, fantasies or fallacies
were, she was going to honor her marriage vows. It
was not a dangerous decision because Adrienne was
risking nothing. Her basic belief in Jake as a good
person sustained her as she sometimes waited by the

window late at night wishing him home to her arms. There were nights of heartbreak and crying but she was going to be damned if she ever let him see it.

Jake might have thought he was pulling one over on her but in reality it was his wife that was gaining the advantage. Her free time gave her the ability to make her way in the business world and become the major financial player in the marriage. The contacts she acquired were giants compared to the contemporaries who populated Jake's world. Unlike Jake, she bragged little about these connections but subtly let her ego-driven husband know whom she could count on in a pinch.

More importantly she began to build a veneer of emotional strength that she never had as a child, a student or a wife. It gave her a tougher shell, made her less needy than other women Jake knew and gave her the tools to deflect the slings and arrows of Jake's wandering ways.

There was no question that Adrienne loved him and would stay in the marriage, but she did so with open eyes, steely resolve and a reassignment of affection for her husband. It was too subtle to notice but every time Jake went off with a new friend and then returned to the fold, Adrienne removed just a little bit of emotional support the man craved. Wise enough not to strip him completely, Adrienne would allow him to realize something was missing but never gave him the satisfaction of knowing exactly what. Some would call it a wife's revenge; others dubbed it as just pragmatic love. Whatever it was, there was an effect on Jake as the years went by.

Adrienne's love mattered a great deal to Jake. She was the steady center of his world. As time went on, Jake began to realize exactly what Adrienne knew all the time, that the two were joined at the hip emotionally which no bimbo could rip asunder. He was in awe of her softness at home but her tenacity in the business world. Her job looked very sedate, but the world of selling books was not for the faint of heart. The influx of the computer age and the high cost of paper had made the industry competitive beyond belief. And the appearance of mega bookstores threatened the existence of independent booksellers. She worked for a medium sized regional bookstore chain. Smaller than the national chains, Booklovers was able to offer customers personal service. She was in charge of ordering materials for the eight-store chain. Adrienne knew her customers. She had an uncanny feel for what they wanted to read and how much they would be willing to spend. Her success gave the marriage its financial stability.

Most marriages like this would be a divorce waiting to happen. A driven career woman who loved the art of the deal and an emotionally needy husband with a wandering eye for a pretty girl would not seem to be the ideal pair. But Jake did his part to keep things going too. He took over many of the household duties to enable his wife to pursue her success. It was not out of guilt but because he truly loved serving his wife's needs whether it be cooking her a gourmet meal, rubbing her feet for hours on the sofa as the couple watched TV or surprising her with small thoughtful gifts. Adrienne on the other hand loved the attention and felt it was the very least Jake could do for her given his behavior.

And so, despite the stresses and self-made pressures, they stayed the course and did not run. The argument could be made that they needed each other desperately but in reality that was not true. By embracing the strengths of the other and by putting their faults on the back burner, they managed to enjoy a marriage that provided each what they needed. As the marriage went on, Adrienne became a stronger, wiser partner while Jake, to the best of his ability, had a renewed appreciation for the gifts his wife brought to the union. There was no doubt Jake would still stray but the marriage would stay pretty much unshakeable because of mutual respect, love, passion and fidelity at least, to the idea of what marriage could be for the two of them. The outside world had a tough time understanding it but the couple stopped caring what the world thought.

The flaw was that Jake still needed a bit more. Adrienne let him try to find it, knowing with great confidence that he'd be back. If Jake had wanted banishment for his sins, he was in the wrong church and wrong pew with Adrienne. She was staying married, no matter how ridiculously he behaved. Ironically it would be two events, baseball and a beautiful woman that would bring Jake back to Adrienne.

Helen Fulbright was atypical of the women Jake carried on with outside of his marriage. In a way she was the closet thing to Adrienne in terms of intelligence and personality. An attorney, she was very thin with an angular face, sarcastic wit and very offbeat sense of humor. She and Jake were thrown together as dinner partners in the wine class they both attended. Their initial mutual dislike of one another turned into open hostility. In a very perverse sort of way, this made the attraction between the two surprising. But their common bond was baseball. As their friendship grew, whatever tensions appeared were eased by the national past time. With Jake it was always about the mind and Helen had never had that type of relationship before. To her, Jake was the ultimate male dog, thinking with his dick and then acting on it. But the twist was Jake never acted on it until he was seduced by the person he was pursuing. To him, this was the ultimate victory of the chase. Helen Fulbright adored Jake but was going to move back to her hometown. She always wondered what a physical relationship with Jake would be like. But neither got around to it because of Jake's reticence and Helen's move. For all intents and purposes her time with Jake would be coming to an end.

The last night they spent together was Game 1 of the 1988 World Series. Beer, soda and pizza were on tap for the evening. The game ended with the famous Kirk Gibson walk off homerun given up by A's pitcher Dennis Eckersley. Just when the Dodgers won that game, Helen leaped off the couch into the chair Jake was sitting on. Looking up at him she exclaimed, "Come to Pittsburgh and live with me. Be my house boy. Cook for me, massage my feet, talk to me like you do everyday. I'll support you in the style to which you're accustomed" she said gazing up at him with her steel blue eyes. Jake was stunned. She was not supposed to be the pursuer. Helen saw that in his eyes. "Okay, okay think about it a few weeks. But look at the women you've been seeing before me, or hell even while you've been with me. A drunk who thinks she's a poet, a couple of medical types who are clinically crazy, and that ex Action News chick for Christ sakes!

Every woman you have pursued besides me is crazier
than a shit house rat. You need normal Jake, you need
a girl like me, someone smart, plain on the outside but
a sex bomb on the inside, you need someone to listen
to jazz with, you need someone to wash your back at
night, you need, you need………" Just then, Helen
fell asleep in Jake's lap. Jake gently picked her up,
carried the snoozing barrister to her room, placed her
on the bed, covered her up and left the fourth floor
walk up. He walked into the chilled October evening
that was illuminated by star-light. He remembered
when he and Adrienne started to date and how they
would each wish upon the first star they saw in the
night sky. Jake remembered dancing to their song,
"When You Wish Upon A Star" at their wedding and
he began to smile and cry at the same time. Mostly he
remembered Helen's sales pitch to him. What Helen
told him was a drunken fantasy, it was everything she
wanted as a woman but would never allow herself to
have in the cold sober light of day. But Jake
recognized the attributes that were listed for him and
examined his choices in the past few years vs. the
woman who was sitting alone at home watching an old
movie on TV. Jake came to the full realization that
every step he took away from Adrienne with some
beautiful woman was not a leap ahead but an
immersion into a pit. Every one who he was involved
with was terribly abnormal and maladjusted. It pleased

him that they needed to be fixed and he fancied himself as the ultimate repairman. Only, the truth was, these women were not fixable. As Helen pointed out, Jake could hardly repair his own broken love life, let alone cope with the neediness of others. As he got older, Jake saw the advantage in playing the percentages just as elder baseball managers had in his youth. Two things were at work here, he was still in love with Adrienne and there was no gain in staying in relationships with insane women. The prize just didn't seem worth the cost he had to pay. He got into his car and went home. Adrienne was in bed. Jake sat up all night thinking.

That morning he went to Helen Fulbright's house. He was always one to hedge his bets. Much to both his chagrin and relief, (another mixed emotion which was a Yanick hallmark) Helen remembered nothing about their encounter the night before except the score of the game. Jake helped her pack her car, she kissed him goodbye and as she drove away Jake knew they would never speak again. Unlike most of his encounters this one ended well. Helen Fulbright showed him in graphic terms what he was throwing away in the person of Adrienne. He went home that morning, crawled in bed with his wife, held her tight and resolved he'd never leave her again. Jake recognized that this was a tall order even for him. So he modified it a little bit. He'd never leave her again but in the event he were to meet someone 25 years younger who adored him and looked like Julia Roberts, well then he'd have to reconsider. But Jake knew in his heart that would never happen at his age and station in life. He was renewing his commitment to his wife Adrienne and would set out to be the perfect husband and help mate. Laying in the large bed in the sun lit bedroom on a fall afternoon, both Jake and his wife would never fully appreciate the timing of Jake's newfound commitment until a few months later. The biggest challenge of their marriage would come not in the form of a drunken floozy but in the shape of an alcohol impaired motorist.

Jake was getting ready to go to the gym when the phone call came. He had just got home from a late client meeting, skipped supper and was donning his Jordans to get some work out time in. Unlike recent times in his life answering the phone was not a crapshoot. No needy woman would be calling invading his home or life and that was a source of great relief to Jake. Lumbering toward the phone, he was struck by the unfamiliar voice on the other end. At first he thought it was a telemarketer. "Mr. Yanick", the caller said, "This is Jean from the County Paramedics Unit. Are you related to Adrienne Kresge Yanick?" Numbed, Jake answered in the affirmative. "Mr. Yanick, your wife has been in an auto accident and is being transported to the hospital. She is conscious and speaking. Is it possible for you to meet us at the accident scene and ride with her to the hospital or else meet us there?" she continued. Jake was in a panic, his hands shaking. He wrote down the address and tore out of the house.

Adrienne was on her way to have dinner with an old friend of hers at an Italian restaurant, The Roman Villa. Traveling south, her car was rammed by an SUV exiting a city park. Her car spun around three times from the impact and crashed into a parked tractor trailer. When Jake arrived Adrienne was strapped to a hard board gurney standing straight up, her head secured so it would stay immobile. His first thought was that she looked eerily like Joan of Arc at the stake. Jake saw fear in her eyes and reacted the best way he knew how. He told her things would be fine, asked her if she could move her extremities and told her he'd meet her at the hospital.

Adrienne was admitted to the emergency room and was given a cursory examination. She complained of head, neck, arm and leg pain. The attending physician who looked all of twelve proclaimed his patient in fine shape and despite her head pain released Adrienne from the hospital. Driving his wife home, Jake tried to say all the right things. He was superb in a crisis and this time he rose to the occasion. Adrienne had been diagnosed with a slight concussion and was told to rest for a day before she returned to work. She was also given the go ahead to resume her running regimen that she followed faithfully. After three days her head pain subsided and she returned to work. The couple did the necessary things like dealing with the insurance company, filing and obtaining police reports and retaining an Attorney. Jake handled the details while Adrienne remained in a confused fog. Both attributed this to her recent injury. and what they thought was her advancing recovery.

As the months went on, Adrienne began to retreat more into herself. Her job that used to be a cakewalk for her turned into a nightmare. Placing orders for the bookstores used to be routine, after the injury many of the customer requests went unfulfilled. Minor tasks became major projects. There were days when Adrienne sat trying to make the decision whether to get dressed or not. Her once efficient organizational skills were all but obliterated. She was no longer able to put together a 3 course meal and wept openly at the least provocation. Jake, the ultimate people pleaser, was bewildered but decided to take over the functions in the marriage formerly handled by his wife. Jake took over the house cleaning and cooking which resulted in a significant burden being lifted off his ailing spouse. His cheerful assumption of these duties helped ease Adrienne's anxiety. However his handling of the family finances nearly put the couple into bankruptcy court. For all of his gifts and talents, fiscal management was not one of them. Still with the problems the couple seemed to get through the trying time.

On the surface, Jake's wife appeared to be fine. But her short-term memory started to fail her and her job responsibilities became overwhelming. Her emotional state varied from crying jags to violent verbal outbursts against people or things that to others would be regarded as a minor annoyance. Jake took it all in stride being as supportive as he could. Adrienne however could not stand herself since the accident. The couple sought advice and diagnosis for the problem in their hometown but it was to no avail. Adrienne at one point contemplated suicide. One night on Public Radio Adrienne had heard about a hospital in Philadelphia that specialized in the treatment of head injuries. Both had denied to themselves that knock on the head could cause such catastrophic fallout. But Jake made the appointment and he and Adrienne drove to the hospital to see if anything could be done. Adrienne was put through a battery of tests that determined she did indeed suffer a brain injury from the accident. A huge rehabilitation program was designed for Jake's wife that included a regimen of exercise, medication and therapy. The couple spent hours mapping out a program with health care professionals and then began to implement it as part of their daily lives. Adrienne's business environment was changed too. The Bookstore built a sound proof office for her newly acquired special needs. Compensatory strategies were employed to have Adrienne regain her former organizational skills that in turn allowed her to keep her position without a reduction in pay. Through it all Jake remained at her side. One therapist told Adrienne that during the time period of brain injury recovery was when a spouse would be most likely to cut and run. Statistics bore this out. Jake was not part of this stat, mainly because with the accident, his wife had become the type of woman he had pursued outside of his marriage: one in dire need. Notwithstanding the love he felt for his wife, Jake's sense of honor and gallantry demanded that he stay with Adrienne. He figured that his loyalty and devotion to his wife were late in coming but decided that it was a fortuitous gift of providence. Adrienne's brain injury ironically would make him a better man and husband. Jake joked that he now had the woman he always wanted, someone beautiful, intelligent but crazy. Helen Fulbright would've been delighted. Jake monitored Adrienne's steady progress. He encouraged her constant napping and rest periods telling her the body as well as her mind needed a rest. He occupied himself when Adrienne was out of commission and hoarding her strength for her job and other outside social activities. The brain injury had changed them both drastically. The pessimist in Adrienne pointed out what she could not do anymore. The optimist in Jake showed her what she was despite the hardships she endured. What was most important was that the two were still a team, undefeated. One day when Adrienne was in Philadelphia for her therapy, Jake zonked out and fell asleep in the waiting area. When he awoke his eyes met a pretty young brunette who smiled at him. The two began to talk about why they were there and Jake fully explained the reasons for his visit. The young woman smiled and said, "There is nothing more sexy than a man who will stand by his injured wife". Jake disregarded the compliment but could not get it out of his mind. Yes he loved Adrienne and had found

his constant and soul mate, he appreciated her more
now than ever after nearly losing her. But to be
regarded as a hero and sexy for sticking with his
mentally beleaguered but improving wife, well that
had to be the coolest thing Jake ever heard in his life!!
Of course had Adrienne's treating physician Dr. Todd
Edwards told him that, he would've instantly ignored
it. But because a stranger, a beautiful one at that
uttered those words, somehow that meant just a bit
more to Jake. And in a way for all his good work on
behalf of Adrienne that was sort of sad.

The top was down on the car, the music was blaring loudly from the CD player. Jake was driving left handed with his right index finger poised to switch the stereo system to the next selection. Adrienne was used to this drill. When you drove with Jake, you'd only hear the instrumental opening to the song. "The Shades of Blue, from 1966, the year that clicked, you know it, you love it, it's called "Oh How Happy", screamed Jake over the motor noise and sounds of traffic. Next selection. "Oh baby, we have got the greatest hits on earth, from 1970, the Ides of March, riding in that black sedan and baby, I'm you're vehicle" was the next song. Turning the corner with the car chugging along, Jake put on the next song. "There's a lot that's going on in this tune, from 1958 the Diamonds and "Little Darling". Jake smiled and was very happy. "One more and you're done" said Adrienne. "Okay", relented Jake, "Gonna make it a good one, from 1975, the Eagles, one of my all time best, actually folks my all time third favorite, "One of These Nights". Right to where the blaring instrumentals ended and the vocals started Jake hit the mark perfectly. This is what he did as a child who loved broadcasting and now as an adult who reveled in those memories. "I still got it!!!" Jake proclaimed boasting about his announcing skills. Adrienne retorted with her usual jibe, "You got it but nobody wants it!!".

The remark was typical of Adrienne and Jake's relationship. She centered him, made him a little less impetuous and brought him down to earth. Adrienne did that to a lot of people. Her even handed approach to things was a throwback to the days when people actually thought things out. She was perfectly happy to sometimes stand in Jake's shadow helping him quietly, steering him in the right direction and watching him grow. Adrienne was extremely close to her father whose temperament she inherited. Unlike her sometimes rigid mother and very gregarious sister, Adrienne tread easily but effectively within her inner circle. Both Adrienne and Jake kept an extremely small close knit group of friends. The two were also not above jettisoning certain ones if they did not return the same things the couple gave. Adrienne's only problem with Jake's circle was that he never really, ever befriended an ugly woman. But even that propensity subsided during her challenging accident recovery.

Adrienne's brain injury changed the couple in many ways. It made Jake more supportive and aware of the true treasure he had in Adrienne. Ironically this devotion would also prime him, not only for his wife but for any other relationship he'd enter into. But neither could not foresee that happening. Jake was truly devoted to his wife and she to him. But their needs were quite different. While Adrienne needed emotional support and things to aid her in her recovery, Jake's concerns were superficial. Adrienne's question was "How am I going to feel?" Jake was, "How am I going to look?" The couple lived a supportive and loving existence. To the outside world, their marriage may have seemed odd. To them, it worked perfectly.

Sometimes when couples face catastrophic events, the change sinks them. Unlike other duos that would be challenged by this, Jake and Adrienne reveled in the changes. Adrienne became more of a force in public, the stigma of the brain injury almost giving her an excuse to be more opinionated and vocal. She used to sit silently when people she deemed as intellectual inferiors espoused stupid, non provable theories. Now she let them have it with both barrels. The new Adrienne was both stronger and weaker. She came on more forcefully for what she believed in but became more stressed and weaker after a fully loaded workday that involved dealing with the public. Jake on the other hand reveled in being the help-mate. The two filled the gaps each had and because of that, their marriage grew despite Jake's eye for women.

Adrienne understood the frustration Jake had in terms of his career. Adrienne had her own problems with her position but at least it was always consistent. Jake was always in the mode of rebuilding various relationships at new places of work. For a person who was as his true friends said, "an acquired taste", this could be exasperating. Adrienne dealt with that side of Jake. But she was also dealing with herself too. She began to see that her role was limited in what she could do in the world and how she could accomplish things. Adrienne no longer felt guilty about not getting things done on time or for not having the perfect home. Her main focus was to get through the day in one piece emotionally and physically. Jake was of great help to her in this aspect of the relationship. As far as her intellectual skills, Jake told her they were still there but needed more of a jump start now. When Adrienne complained that she could no longer react as nimbly as she once did before, Jake's only comment was "Now you're like the rest of the world".

During Adrienne's recovery Jake worked as a substitute school teacher. He was very popular among the students but the openings for his skills were just not there. As his wife got stronger, Jake decided to take on a new career, one that he could carry with him into his old age. Every Sunday, as Jake and Adrienne rode the highways of Northeastern Pennsylvania, Adrienne had to listen to the same staccato voice talking up the instrumental leaders on the CD player. As Jake intoned his faux broadcasts and recited verbatim radio ads from years gone by, Adrienne suggested that her husband get back into broadcasting. For a while the suggestion like many of hers to him had fallen on deaf ears. But rather than nag or pout like other women, Adrienne let the thought settle into Jake's mind. She used this tactic in her firm, tactful encounters with disgruntled customers. Plant the seed and then let them think it was their idea all along. One day as Jake played some Temptations on the CD, he said to Adrienne, "I saw an ad that looked pretty interesting in the daily newspaper for sales at Power 108, I think it might be a good idea for me to apply, what do you think?" he asked as the song, "Just My Imagination" blared on his car stereo, Adrienne, leaning against the car door, adjusting her body to face him said as they rode along, "I think that's one of the best ideas you've ever had".

Jake carefully took the resume and faxed it from the old machine to Power 108. He was tired of working for the tiny newspaper owned by a former record producer who really had no concept of the local news business. Jake needed a change in jobs very quickly. Plus Adrienne was tired of Jake bringing home cash dropped into his briefcase by the misguided businessman. Concerned there would be tax troubles, she urged Jake to get another position.

For close to 15 years Jake had avoided his first love-radio. Now he was sending out a resume to work for Power 108 as a sales rep. He wanted a product to sell. And Power 108 was one of the most well known stations in the market. The success of the station came about because of consistency in format, promotions and logo. The Power 108 logo, navy blue outlines with red letters against white was on every car in this section of Pennsylvania. It never changed. On the surface it was a brilliant marketing ploy. It was the anchor of an ever-changing radio market. Below the surface though the real reason for the lack of change was the penurious policies of Big Bob Little. The radio station always lost money so any new investment in a promotion was unthinkable. In a strange sort of way, this cheapness paid off.

The morning team of Thomas & Jefferson were familiar voices with their wry antics and practical jokes. Plus the classic rock music of the 60s was now what the adult consumers between the ages of 25 and 54 listened to. Jake felt that this was a good career move for him image-wise. Adrienne thought a stable paycheck with health care benefits would be a good thing too.

For two weeks Jake waited for a response to his fax. Finally, Wally Peterson the sales manager from Power 108 called to set up an interview. Unlike many job applicants, Jake enjoyed interviews. It pumped him up plus gave him an opportunity to talk about himself. He loved the questions that required insights and fresh thinking. Essentially it was a way for Jake to intellectually show off. His meeting with Peterson was filled with bantering, jocular humor and theories on broadcasting. Jake left the Power 108 building convinced he had the job.

An entire month went by until Jake heard from Power 108 again. It turned out that Peterson's father had passed away. Jake's second interview came about only after he had called the station on his own. On the day Jake came to that meeting, he met Pete Cassidy, a man dressed in a suit but wearing a Cleveland Indians hat. Jake later learned that Cassidy wore the hat while he waited in anticipation for another hair piece. Easily talking about baseball and Jake's beloved Cleveland

Indians the job applicant began to make an impression with the staff. Cassidy was given the job of giving Jake a tour of the radio station. The facility was something out of old time radio with a huge 200 seat auditorium as well as cavernous studios that housed semi-modern equipment. Jake began to recognize some of the radio equipment and began to catalogue it for his tour guide. "Oh shit" said Pete to Jake. "You really love radio don't you, I mean you know this stuff, the equipment and all, that's a good and bad thing". Jake asked Cassidy why. "Well, if you know and love the business, in sales you come across as being genuine and that's a good thing. But if you have such a passion for it, sometimes the stuff you see here will drive you nuts". The tour began in the lobby and continued through a circular pattern passing various studios, offices and facilities that looked like they were allergic to both broom and brush. After completing the full circle of Power 108's facilities including its AM station and FM Oldies outlet, Pete deposited Jake in General Manager's Tim Higgins' office where Wally Peterson sat waiting.

The two shook hands and Peterson explained that this was the final interview process. He intimated that if Tim Higgins thought Jake was okay, Jake had the position. Wally Peterson was a strapping blond young man who was a chef in another life. He ascended quickly to the position of Sales Manager and reminded

Jake a little bit of Wally Cleaver from the "Leave It To Beaver" program. The sales manager combined an earnestness and wry sense of humor that served him well in his position. Jake was looking forward to working with Wally. He felt comfortable with him as his boss. His thoughts were interrupted when Tim Higgins entered the room. Higgins was a thin man wearing a sport coat with a huge shock of brown hair topping his frame. Higgins explained all about the radio station, told Jake his plans and interrogated Jake on numerous sales scenarios. Rising to the occasion, Jake began to intellectually preen but stopped short a few times, when he read (accurately) that Higgins was not interested in being over-shadowed. After an hour, Higgins looked gravely at Jake and said, "Now comes the hard part of the interview, understanding a client's humor. I'm going to tell a joke to Wally here and how you respond will decide if you get the job," said Higgins looking intently at Jake. Jake nodded nervously. Wally Peterson said to Higgins, "Did you hear about the butcher who left his wife?" Higgins arched forward and said, "No, I most certainly did not". Peterson continued with the punch line, "Well he ended up going to clown school!!!!!". The two men laughed uproariously at the joke. In real fact it was no joke at all but the two men were slapping their knees and had tears in their eyes. While Jake thought the joke was stupid, he laughed anyway at the sight of these two men carrying on. As quickly as the laughter began, it ended just as soon. Jake was still chucking when Peterson looked at him and said "It isn't that funny, are you some kind of dick?" And at that point Higgins went into another fit of laughter along with his sales manger. After what seemed an eternity Higgins stood up and said to Jake, "welcome to Power 108". Peterson added, "We expect big things from you young man" Jake found that amusing since he was 8 years Wally's senior. As Jake rode down the elevator, he felt good about the fact that he was back in broadcasting, albeit sales. He would have a stable weekly paycheck, health care benefits as well as a normal 8am to 5pm existence. As he went outside and walked down the street he turned to look at the radio tower on top of the storied old broadcast building. When he was a young boy at Christmas he'd take the bus to see the tower lit like a tree. This was going to be a new start for Jake's career. As he entered his car he noticed a young woman in a short skirt walking toward the radio station. He nodded hello and she smiled back at him flirtatiously. Jake surmised she was an employee or a prize winner, either way he looked at the incident as a sign of good things to come. The new job at Power 108 would prove to be life changing for him. It would confirm a few things he knew about himself and reveal a few he didn't.

PART TWO

Jake's first day at Power 108 was anything but a smooth start. He was put in a dingy office and told to make up a client list of 100 business places that he wanted to call on. Taking off his trademark double breasted suit coat, Jake set out to make his dream list which he was sure would make him rich. Throughout the day no one came and checked on him. At the end of the day he went into Wally Peterson's office and handed him the list. Peterson went through it in a matter of minutes, crossing out 96 of the 100 names Jake had painstakingly added. "They're all taken, here's a different phone book and start up again tomorrow" said the genial sales director Peterson. Day two was no different but this time Jake had the opportunity to meet some of his co workers. Amanda Dickens started the same day as Jake and she was given the job of selling the American Standards AM station. Jake was a little jealous because he did not particularly like classic rock and preferred the good old songs. But Peterson told him more money could be had with Power 108. Amanda joined Jake in the office and they both worked at their lists. "You know this is bullshit" Amanda declared after 1pm. "Just do it" said Jake. "They most likely have a plan for us". Pete Cassidy came in to check on the two rookies and

Jake engaged him in talk about the Indians again. One by one that day Jake met the sales reps who seemed very friendly and effusive to the new guy. The only person who seemed distant was Jody Mecklenburgh. Jake was at first insulted by this because he was told she was the top producer plus friend and mentor to one and all. It bothered him that she was cold. Jake later found out that on the day he started at Power 108, Jody was going through a painful personal situation in her life regarding an aging parent.

At the end of day two, Wally Peterson called him into the office. Peterson said that the company was enrolling every sales rep in a training program that would maximize their earning potential. The 8 week program was called the Radio Selling Associate degree or RSA. Jake readily agreed to the program and eagerly accepted the terms of the weekly assignments. He was only too willing to show off his knowledge but at the same time was grateful he did not have to work for the tiny weekly paper where he wasn't sure if he'd get paid on time or at all. Jake's sales counterparts were not as enthusiastic as he was. All griped about the fact that there were night time assignments and were not happy. It didn't help to have Tim Higgins address the weekly sales meetings calling the reps "Lazy and used to working in a country club environment". Against this backdrop of low morale, unhappiness and disorganization, Jake did what he did best. He cheerfully endured and put a positive face on just about everything. Wally Peterson, and to a certain extent Higgins appreciated his support while his co-workers were thankful for the cover Jake provided them by his upbeat company attitude.

After a month on the job, Jake finally hit the road singing the praises of Power 108. He rode first with Pete Cassidy who explained in brief detail what his career would be like. "We're like a baseball team" said Pete driving his huge cherry red Buick. "We all have our roles, Tracey's the hot chick with the good bod that can get gyms on the air. D.J. is the bulldog who when a customer shoots him down the first time, goes back and deliberately asks for more money. Jody is the top seller and gets all of the grief but big orders too. I'm the seasoned veteran who knows the business inside and out and I see you as a type of transition guy, a bridge between the young people on this staff and the entrenched ones because of your personality", recounted Cassidy. Jake thought Pete Cassidy's observations were right on and was comforted by his perception of what his role would be at Power 108. This assignment was nothing new to Jake, all his life he had bridged different worlds. Even in high school, he was embraced by diverse elements of his class because he made no moral judgments and offered his sunny disposition to all who wanted to bask in it.

Another thing Jake enjoyed about the job was the interaction with the on air staff. An old radio hand himself, Jake was given the opportunity to work weekends as a board man for the oldies station which carried the NASCAR races. Armed with some technical expertise, Jake helped set up remote broadcasts for Power 108 as well. His knowledge of politics made him a popular mainstay during discussions of national import and his handle on sports endeared him to the hard rockers Bulldog and Fontana who manned the afternoon shift at Power 108. Fontana asked Jake if he wanted to get in on an in house rotisserie football league. Leaping at the chance, Jake confounded many of the other participants by some of his picks. The method behind his madness was to pick uniform colors, not necessarily the players who were offered in the draft. However as the season progressed his football judgment proved vindicated. One day, three months into his job, Jake received an urgent message from Wally Peterson while he was on the road. Jake rushed back to the studios sure something was wrong. On the way up to the station, Jake grabbed a copy of the Scranton Record, a perk for all of the employees in the building. It was a knee jerk reaction to the situation but if he was going to be fired, Jake at least wanted a jump start on the classifieds. Entering the lobby, Jake was met by a grim faced Wally Peterson. He motioned to his office, escorting Jake inside and shut the door behind him. Jake steeled himself for the bad news. Wally Peterson sat behind the desk, eyes down cast and said "We have a serious situation that I need to talk to you about that requires your utmost cooperation". By this time Jake's insides were tumbling like an acrobat's. He stared intently at his boss. Peterson brought his head up, looked at Jake and intoned the words, "Keenan McArdle!" Jake looked at him blankly. "I need to obtain Keenan McArdle in the Fantasy Football league. I'll give you Bret Farve, Hugh Douglas, Jerry Rice and Marshall Faulk. Even up. Four guys for one. You're number three in the standings, this could put you over the top into number one" said Peterson sweat beading on his forehead.

"What place are you in?" asked a relieved but mildly shocked Jake. "I'm dead last man but the way I calculate it, even with losing those four guys I can jump from 17th to 4th place in just one week, " said his sales manager. "Why not this" Jake suggested. "I'll give you McCardle, you keep your 4 guys, let me pick a replacement player and give me the Brian Besser Auto account." Peterson looked at him and said, "Are you suggesting I give you a great account in a trade for a Fantasy Football player? That's crossing the ethical line Yanick, I thought you were a better man than that, get the fuck out of my office". Jake tried to explain himself but Peterson was having none of it. Jake went back to his desk and actually began to peruse the want ads in the paper. A half hour later Peterson walked in and threw the Brian Besser Auto account folder at Jake. "You keep Rice and Farve, I keep Faulk and Douglas, I get McCardle, you don't get a replacement draftee and make sure you call John Batt, Besser's agency down in Atlanta tomorrow on this file here, he'll be expecting your call" said Peterson. "Okay" said Jake putting aside the want ads and looking at the lucrative file which was bestowed on him by his boss. Jake smiled to himself as he said slowly to himself out loud, "Thank you very much Mr. Keenan McCardle whoever the hell you are!!".

Jake enjoyed the pace of his work at Power 108. The lowest rung on the ladder was a tough place to be but he worked hard at moving up. A requirement for success in the radio industry was developing new clients and Jake tried hard to close new deals. His constant participation in the RSA seminars did not go unnoticed by his superiors either. The rep began to forge professional friendships with Tim Cassidy, Jody Mecklenburgh as well as their mutual friend from Shawnee Broadcasting, Jim Poppinaro. The busy work schedule plus the addition of joining a gym kept Jake's opportunities for womanizing at a minimum. The closest thing he had to an assignation were his weekly lunches with a Power 108 intern named Heather Spence. She was all of 23, tall, thin, nubile with a cutting personality. Heather and Jake were thrown together in his first week at Power 108 in that dingy office, and bonded. Both talked about many things during that period and when they lunched, Heather gently chided him for looking at older women instead of ones her age. Jake told her that at his age he was certain no one younger would have anything to do with him but Heather told him not to rule that out entirely. This flattered him to no end but he promptly forgot about it when Heather returned to school to finish her degree.

All of his life Jake possessed a sunny optimism that saw him through most things. However there was a two edged sword to this gift. Jake was so hell-bent on making himself and others feel good that he missed the nuances of negativity that at times precipitated a huge problem. Such was the case at Power 108. Jake was so grateful for his job that he was oblivious to the mutinous conditions at the radio station. The team of Thomas and Jefferson were not happy with the extra work required of them on personal appearances. The program director's people skills were non existent, and the station's revenues were down. Poor Wally Peterson was being blamed for the slide in fortunes and expressed his dismay to Jake one day in their weekly meeting. "These sales people are my friends" Wally told Jake. "And they aren't taking me seriously, they're not working and I know they're taking advantage of me". Jake was about to respond but felt Wally needed to vent. He got the impression that Tim Higgins was blaming Wally for everything wrong with the station and he soon learned that his theory was not far off the mark.

In the meantime, things at Shawnee Broadcasting down the highway were also in turmoil. The stations were bought by the mega giant Fortress Broadcasting and most of their sales people were unhappy with the changes. Jody Mecklenburgh got daily reports from Jim Poppinario about the trouble, but it was agreed that Shawnee's concerns were small time compared to the chaos at Power 108. Tim Higgins was storming around the facility doing a psychotic two step. On one hand he denigrated his staff ranting and raving at their incompetence. Then shifting gears he played games of hide, seek and scare with employees all the while laughing like a maniac. No one knew what to expect of him or his leadership anymore.

Despite these problems, Power 108 held its Radio Selling Associates seminar for local business at a nearby hotel. There were over 150 broadcast clients there along with 10 radio reps from other stations who wanted to see what the alternative rockers were up to. The hostility and tension were evident in the room. The only comic relief came when Penelope Hartz sashayed into the gathering and Jake made a beeline to meet her. Jody Mecklenburgh, in whom Jake confided his fidelity failings whispered loudly after him, "Jake

Yanick, stay away from that". Other than that tidbit, the seminar seemed like a death march with the current management leading the parade.

The much ballyhooed business that was supposed to be generated from the seminar never came. Power 108 struggled on into the holiday season. The radio station hosted a huge Santa Parade and Jake drove his convertible in the cold winter air with AM morning host Clyde Kozer and Fontana riding in his back seat waving to the crowds. At one point in the parade Heather Spence, the intern materialized to greet the trio. As the car idled Heather complained of the bitter cold on her ears. Jake quickly took off his warm stocking hat and gallantly offered it to the pretty young girl. She eagerly accepted giving him a buss on the cheek. Fontana looked at Kozer with mock disgust and said to Jake "We got a new motto for you...... "Anything for a chick!" All three laughed but Jake knew deep down how true Fontana's comment was.

On the day after the parade, at 4pm, Wally Peterson called his sales staff into a meeting and announced his resignation. The only one in the room stunned was Jake who had not seen this coming. Most of the Power 108 staff were used to this and truth be told, numb to it. Peterson said his good byes to the staff and went on his way. Jake went to a bar that night and ran into Jim Poppinaro. Both talked about the events at Power 108, agreed to get together for the holidays and ended the evening by speculating who the next sales manager at the station would be. Poppinaro said the most likely candidate would be Jim Duncan, the recently deposed sales manager from Shawnee Broadcasting. Jake remembered Duncan from his college days when he interned at Shawnee Broadcasting. He hoped that would put him in good stead with his new boss. A few months of job continuity was all Jake had under the Peterson regime, now a new era would begin and along with it the uncertainty of proving himself to a new boss.

The paths of Jake Yanick and Jim Duncan crossed once before. Jake was a college intern and Duncan was a Vietnam War vet who applied for a sales job at WSUN radio, then the gigantic number one radio station in the market. In the 60s it wasn't easy to be hired as a radio sales rep, especially at the number 1 station in the market like "The Nifty 1050". One had to have at least five years experience before they even got a look. Duncan, not knowing this rule walked into the Shawnee radio headquarters and asked for a sales job. Taken aback, the management rebuffed him initially and then to add insult to injury, asked the young vet exactly what qualified him to work in the then prestigious organization. Duncan said evenly, "I don't want you to hire me because I'm a returning vet but I do think you should pick me because I served as a watch commander. There is no set job description to be one of those guys except that you must be prepared for everything. And it seems to me in a sales job you have no idea what the day might bring, especially if you have a demanding client. The reaction to anything that can be thrown at me is the main reason why you should give me this job". Amidst much ballyhoo, Duncan was hired and parlayed his low key, intelligent style into a successful management career which took him to various parts of the country including a stint in the mid 1980s at Power 108.

The hallmark of Duncan's success was that he knew the two things reps craved were continuity and consistency. He hired people with his gut. If they had heart and determination he instantly gravitated toward them. If they were caught being lazy, made him look bad, or did not follow his program, Duncan let them go without a blink of the eye. Anyone who worked for Duncan and followed his rules would have a career for life. At Shawnee Broadcasting Duncan had built a team of diverse sales professionals that broke all financial records in the market. If Duncan asked them to march barefoot through a freezing blizzard, every rep, to a person would acquiesce to his wishes. When Duncan was hired by Tim Higgins to replace Peterson, the phone calls started coming in to Power 108 the very afternoon word got out that he was hired. Reps like Jim Poppinaro, Penelope Hartz, Don Norris, and Kenny Kelso rang the receptionist at Power 108, leaving their names and call back numbers for Duncan. It was a clear sign of unconditional loyalty and blind confidence. They were ready to give up their present livelihoods to follow the deposed boss into uncharted territory.

By the end of his first week, Duncan had recruited 8 members of the Shawnnee sales teams. This meant that the Power 108 radio stations had to make room for the new staff by eliminating some currently entrenched players. Duncan rarely fired anyone mainly because his program, while simple was very rigid. Upon seeing Duncan's plan, a seasoned sales person would know then and there if they could become a member of "Team Duncan". By the end of the second week, more than 5 Power 108 reps left the station.

On paper Jake and Duncan should have gotten along fine. When Jake was in college, he interned at "The Nifty 1050." While he was thrilled to be in the company of world class broadcasters like Little Johnny Walker and Tommy McMurtry, he also got a tour of duty on the sales force. Jake remembered clearly the first time Duncan, as a rep himself drove the intern to Kragan's Kashway in the Poconos. Duncan had no recollection of Jake or the incident. With Jake's newfound love of career rigidity and formula plus Duncan's willing imposition of it when it came to radio, the conventional wisdom was that Duncan and Jake would hit it off. They did not.

All of his life Jake had to work for acceptance into any circle he attempted to enter. He maintained that it was his physical appearance. Pete Cassidy knew otherwise. Cassidy dubbed Jake as "an acquired taste", one who grew on others. Cassidy felt that Jake's booming personality and GQ type appearance in a non-fashion-model type package projected an affected front. Once people got to know the real Jake their perception of him as a preening, pompous know-it-all melted away. Both Cassidy and Jody Mecklenburgh were appalled when they heard that Duncan wanted to jettison Jake from Power 108. For whatever reason, Duncan had no use for Jake Yanick. One night shortly before the Power 108 January Holiday party, Duncan called Jake into his office and told him he had a great deal of work to do in order to survive. Jake was devastated. Quietly he withdrew into a timid mass of despair. His sales numbers took a major dive. But it didn't last.

Whatever one had to say about Jake Yanick the one thing everyone would agree upon was that he refused to be defeated. Like winning the heart and mind of a beautiful woman no one thought he could attain, Jake persevered all the more when it looked like he was going down for the count. The more impossible the task, the harder he worked. Duncan presented him with a formidable roadblock and Jake set about chipping at the cold hard stone before him. Tim Duncan was appalled at what he found at Power 108 in terms of sales strategy. There were some reps using old school methods, others like Jake utilized the Wally Peterson inspired RSA scheme while many floundered around with no clear direction. At Jim

Duncan's first meeting, he gathered all of the sales material everyone was using and threw them into a huge garbage can in the middle of the stage in the Power 108 auditorium. Duncan then told everyone he was starting from scratch no matter how much people made. He had the support staff design Orange loose leaf binders filled with sales maxims he either appropriated, thought up himself or refined throughout his career. It was elementary work that insulted some of the seasoned reps. People like Pete Cassidy were in open revolt feeling Duncan was talking down to them. Duncan for his part saw that Power 108 was so far down, it had to go up just by osmosis. But like a successful political candidate, the radio station had to project one message instead of many. His plan was met with great reluctance and a few reps derided Duncan behind his back. Jake was way past the point of thinking he knew everything even though he projected that image. After Duncan told him his head was on the chopping block, Jake instead of retreating to the back of the room during sales meetings took a seat next to Duncan. He dutifully wrote down every single pronouncement his boss made. Slowly Duncan began to warm to Jake. Little things meant a lot to Duncan. One time during a projected blizzard, Duncan told everyone not to return to the station for the afternoon wrap ups. The foul weather never materialized and Duncan expected everyone back to work because the roads were clear. No sales rep returned except Jake Yanick. The glacier between Jake and Duncan melted one morning when no member of the sales staff had memorized Duncan's homework assignment. Against the back drop of smoldering anger by his sales manager, Jake calmly raised his hand, stood up before the group and gave the entire 5 minute "Feel, Felt, Found" sales presentation so embraced by Duncan. Jake was flawless, every single word memorized, every nuance accented just as Duncan wanted. After he was finished Duncan looked at Jake and simply said "Thank you". Once the meeting was over though and the reps were going back to their desks Duncan commandeered the loud speaker in the station and effusively praised "Jake Yanick is the man of the hour, the most brilliant student I ever molded and shaped!!!!!" Both Kenny Kelso and Don Norris, two Duncan recruits from Shawnee, sauntered over from the Oldies sales side and told him that this action by Jake was "huge". After this day Jake's relationship with Duncan was marked by mutual respect, admiration and kindness rarely seen in a boss/employee relationship. Duncan and his wife even sent a sympathy card when Jake's beloved dog Monty passed away. Jake had mentioned to Duncan that he memorized his sales speeches when he took his ailing pup for a walk. Unlike the earlier incident between the two men at Kragan's Kashway, Duncan remembered this.

Throughout the next year, Jake's career at Power 108 remained stable. He did exceptionally well selling for the AM Popular Standards station as well as Power 108. Duncan aided him immensely by forgiving an outstanding draw against salary and giving him a heads up on new business accounts that wanted to use Power 108. Despite his rocky start, his wife's rehabilitation from a brain injury which sometimes consumed him, and the daily grind of getting new advertisers Jake was riding high as one of Duncan's team members. But when Jake had no crisis in his life and things were handled, his focus and eye began to wander. This time it was in the direction of a tall blonde radio rep working for the competition down the road. During lunches at the 747 Diner, Jim Poppinaro, the conduit between Power 108 and the new Fortress Broadcasting company stations provided Jake with the details of the intriguing Ms. Penelope Hartz. That would be akin to giving a can of gasoline to a pyromaniac.

Jim Poppinaro was a truly unique individual. He was an imposing man physically with dark, handsome features that would make him look at home in Venice. He grew up outside of New York in a suburb. His father, a policeman, did not want his son involved in that occupation. From the start Poppinaro loved politics and radio. A devout Republican, Poppinaro had a great appreciation for radio news. Schooled by Holy Cross fathers, Poppinaro eschewed their campaign to have him enter the priesthood and decided that broadcasting was going to be his career. Unlike others involved in the business, Poppinaro had an over inflated idea of just who could qualify to be a radio sales advertising representative. He had such an exalted view of the trade that he earned a Masters Degree in Business/Corporate Administration to prepare him for the career. His first stop after achieving his degree was Power 108. He teamed With Jody Mecklenburgh to bring the rock station to parity and market respectability in terms of revenue. The personality he conveyed as well as his ability to tell a yarn earned him the nickname "Poppy." Poppy heavily relied on Jody for friendship. Poppy and Jody were like a long lost brother and sister. Their enduring kinship made them recognizable in the market as mentors to new radio reps. One aspect of this frustrated Poppy very much because there were no clear educational requirements for radio sales people. Poppy got his masters thinking it would be needed. Much to his chagrin he found that in a way, even at the management level, he was overqualified.

Poppy was a great guy to have at any gathering. His fast wit and sharp memory gave him instant recall of entertaining stories that enthralled his audience. Poppy was known for his performances but equally famous for his OCD tendencies. Extremely fastidious, Poppy once rented a hotel room in Vegas just because he did not want to use the public rest rooms. He constantly washed his hands raw, then after leaving the men's room walked down the corridor with his hands turned upward like a surgeon going in to operate. He used radio station restaurant trade policies as a personal fiefdom. Poppy dined out almost every night and made certain that his clients had more than enough promotions to make up for his meals. He was a master at it, but more importantly his clients always had good things to say about him. Poppy's time at Power 108 was so successful and lucrative that he was recruited by Shawnee Broadcasting to start up its

Urban hip hop station. Poppy acquired clients for the new facility by charm, persuasion and by his relationship with his fellow rep, Jody Mecklenburgh. Though working at competing stations, both doubled-teamed unsuspecting advertisers to get huge buys which made them both successful and fairly wealthy. Poppy used Jody as a social crutch. He'd accompany Jody and her husband to various events. Poppy's relationship with women was one of awkward wanting, failed attempts and unsteady assignations that yielded marginal results. Poppy, handsome and vigorous always got the first date but rarely had an encore. This was in stark comparison to Jake who had to lobby hard for the initial offering but then had no problem with the follow up.

Jake first met Poppy at a remote at Dixon Furniture Outlet. DFO was Jody and Poppy's mutual client. Jody asked Jake to bring the pizza for the broadcast featuring Thomas & Jefferson. These remotes were numerous because of the relationship Jody and Poppy had with the buyer. No more than 12 people showed up at any given time during the program and almost always they were the same individuals looking for a free outing featuring CDs, pizza, soda, and the omnipresent Power 108 bumper stickers. Despite that, the client seemed happy with the buys, Thomas & Jefferson got a talent fee and Jody and Poppy flourished.

Entering the store with the pizza the first thing he spied was Jody hitting a large man outstretched on a sofa. Poppy was making himself comfortable. "Quit hitting me will ya?" he screamed. "Poppy" Jody said in a conspiratorial voice. "The store manger doesn't need to see your fat ass and shoes on his sofa. Now get up". Poppy complied. Jody introduced Jake to Poppy. Jake instinctively put out his hand but Poppy refused it. Jody explained about Poppy and Jake, always the first to smell a snub, reluctantly understood. Both men sat and conversed about radio, politics, the state of the economy and the world. They both found a common ground of intelligence that was rare in the world of broadcast sales. After the remote, Jody and Poppy invited Jake to Sirens for a drink.

Sirens was a downtown sports bar located caddy corner from Power 108. Most of the local politicos, sports figures and media people hung out there. It did not matter that competing radio reps drank together or for that matter slept together. There were no secrets among the sales people except for how much money each received from a client. This was sealed information kept under lock and key. No one knew anyone else's budget. That lack of information ironically kept everyone competitive. Jody, Poppy and Jake sat down at a table and began to rehash the idle gossip they spoke of earlier. Poppy ordered a Manhattan, Jody and Jake ordered a diet soda. As they conversed, Poppy's attention wandered over to the buffet table. "Who is that?" Poppy exclaimed loudly. "That's Stacey Macey, she works with us. She's a new rep. Look Poppy, she's over there with Penelope," said Jody. Poppy sat upright, cupped his mouth with his hands and bellowed across the room to Penelope, "I love chicken breasts, I brush my teeth with Crest, but when all's said and done, Penelope's hooters are the best". Both women at the buffet table turned around. Stacey looked stunned, Penelope, at first outraged, smiled at Poppy. The tall woman began to make her way toward their table. The only way to describe Penelope's walk was that of a strutting model who was proud of what she had. Stacey followed behind her. Both women were introduced to Jake, stopped and talked shop for a while, bantered and flirted with both Jake and Poppy, then went back to their table. There was silence as the women departed. This worried Jody. She knew that any absence of talk from Poppy was allowing him to do something more dangerous than speak and that was to think. Finally, Poppy said, "Wow, that Stacey is a looker. I'd really like to get to know her better but I have no shot". Jody readily agreed. Jake said, "Are you kidding me? Of course you have a shot……….." Jody jumped in and said alarm raising the level of her voice, "No he doesn't. Leave this alone." Jake ignored her and went on. "See Poppy with a woman like her, you have to engage as a general would in a war. All those civil war generals, they had a plan. A consistent plan that was slow and steady in their pursuit" said Jake. Jody had her head in her hands at this point. "Right, right" said Poppy getting very excited. "A woman like her needs a war waged to win her heart" added Jake. "But I'm not good at strategy", countered Poppy. "I am" said Jake. Even though he was married, Jake reveled in helping other men win women. Throughout his marriage, Jake strayed but not for the reasons most men would. Jake saw the pursuit of beautiful, unattainable women as a vindication of how he viewed himself physically. The more beautiful the woman, the harder Jake pursued her. He was a master at it. But then when the chase ended, Jake was more than content to live his life with Adrienne. Jake was discreet but numerous times, particularly after he attained the woman and lost interest, repercussions would occur. They were minor but unsettling like having notes left on his car saying "Hope you're having fun" and "Die bastard die". Jake wanted to keep his marriage going, and he truly loved Adrienne but he could not resist the chase. To help out a fellow traveler like Poppy would only add to the intrigue.

As the two huddled, Penelope Hartz stopped by on her way out. Poppy bolted upright. Penelope said a few things and made a very big deal of brushing crumbs off the front of her ample bosom. She then seductively handed over her card to Jake while both Poppy and Jody watched. They had seen this act before. Jake graciously accepted and the tall blond strode out the bar with most of the men who were not acquainted with her giving her the eye. Poppy adored Penelope but couldn't get himself in gear to pursue her. He was convinced the two would be together but needed time. Poppy actually fixed Penelope up with men he hand picked to keep her occupied but not marriage ready. Poppy found Jake, a married man who loved the chase and not the conquest an ideal candidate to keep Penelope's motor running while he schemed to obtain her affections.

With Jody looking on disapprovingly, Poppy said he'd advocate for Jake with Penelope if Jake worked the war room to pursue Stacey. Jake thought he was getting too old for this type of gamesmanship and was going to refuse. Then he looked out the window and saw the Penelope Hartz strut. Despite himself, his commitment to his wife, his embracing of an uneventful life, Jake accepted. While the two boys made out their battle plan, an extremely worried Jody Mecklenburgh put aside her diet coke and ordered a double scotch. She knew this was not going to end well.

Poppy went to work to get Penelope and Jake together. For his part, Jake asked Stacey to check over Poppy and she agreed. The initial foray between the two turned into a disaster with Poppy nodding off in the middle of the dinner. Jake and Penelope's match went much smoother. Always one to judge a situation and then adapt, Jake (after meeting Penelope at a mall shortly before the holidays) found that like most women in business, Penelope wanted to be taken seriously. Since Jake's career in radio sales was brief in comparison to hers, he decided he needed a mentor. Penelope Hartz would fit that bill.

For her part, Penelope was charmed by Jake's interest, his easy going demeanor and his total focus on whatever she was saying. Jake utilized one of his greatest tools with women, and that was "the gaze". This technique was a long standing part of Jake's bag of tricks. He developed it when dating an attention hungry ex weathercaster when his wife had thrown him out years before. "The gaze" had Jake's elbows on a hard surface, his hands lightly cupping his chin. His body leaned forward slightly and his line of vision concentrated directly on the woman's face. There was no movement whatsoever, just an intense, locked in-stare that portrayed his interest. Three naked fan dancers could be walking by, but Jake would be focused on whatever words were coming from the woman seated across from him.

Penelope and Jake first met for lunch. It went well. Both told their stories, talked about the people they worked with, bantered about mutual clients and shared stories about their child hood. Jake found Penelope to be easy on the eyes, very smart in business and very religious. For her part, Penelope's take on her rival rep was that he was non threatening, easy to be with and conveyed a sense of security she had not seen in most men. The two started sharing stories and by all accounts a nice friendship started to bud. The two met every week for lunch. Both looked forward to the meetings. It was a safe relationship for both of them-no physicality, plenty of intellectual stimulation, no pressure and plenty of laughs often at the expense of their co-workers.

Poppy monitored Jake's progress in the Monday lunches the two men shared. This was a type of re-hash of game day, as when the coaches would have their Monday meeting after the big Sunday football game. Poppy, essentially living vicariously through Jake, pressed him for details and urged him to "take it to the next level". The trouble was that Jake had no desire to go to that area. The last thing he needed was an emotional attachment to complicate both his professional and personal life. In his way, this was Jake's attempt at fidelity to his wife. He viewed it as a weaning of his womanizing tendencies. It was not full blown faithfulness but on the other hand it wasn't out and out adultery either. Still, despite his reluctance, Poppy pushed. Jake ignored his pleas, enjoying the comfort of a lunch time matinee with a Suzanne Sommers look-a-like and tending to his ailing wife at night.

Despite his faults, Jake worked at being a kind man. Growing up in a poor but generous family, Jake saw the value of the extra effort and sweating the small things. He was the only radio rep to attend wakes of clients, send birthday cards to their kids and remember little nuances most people forgot. Penelope had given him a photo of herself and celebrity Richard Chamberlin. Excited at meeting him, she made copies for all of her friends and associates. Jake had it blown up into an 8 by 10 and on a rainy Saturday night drove to Bridgeport, Connecticut to have the star of stage and screen personalize an autograph on the photo. Jake presented this to Penelope on her birthday. To Jake it was a simple thought that had not cost him much money but gave him an intense feeling of satisfaction. It was a unique thought and gift no one else had bestowed. For Penelope, it was a token of esteem that brought tears to her eyes. She was amazed at the lengths Jake went to for this birthday gift. When Penelope attended her Friday night soiree with Poppy and her cronies (Jake avoided these noisy Friday gatherings primarily because he wanted to spend time with Adrienne and because he did not like to go to bars) she broke down in tears when she described the gift. "He reached me where no man has ever gone in a long time, he touched my heart but more importantly, my soul" she intoned. Kenny Kelso, Poppy's former co-worker at the station, a very handsome babe magnet rolled his eyes and laughed at his friend uproariously. Downing his martini, he turned toward Poppy and said sarcastically, "Poppy, have you ever reached into Penelope and grabbed anything?" Poppy was becoming alarmed. He had never seen Penelope like this before. Usually she made sport of her numerous suitors, but she didn't do that to Jake. Poppy who used Jake as a decoy now found that his plant was generating more interest than he could have imagined. This concerned him.

Both Poppy and Jake loved beautiful women. Unlike Kenny Kelso, both had to work to get the women to notice them. Poppy envied the way Jake went about his pursuit of women. While Poppy rushed right in and flopped, Jake methodically built himself up as the indispensable man no modern thinking woman should be without. The major difference was that Poppy cared too much about the outcome and Jake cared too much about the chase. The end result meant nothing to Jake. Had Poppy understood that, he would never have set into motion the events that for a while fractured the friendship between Penelope and Jake.

No one quite knows how it all started but all agree it was Poppy who was at the center of it. One cardinal rule Penelope had with everyone was that no one invaded her privacy at home. Jake wholeheartedly agreed with this concept. The two referred to their homes as their "castles of solitude". As corny as it sounded, it made perfect sense to the two radio reps who always had to be "on" during their work days. Neither Jake nor Penelope would even think about violating that trust.

One day Jake got a call from Poppy at Power 108. "Jake" said Poppy. "I have an emergency, rather Penelope does. It's urgent. She's not in the office today but she needs a dub dropped off for "Flannery's Market", can you do it?" Jake who had been accustomed to picking up tapes at rival radio stations readily agreed. Queenie Foxx, one of the sales managers at Fortress Broadcasting joked that Jake seemed more like an employee of their operation than 108's because of his frequent visits to pick up tapes. But there was a catch. Poppy told Jake he needed to take the tape directly to Penelope's house. Jake thought that odd and told Poppy so. Poppy persisted and said "It was a matter of life and death that Penelope received this tape". Jake agreed and Poppy gave him directions.

There are still differing versions about what happened. Penelope, who was off on the day in question was doing exercises in a spandex outfit when Jake arrived at the door. She claims she tripped on a piece of rug and fell toward Jake hitting her chin on his nose as he stood in the doorway. Jake claims that the big woman cold cocked him in the face, calling him a stalker and threatening to call the police if he did not get off her property. Either side you believe, Jake wound up with a bloody nose that stained his prized white DKNY shirt a violent red. When Jake showed her the dub of "Flannery's Market" Penelope informed him she was not the rep for Flannery's and that he should hit the road.

This little incident would have ended there had Jake not confided in Poppy about it. Poppy then related the details to Penelope's female sales rivals at the station who were only too glad to gossip at her expense. By 8am the next morning, Poppy had the story about Jake's assault from Penelope throughout the market. The spin was that Penelope was appalled that anyone had seen her "out of uniform". When Penelope came into the office, Poppy took her aside and claimed Jake was spreading the story. By late afternoon at Power 108, Jake's Manager Tim Duncan, a close friend of Penelope's took him aside and told his employee how upset she was that Jake was spreading stories about her. Jake was mortified.

Duncan, when he took over the reins at Power 108 still had working knowledge of what all of his former reps were doing. Jake related to Duncan what had happened and both men concluded that there was the hand of Jim Poppinaro in this mess. Duncan volunteered to call Penelope and set things right. Jake accepted the offer. A few days later, Duncan told Jake he had spoken to Penelope and that he had fixed things for him. His boss recommended that he phone Penelope to resume their friendship. Duncan, unknowingly had overstated the case. When Jake called Penelope he was greeted with an icy reception. Their strong friendship would one day resume. But for a while, both Jake and Penelope stayed at odds. Jake had become what he did not want to be in her eyes and everyone else's. He did not want to be a failed suitor because in his mind he was not. But the perception was there. Fall had turned into winter and two friends became casualties in a silly battle that existed because of this incident. Penelope barely looked at him when they had mutual business in the market and in a fit of pique, Jake stopped talking to Poppy. It wasn't until a Christmas party at Jody Mecklenburgh's husband's office that Poppy and Jake spoke. Poppy admitted his true feelings about Penelope and admitted he was worried about Jake's tactics toward her. The two men decided to forgive and forget and vowed to learn from this lesson. There was one nagging concern though for

Jake. Image. Most men didn't care what other women, especially the discarded ones thought of them. Jake's fatal flaw was that he did care. A lot. As the holidays approached, he mourned not so much the loss of a friendship but the chink in the armor disguised as his image. He was confident it would be repaired some day because Penelope was a fair and good woman. But time was the only way to heal this rift.

The social event of the entire season for broadcasting people was the Mecklenburgh Super Bowl party. The gathering was everything Jody and Jerry were, generous, friendly, gregarious and fun loving. In the competitive cut throat world of broadcasting, the party was a one time oasis of good solid fellowship. Sales reps that routinely stabbed each other in the back were pleasantly surprised to see that away from the media, these people actually were loved by either a spouse or a kid.

The party was going to be difficult for Jake because of the presence of Penelope Hartz. Penelope was the type of woman who made men crazy. In her 50s, she was tall, bright, engaging but had two annoying habits. One was that she acted dumber than she was and the second was that she was an incredible flirt. She would take a relatively worldly man and turn him into a 12 year old boy. Much to Jake's chagrin and shame, she did that to him. Jake, vulnerable for excitement after being a care-taker to his ailing wife leaped into the Penelope situation with gusto. He found her bright, engaging, but very volatile and passionate in her beliefs and ideas. Jake didn't like that aspect though, Jake liked the boredom of a friendship, the sameness.

Penelope on the other hand fed off the attention of many male suitors. She had been engaged 6 times but broke them all off at the last minute. It was said that she took a man to the edge of the creek but never allowed him to drink. When she was with you, Penelope was with you. But when she was bored of a man's shtick, she cut him off cold turkey. That was difficult for anyone concerned about image. To Jake, image was everything and Penelope had provided a wonderful and glamorous addition to that aspect of his personality. Jake's meetings with Penelope abruptly ended when Poppy, getting worried about Jake's intentions created a nasty misunderstanding with a mutual client of the two friendly but rival radio reps. Jake did not miss Penelope but missed the attention she gave him. He knew this friendship would be fleeting because he understood Penelope's monumental need for up close attention, a commodity he had no desire or energy to provide.

Jake didn't think Penelope ever realized what she did to various men like him but all her male victims certainly did. For Jake it was the embarrassment of being so goofy around her. Jake was too old for that type of infatuation. The key here was to make it appear that the Penelope Hartz situation had no effect on him. He had heard that every man had a Penelope Hartz recovery strategy and to save face, his would be two fold. The first part was to avoid her altogether and the second was that if he could not do the former, he'd have company whenever he encountered her. This meant he had to get someone female to accompany him to this Super Bowl party. Making this happen was easier said than done. His choices were very limited because Jake had been out of action for some time on the "lady front". Plus, Adrienne was still unavailable for huge social events due to her continued recovery.

A month prior to the party, Jake asked several women he knew to go with him. The obvious choice would be Jake's wife but for his spouse the entire month of January was spent on the couch in fits of sleep and depression. She was paralyzed by her inability to accept what she could accomplish mentally before the accident.

While Jake tended to her needs, he tried to get her socially engaged. Each time he tried to suggest something new, it turned into a disaster. The setting was either too loud or crowded and her recovery time from each tried foray would take days. Jake, while loyal to her, was on his own socially. Unlike other couples, Jake and his wife were not joined at the hip. It was common for the couple to go their separate ways via business trips, meetings and the like and reunite for quality time. The accident had turned that time into constant rehab and rest. And while Jake looked at it as a labor of love, it still was a labor. With his wife out of commission, Jake tried other female friends. A male buddy would not do. He had to make the point to Penelope that he was not like the other panting suitors pining away for her in solitude. Every person Jake asked either had plans, avoided the subject with him or just said no. Jake even lowered himself by stopping off at various happy hours that yielded disastrous results. It was the day before the party and Jake had not found anyone to accompany him. Like he did every day, Jake went to the gym. Always a big man, Jake was haunted by his size, his perception of himself as not handsome and the way his clothes fit. Jake could handle a brain injured spouse, a screaming client and solve most any problem with aplomb. He was strong in those areas, but weak in his comfort with his physical appearance. On the way to the gym, Jake thought at least he'd look half decent at the party, but nothing could change the fact that he would be going alone and he was sure Penelope Hartz would make note of that fact.

The gym Jake went to was a cardiac rehab center run by one of the hospitals. Jake went there to sweat and lose some weight, nothing more. His wife had introduced him to the modern facility. Jake liked his gym routine because he didn't have to be the big friendly media guy, he could sweat and grunt in anonymity. He struck up few conversations but recently had begun talking with a gangly girl who once approached him with concern while he was on the stair master. She thought he was having a heart attack. This tall woman with the engaging smile and Julia Roberts giggle was going to be Jake's last stand. Furthermore, he was going to try a novel approach this time, unusual for any man, especially one like Jake. He was going to be brutally honest with her. She sat down on the stationary bike next to him looking disheveled and awkward as always. Their conversation was compact with the young lady doing the asking and Jake responding.

"Hey.

Hey.

Wearing the Packer shirt today, they going to win tomorrow?

I hope so but I wouldn't care if Elway won.

Hey, Elway's cute.

Sure he is. That's always the key to victory.

Who crapped on your English muffin this morning?

If you must know, I'm a bagel man myself. But I have to go to a thing tomorrow and I don't want to go by myself.

Wow, I have to go somewhere tomorrow and I'm gonna be hating it too!" This time Jake asked the questions.

"Where do you have to go?

Well, I have three brothers and they are all married to these hideous women who hate me. They're having this annual Super Bowl party. It is a huge deal with hundreds of people I don't know and a few I do."

Instantly Jake deflated. Still another woman with plans, another dead end in his quest to show up Penelope. This time though a ragamuffin in ill fitting gym clothes was refusing him. How low could he go with this streak. Still, he decided to soldier on and present his plan.

"I have to go to this party with all the people who work in my industry.
Which is...............?
 Radio and TV, I work for power 108.
 My family is in the demolition business. I love Power 108. Billy Jefferson lives the town over from me. He's a scream. Sounds like fun. Why don't you want to go?
There's this woman that's going to be there. Our friendship ended badly. I don't want to go alone, I just don't want to walk into that party and have

her see me solo. I know it's dumb but I don't want to go alone.

You realize that you are acting very immature about this, right?

Absolutely!" This time, the red headed girl turned interrogator.

"This woman, did you treat her well?

Yes, very well.

Was she erratic in her actions?

Sometimes.

Did she have kids?

Three boys.

That explains it.

What?

When a woman has children, especially boys, the mental stress of the birth saps her energy and even some of her intelligence. As she ages, the woman's behavior becomes more erratic. You compound that with someone with an ego and you got problems.

Where did you get this stuff?

Italian scientists did a study of afterbirth and placentas and determined this was so.

You're nuts.

Hey, I'm not the one looking for a date to show off because I'm immature!

Point well taken. You want to go?

Well, let me ask a few questions.

Okay.

Have you ever been arrested?

No.

Ever hit a girl?

No.

Favorite song?

Will You Still Love Me Tomorrow by the Shirelles.

Love the kettle drum at the start of that song!

I do too. My second favorite song is.......

Don't care. Next question. Is your mom alive?

Yes.

Call her every day?

Yes.

Do you go to church?

Every week.

What type of cologne do you use?

Polo.

Okay, meet me at 4pm Sunday at Flannery's grocery store on Shadow Avenue. I'll see you there.

Where do you live?

In Simpson. About twenty five miles from here.

How did you wind up working out here?

Using my girlfriend's pass.

So you're real name is not Kimberly?

No it's Bernice but I hate my name. It's an old ladies name!

So what do I call you?

By my name, you dope! Bernice.

I appreciate you going. I hope you don't feel I'm using you to do this.

Hey, as long as there's good food, I don't care. and besides, I may ask you to come to my family's Super Bowl deal afterwards.

Sure.

You realize you are being very immature though, right?

I do.

Okay, as long as we got that straight."

Jake was elated. He would not have to walk into that party alone with Penelope and her posse of ordinary looking girlfriends chattering about how she pulverized his sorry emotional ass. Jake would walk in, nod a curt hello to Penelope, signal that he was doing fine without her and then waltz back out again.

Sunday came and Jake got ready for the party. He drove to the designated meeting spot and commenced to wait for his date's arrival. On time as usual, he settled in to wait. When 430pm rolled around, Jake got a bit concerned but then remembered he was not dealing with a sales rep nor a rocket scientist in the person of this Bernice, a.k.a. Kimberly. By 5pm, when there was no sign of her, Jake became worried. By 530pm, he was frantic. No sightings at 6pm either, by then he was beside himself. Jake considered himself the biggest loser on the planet. Bernice was right, he was not only immature but pretty pathetic. It took a kid in a gym to show him that by standing him up. His plan now was to go across the street to the

Sheraton hotel, use the bathroom and then go home to watch the game. Penelope had won her emotional war with him. The saddest part was that she was oblivious to the energy she caused him to waste in this endeavor and the pain that it caused him. As he walked out of the hotel, his cell phone rang. It was Bernice.

"Hey, it's me, I fell asleep in the bathtub. Do you still want me to come?

You fall asleep in your tub, Gosh I do that every couple of days, I thought I was the only one who did that!

No it's quite relaxing. Kind of like being in a mother's womb.

You're really fixated on this baby thing, huh?

Do you still want me to come and what do you want me to wear?

Yes I do and wear what you'd wear on a date.

I used to date this guy Richie who owned a lube shop so should I wear the beige coveralls or the navy?

Could you change a car's oil?

Sure but I know you can't.

Yeah, you're right. Wear what you wear when you want to....oh wear whatever you want.

I'm getting dressed and I'm on my way".

Jake looked around in disbelief and realized the

night was not going to be a total loss. About 20 minutes passed when he saw a red Escalade careering down the road. The car pulled beside him and Jake was stunned to see his gym buddy transformed into a Cinderella. Her red hair was flowing over her coat, her legs were longer than he had remembered seeing on the bike at the gym and her smile lit up the parking lot. She wore a navy skirt, pale blouse and looked like she stepped off a model's runway.

"How do I look?

Beautiful.

Really?

Yeah, how do I look?

You look nice. Do you dress like this all the time?

Pretty much.

Nice, now sir, what are my instructions for the evening?"

As Jake's car pulled away from the parking lot and headed toward the festivities on Doe Road in nearby Moscow, he simply said, "Just act as if you like me".

"Oh Christ" she answered, "you didn't tell me it was going to be this freaking' tough".

The party was hopping by the time they arrived. People were spilled out into the January cold at the house drinking all forms of alcohol, eating food, and watching the game on a myriad of TV sets set up by the hosting couple. They parked a block away and went through the back door. Jake let Bernice go first to guide her from behind winding their way through the crowd to see their hosts. Bernice had made him stop at a convenience story to get Jody flowers as a gift. When the two entered, there was a buzz but then it lowered when people saw them together. Quiet murmurs began to circulate as they made their way from the massive deck area to the inside of the home. Just then, the quiet was shattered by the unmistakable voice of Penelope Hartz who screamed at poor Jim Poppinaro, or Poppy as he was called. "You perverted sick bastard, we're leaving". The front door slammed hard and Penelope was out the door. She had not even seen Jake!!!! All this energy, all this planning and she went out the front door while Jake was coming through the back door!! As they entered the living room, the duo encountered Jody who while graciously accepting Bernice's flowers filled them in. "Poppy just called Penelope a lesbian again because she went to see "Titanic" with her girlfriends instead of him. So she just caused a scene and flew out the front door," " said Jody juggling the flowers and her 2 year old daughter. "You mean we missed meeting her?" Bernice asked grinning an impish grin that spoke volumes. Jody, figuring Jake's original motives nodded knowingly and said, "Yep, you missed her". At that point her baby started to grab at Jake and Bernice said "Babies like him huh?" and Jody proceeded to tell Bernice how Jake was an unofficial uncle.

"Pretty cool" commented Bernice.
At that point Jake left Jody and his date to talk while he got some drinks. Poppy approached Jake filled with too much wine and still stinging from Penelope's latest rebuff. "It's too bad Penelope didn't see you with that babe" he said loudly. "Is she a hooker, how much you paying her?" "Poppy, she's not a hooker and the reason why Penelope left is you called her a lesbian again. She was storming out the front while we came in the back," Jake said. Poppy continued, "Hey she's nice, she's not the girl from the gym, that girl was really homely and real tall, like a big old rag doll, I saw her there once when I was waiting for you".

"That's her", Jake replied. Just then Poppy screamed over at Bernice at the top of his voice "Hey, hey you over there, you're not as bad looking all dressed up as I thought you were. I thought you were pretty ugly there but you look nice!!!". It was another Poppy outburst, a symptom of his innocence and his OCD disorder. In shocked silence people waited for Bernice's response. She grabbed her heart and said, "At long last I can rest well at night because such a master gentleman says I made the cut". Doing a mock ballerina bow, she blew him a kiss and said, "I now have the broadcasting seal of approval." The stark contrast between the way Penelope and Bernice responded to Poppy was not lost on anyone.

The two then made the rounds of the party. All eyes were on the dumpy little fat guy with the glasses and this tall, friendly and energetic woman. She charmed the men talking about sports, banished any envy of the women there by complimenting them on what they were wearing and enthralled the young kids with that smile that came so natural and easy. She swapped recipes, listened to the stories of radio and TV folk and of course shared her theory on women's intelligence vs. childbirth with anyone who would listen. Two hours went by and Jake had no thoughts whatsoever of Penelope Hartz.

After two hours and 15 minutes the couple decided to take their leave. Donning her coat Bernice broached the subject about the rest of the evening.

"Wanna meet my Super Bowl demons?

Can I?

Absolutely. Just know that I think my dad is a year younger than you, my brothers will try to get you to say dirty Italian words to my gram and my sisters in law will tell you how stupid and pathetic I am. Can you handle all that?

Only if I can defend your honor.

Cool."

They said their goodbyes and Jake could tell that this party was going to be media gossip for weeks on end . He knew everyone would be talking about his party guest. But it didn't matter now, Penelope Hartz didn't matter after this night. What mattered most now was going to Bernice's party and being as protective, charming and as wonderful to her as she was to him. This was going to be Jake's mission for the rest of the evening.

The night was freezing cold and some ice had formed on the road. They walked up the street arm in arm, being careful not to fall, in effect, holding onto each other for dear life.

"Well, how did I do?" she asked.

Jake responded, "Wonderful. Just wonderful. Thank you for acting like you wanted to be there."

Just then, Bernice grabbed Jake with force and spun him around on the ice. It was the first time he had an appreciation for her size and strength. She held his face, kissed him and looked deeply in his eyes and said, "I wasn't acting".

On that night, under the cold frigid stars is how Bernice and Jake began.

The night, for Jake was a huge success. Now he had to keep his part of the bargain and go to her event. It was only fair, he had promised. He did find it odd that he was even needed. As he drove, he glanced over at her sitting in the passenger's seat. The moonlight and the highway lights shone on her face, giving her an angelic quality. That moment took him back to the days when he and his wife would go to the movies and the light from the projection screen reflected her beauty. It had happened once before with Adrienne in a crowded movie theatre in New York. He had not had that feeling in over 15 years but here it was again tonight.

"Tell me how to get there" he said breaking the silence. "No problem, just keep driving. I'll navigate you there" she said. "what about your car?" Jake asked. "I'll have it picked up Monday morning on my way to school, we have people who do that stuff for us", she offered adjusting her lipstick in the car mirror. "Who's us?" Jake asked. "The family, my family, the people you're meeting tonight. By the way, do you have your gym bag in the car and do you have a bathing suit in there?" she asked. "Yeah" said Jake "are we going swimming?" "If you want," she continued, "There's a Jacuzzi and heated pool in the third house, my brother P3's house". "Whoa, whoa, whoa" said Jake, "what type of party is this going to be, is it going to be like a pub crawl or something?" "No, it's the annual family Super Bowl party. It goes from door to door, we all live on the same street. And we just go from house to house, up and down the street, dwelling to dwelling" she told him.

Just then Jake hit a patch of ice and momentarily the car slid on the roadway. Slowing down, he said, "Fill me in on this deal, give me names, dates, details". "Okay" she said turning toward him and crossing her long legs Indian style in the car facing him. "My grandfather bought this street in the 40s and built a house on the corner. Then when my dad and mom married, they built a second house. So when my dad, Primo the second built his house, his brother, my uncle Rocky moved next door on the lot and built another house. When uncle Rocky went away, my oldest brother Primo the third bought the place and moved in with his wife Romayne." "Where did Uncle

Rocky go?" Jake asked. "He had a little trouble with the government but he'll be out and about in a few years" she said without batting an eyelash. "Then when my brother Danny married his wife, Rose Marie," ...... Jake interrupted her, "You mean Rose Marie from the Dick Van Dyke show?" "Who?? What are you talking about, this is Rose Marie, Danny's wife, follow the story will ya" she screeched. The first faux pas of the evening brought the realization to Jake that his cultural points of reference didn't mean a hill of beans to this younger woman in his vehicle. "Anyway, Danny marries Rose Marie and they build a house on the street. So after my third brother Eddie gets married, he and his wife Roxanne build a house. Every holiday, even Super Bowl Sunday we block off the street and have one big party, moving from house to house." "With all that traffic, where do we park?" Jake asked. "Oh in the vacant lot next to Eddie's house. I'll show you. We park there and then we start at my gram's house and work our way up," she said. "Am I going to have fun at this thing?" asked Jake. "Oh you'll have great fun, I won't though. The family invites business associates that constantly ask me why I'm not married and refer to me as the "angel".

"You do fit the description you know" Jake countered not resisting the opening. Glaring at him, she said, "Puhleeze old man, I swear I'll get out now if you keep that bullshit up" her long arms folded in a defiant manner. "And then there are my hideous sisters in law who do everything in their power to make me look stupid and ugly, oh yeah this is gonna be real fun for me", she continued.

Jake got very concerned. This girl was counting on him to make a positive impression, to make her look good. He was scared. How in the world was a short, dumpy looking, balding old guy going to save this kid from this family event? Right away he began to panic. Always insecure about his looks, he compensated by buying good clothes and charging into a room bowling people over for better or worse with his personality. That said, he never felt comfortable in his physical skin. And now, here he was with a beautiful woman half his age meeting her family, using him as a tool to draw less attention to herself. If she was ridiculed before, this was going to be murder on her. He had to make this work for her.

As they pulled onto the street, a police car's flashing lights greeted them. A uniformed officer approached along with a young man with a ball cap pulled past his eyes. "Hey sis" the man in the hat said, "The family's waiting on ya. Everybody's asking about the "Angel"!!!" "Hiya Danny" she hollered, "This is a friend of mine, Jake Yanick. I'm bringing him to the party". Danny looked at Jake up and down, spit into his hand, wiped it on the back of his pants and offered it to Jake who shook it. "How's it hanging tonight bro?" he asked grinning like a maniacal serial killer. "All right" said Jake. Danny looked at Jake again, and waved them onto the parking area. As he did, Danny began reciting the lyrics from Edgar Allen Poe's "Raven" and laughing. "Wow" she marveled, "Danny really likes you Jake!!" "How can you tell?" he asked, "Well for one he cleaned his hand off to shake yours and he never once reached for his gun." Smiling that winning smile that seemed to light up the night sky, she proudly said, "I think this is going to work out just fine tonight. Come my handsome archangel and meet this little angel's personal set of demons."

As they walked down the street from the vacant lot, Jake looked at all of the homes to his left. They were well appointed but unobtrusive in nature. The lawns were well kept and neat even in the dead of winter. He noted that his date for the evening was going to start with the very last house on the end and then intended to work their way back to his car. That structure appealed to Jake's sense of order and neatness.

"We're gonna see gram first" she announced holding onto his arm as they walked toward the house. "My family's events are well organized. In this house you'll meet my gram, my mom and all the ladies who are doing the cooking for the party. They transfer the food to the other houses or else bring more when they are signaled," she added. This blew Jake's mind. While he was doted on all his life by a mother and sister who seemed joined at the hip and adored by a wife who loved him no matter what he did, his legs would have to be amputated before any female fetched anything for him.

As the door opened, aromas attacked his senses. It was like walking into an Italian bakery of sweet smells and delicious temptations. There was no TV on with the football game playing but rather the muted strains of Frankie Laine coming from a radio set on an end table. They both stood there quietly until the silence was broken by an ear-piercing squeal. "Angel, where have you been tonight, one of the biggest nights of the year and you're gallivanting around dressed to the nines. You break your grandmother's heart when I no see you here cooking and helping out for the men" said the short, red faced woman wearing an apron that read "Cooking staff of the Vatican". "Gram", Bernice said smiling, "I had plans tonight. This is Jake, Jake Yanick, we went to a party together and then I invited him here tonight." Jake extended his hand to the older lady but she ignored him focusing on her grand daughter. "I just wanted you here because you light up this place when you're here, you know you're not worth a damn in the kitchen with us anyway, I mean everything you try is terrible. But we want to keep track of you" she said. Turning to Jake, she said, "What is it, Jack", Jake answered, "No, I'm Jake, not Jack. Jake Yanick. Very nice to meet you Mrs. uh........uh". It had never occurred to him to ask what his date's last name was let alone her grandmother's name. "Vitaaahhhlleee" the old woman replied stretching out the letters. "You are a big old man here with my angel but at least you are a man. Do you work?" she asked. "I work in broadcasting, work for Power 108". "Teenage music, terrible stuff, I listen to beautiful music, Sinatra, Tony Bennett, Caruso, not junk" she said smoldering. Jake looked and saw his friend's proud confident shoulders drooping in uncertainty. It was time for a long pass into the end zone. "Mrs. Vitale, what about this song?" he asked taking her by the hand, posing to dance and starting to sing, "Lazy Mary you better get up she said I'm not able, lazy mary you better get up we need the bed sheets for the kitchen table" he sang out swinging her around. Much to his surprise, delight and relief, she sang back "La La La, La La La" and laughed uproariously at herself and Jake. After a brief interval, she invited Jake and her granddaughter to sit while she fetched them some food. Jake had done something he was good at, breaking through to people who initially did not like him. His date was really taken by that aspect of his personality.

Just then her brother Danny, his hat pulled over his eyes came in the house for a flashlight. He leaned over Jake's shoulder and said, "Want to impress my gram? I'll give you a word that will make her adore you. She'll think you're a regular paisan. Just say the word merdata. Merdata, got it?" Danny asked. Jake nodded yes and watched as Danny grinning a self satisfied smirk left the house. "Tell me Bernice", Jake said, "why did your brother tell me to call your gram a pile of shit? Does he think I'm so dumb that I don't know some Italian?" Bernice laughed and said, "He is such a jerk, see what I mean, they're all crazy, they drive me nuts". Looking toward the closed door, Bernice was more than enthused about the first impression Jake made on the most senior member of her clan. "Wow, my grandmother really took to you" she said.

Wait until she gets mom. They're all in the kitchen cooking and baking for the men" she said taking off her coat and hanging it on a coat hanger next to a huge religious statue of what appeared to be the Blessed Mother. "Hey, were you at all upset that she kind of downgraded you in front of a perfect stranger tonight?" he inquired leaning forward. "Oh that's nothing. Wait until you meet the rest of them. I've been getting it every day since I was a kid. On one hand they call me their "angel" and on the other hand, I'm ugly, stupid, a whore, you name it. I can't win with them and I guess I just wanted to bring someone here to give myself a reality check to see if they're right. This is the only family I have but going to school has opened up some new ideas for me. They love me, but I'll be damned if I'll ever know it. Notice how stiff I get around them? My gram that cradled me in her arms when I was small makes me feel so bad sometimes. I just don't get it" she sighed. Jake was now in his element. A beautiful damsel in distress, a gorgeous Cinderella beaten down by wicked stepsisters, this was his forte. He leaned forward and looked deeply in her eyes and said, "Before I leave here tonight, all of them will see you through my eyes". She smiled and mouthed the word "thanks" to him as they sat waiting for the canoli patrol to make an appearance.

"Well, well, well" said the sturdily built woman about Jake's age coming from the kitchen with her mother and what looked like a six pack of Italian matrons all wearing aprons with their hair collectively pulled back in buns. "You're the beanpole's date for tonight huh, what do you think of how she dressed for you. Look at that blouse, look at the skirt, she looks like a cadet from St. Casmir's o do you old guys like young girls who dress up like schoolgirls?" Jake was momentarily taken aback because I never thought of his date in a sexual way until her own mother put the thought in his head. He imagined this tall drink of water in knee socks and saddle shoes and his min drifted for a bit. "I think she looks just fine, uh, Mrs. Vital She's a very nice dresser", Jake countered. "Well, she has work with what she gots ya know?" said her mom. Jake immediately saw what his friend meant. Nothing she did seemed right. His chest pumped up for battle.

Surveying the room, he said, "You know I always de with people on a first name basis. If you don't mind, can I have all of yours, let's start with the oldest, Mrs. Vitale, ca you do the honor for me?" The elder lady, obviously charmed by the attention took to the task with vigor. "Wel my name is Bernadette, I was named after the saint. This i my daughter in law, Bernadine, she was named after the P Boone song. And you of course know our little Angelina here, Bernice. We named her after both of us. But since she's never measured up, we call her "angel" after her middle name," she said. It was all Jake could do to keep from laughing out loud, this family was obviously committed to monogrammed sheets and towels. The old lady continued introducing the cooking posse. "This is Betty Spinnini my sister in law, this is Beverly Spinoza my neighbor up the street, this is Barbara Spinetti our across the street neighbor, this is Bertha Spinutti and last but not least this is Katie Finnegan, my wonderful late husband's bookkeeper" she said with a flourish. Looking over at the hunched over Mrs. Finnegan, Jake said, "How'd you get in this crew?" The elderly lady replied, "I know where they keep their money". After the introductions, Jake rose to the occasion and for the next hour regaled the cooking ladies with his take on the Papacy, the saints, recipes for Italian cooking and his views on the one they referred to as the beanpole. He could've stayed a bit longer but the next destination was calling and he had to meet the occupants there. As he and Bernice left the house, carrying a large stromboli for the next stop, her grandmother asked Jake what he would do if he could talk to God tonight. Jake thought long and hard a minute and then said, "I'd ask him that no child ever be hungry again in the world and that what I felt here tonight with all of you could be bottled and distributed throughout the world. Hearing this, Bernice rolled her eyes in amazement but it brought a tear to the eye of Bernadette. Which is exactly what Jake was going for. They left the cooking house and were on their way to the game house for the second stop of Super Bowl Sunday, Vitale family style.

The two partygoers made their way to the second house sans overcoats. "What's behind door number 2?" quipped Jake. As they went up the two small steps of the patio, the door was opened wide by the biggest man Jake had ever seen. Standing 6 feet 9, with wavy black hair was Bruno, better known as Bruce. At first wary seeing just Jake, his face broadened into a huge smile when he saw Bernice. "Hey Beanpole" he cried picking the 6 foot girl up by her arms and dangling her like a rag doll in a windstorm, "where ya been tonight?" "I had a commitment with my friend Jake, Bruno this is Jake Yanick and then we went to see Gram and Mom. We have some more food here. Are you going to let us in with this food or you gonna block the door all night?" she said holding her hand on her hip. "Come on in" he said gesturing to her. As an after thought, Bruno looked at Jake and grunted, "You too".

The kitchen area was set up as a make shift bar with Bruno guarding the stash. On a table were various dishes of food that included sausage, peppers, pizza, pastries, cheeses and fruits. The food table was manned by a buxom bleached blond named Lorraine who wore a satin jump suit which accentuated all of her curves. She stared at Jake, looked him up and down and glared at Bernice. "Hello Beanpole" Lorraine said, "Hiya bitch" Bernice said as she led Jake out of the kitchen and into the dining room. As they passed her, Jake heard Lorraine say, "Love you too honey". Bernice glared and led Jake away. Jake later found out the true meaning of this little drama. It turned out that the well built woman was the former mistress of Primo Vitale I and as per his wish, the family took care of her long after he was gone. In a weird sort of way, Jake found this admirable. Bernice however did not.

Through the hallway hung pictures of the family that seemed to scan 75 years. Graduation and wedding photos adorned the walls as well as a few baby photos. Jake tried to search the wall for Bernice's photo but was interrupted by a booming voice coming from the dining room. "Hey kiddo, where ya been?" said a rather large, robust man with an uncanny resemblance to a tired looking Al Pacino. "Daddy, I was at the library this afternoon, then I took a bath, then I met my friend Jake, then I met his friends, then he met Gram and Mom, then he met Bruno and the lady we call the "L" woman, now we're here to see you!" said Bernice. Primo II looked over at Jake and said, "Shit you must be pretty tired after all that. Is she behaving?" Jake nodded yes. Raising an eye brow Primo II said, "And you?" Jake nodded a quick yes. The father invited them into the living room. What Jake saw there rivaled anything he had seen in Vegas. A large screen TV was set up with the game on. To the left were 2 TV monitors that showed horse racing results from two racetracks, on the right were 2 more monitors, one set to ESPN, the other to CNN. The sunken living room was filled with folding chairs and was totally devoid of other furniture. A small desk with a phone and an adding machine was the only concession to Ethan Allen. Around the room sat big burly men who were introduced to Jake as "associates" of the family. All of them, to a man, kept their eyes on the game, oblivious to Primo's daughter and her new friend. At the desk sat a bespectacled bald man by the name of Silvio who constantly took phone calls and jotted things down on a note pad. The phone rang incessantly. "As you can see" Primo II said to Jake, "we take the game pretty seriously. Who do you like tonight?"

"The Packers, love the Packers" replied Jake. Bernice beamed. "Hey me too, I love the Pack, this team isn't like the old teams I remember though," said her dad grabbing himself a piece of cheese. "I hear ya"

Jake offered. "You can't beat guys like Hourning and Jim Taylor and Jerry Kramer, nothing like him". Primo enthused said, "And how about Jim Chandler, one of the best place kickers I've ever seen". Jake countered, "And what about Herb Adderly, Jesus he was fast wasn't he?" "Yes he was and you know" all of a sudden Primo stared at Jake and Jake stared back at Primo because both men came to the ultimate realization that they were thinking the same thing. Primo clenched his fist at his side, Jake gulped hard. Men bond seriously on sports, especially boyhood idols. The sports idols become known as "my guys", the heroes we root for and against. Every generation of men has "their guys". For the first time that night, for the first time ever the age difference between Bernice and Jake became evident when Primo realized that the Packers of his youth were also the "guys" of Jake's. It was an awkward moment that only the two men felt and understood. Bernice broke the tension by saying, "No player you guys are talking about could beat that Denver QB Elway's butt, both literally and figuratively." Primo looked at her and in feigned shock said, "My money for your college education is paying off, you're talking real good there kiddo". Bernice thanked him for the compliment. "Have some food" Primo said to Jake and his daughter. "Kiddo, get Jake here a plate". As Bernice went toward one of the tables filled with food to fix Jake a plate (which incidentally continued to blow Jake's mind) her father fixed a stare at Jake, grabbed his arm and said, "She's a good girl, I hope you know that". Jake took the father's arm off his own, placed his own arm on Primo's shoulder and looked him in the eye and said, "I know she's a good girl, more than most people in this house realize, and incidentally I'm also a good man". The father looked at him, smiled weakly and said, "Good". Of course, it didn't occur to Jake that Primo might have disputed this literal definition of "good" had he known about Adrienne.

Bernice brought them food and both sat down on the steps leading to the upstairs of the house. As they ate, Jake asked her where her room was. "In the basement, they keep me tied down there" she said. "C'mon" said Jake, "I bet you have the whole floor to yourself like a princess". Bernice gulped some beer down and said, "I do have a nice room and my own bathroom. Want to see it?" "Sure" said Jake. "Well you can't buster. It's one thing to meet the family the first time out but to see my bedroom, my boudoir, my palace of privacy, my solitude, no way" she replied picking at some dried meats and onions. Jake looked at her and said, "So the room is a mess, clothes all over the place, huh, big ring around the tub, right? Worried that I might think you're some kind of slob, correct?" She took her long tapered hands, took his chin and placed it in them and simply said, "You are correct sir!!!". They both laughed and returned to the big room to watch the game. The room was smoke-filled and dark and as they watched, he saw the reflection of the TV shining on her face. She did not see him watching her smile and selfishly he did not want to engage her in conversation. He just wanted to drink in the vision of her beauty. But still Jake had the urge to ask who were these men, what were they doing, were they booking the game, what was the point spread and would they get raided? Jake had all those questions but refrained from asking them. The third quarter ended and Bernice excused herself. Jake sat next to three guys named Paul, John Paul and Francis Paul, all of whom seemed to be inhaling the food at a breakneck speed. Jake could swear he heard someone fart but couldn't be certain. Finally Bernice returned with his gym bag she retrieved from his car. "I'm going to my messy room to put a suit on, you change in the bathroom down here" she said. "Pardon me" said Jake. "We are going to phase 3 of the Super Bowl party, we're going to the heated pool and hot tub over Primo' III's house, next door. Are you cool with that?" she said smiling at the shocked expression on Jake's face. "Well I don't know, I'm kind of nervous, I don't know you guys" he stammered. All the insecurities of his body were coming back to haunt him in one fell swoop. He started to make every excuse under the sun. She sensed it and said, "If we don't do this tonight, you may never get to see me in a bathing suit". Then her brow furrowed and she intently looked at him saying "but more tragically, if we don't go in that hot tub, I may never see you in a bathing suit either. You can't ask me to live with that now can you Mr. Yanick?" There it was again, that smiling face that lit up a room. He got up, grabbed the gym bag and proceeded to the first floor bathroom to suit up. In a few moments, he'd be walking half naked into House number 3 with a room full of strangers watching the last quarter of the Super Bowl. Jake was excited, confused and really wished he hadn't eaten so much at Gram's house. But what was done was done and he patiently waited at the bottom of the steps for his leggy young friend to take him to the next level of football enjoyment. It was turning into a night that even in his wildest dreams he never allowed himself to imagine.

It was cold as they crossed the pathway to the third house. Floodlights illuminated the dark winter skies but for all Jake knew, this could've been Cancun on a chilly night. At least 30 people were in the pool, all in various states of undress and drinking heavily. Two huge kegs of beer were set up on the patio and at the edge of the pool was a bar that had more than twenty types of premium liquor. Behind the bar was Primo III, a tall, gangly man with a ready smile and gregarious manner. His demeanor was more in sync with Bernice's than Jake's earlier introduction to their brother Danny. "Hey kiddo" he called out, "where ya been?" "Making the rounds of Super Bowl Sunday with my friend Jake, Jake Yanick. Jake, this is the man we refer to as P3, my oldest brother" she said. Jake took his hand, shook it and noticed the family resemblance. "So you're the guy that was having the heart attack, huh?" asked a smiling P3. Surprised, Jake at first hesitated but then recalled the incident. "No, I was on the stair master at the gym and you know how they have the red readouts, she thought I was having an attack because the red was reflecting on my face. She was quite concerned, we had a laugh about it" said Jake. "Yeah" added Bernice, "and I was using a fake name too, as if that never happened in this family. Tell me P, is your lovely wife Romayne here tonight?" "Bernice, now don't you two get into it again. Why can't you get along with all the wives. Give them a chance to like you" said her brother. "Give them a chance" bellowed Bernice, "they go out of their way to insult me, make me feel bad, ridicule my choices, undermine me, make me feel stupid and small, you know that". "Oh I think you're exaggerating here a bit" said P3 pouring two Baileys for Jake and his sister. Just then a short, well built brunette with a bouffant hair style that seemed to point toward the skies emerged from the pool. Dressed in a lime bikini she sauntered over to the trio by the bar. "About time you got here beanpole, God knows we couldn't get through this night without the Queen of Sand Street. But I guess our little college girl had to study sooooooo hard. By the way hun, where'd you get that bathing suit, borrow it from Bess Myerson or something?" she said to her sister in law. Looking over at Jake, seeing him in his bathing suit she said, "Hiya tubby, what's shaking tonight?" Bernice lunged toward Romayne and Jake and P3 stopped her. "Do you see what a bitch she is to me? You can't even hide your contempt for me can you?" in anger she exclaimed. "Nope" said her sister in law. At this point, Jake jumped in. "You know Romayne, by the way, I'm Jake Yanick but you could call me Chunky instead of Tubby, I appreciate you complimenting Bernice like you did, I'm just sorry she didn't see it that way" noted Jake. All three of them looked at him with astonishment. Jake continued looking at Bernice, "And to say that your suit looked like Bess Myerson's, well I'll have you know that Ms. Myerson was one of the all time beauties of the 20th century. It does not surprise me Romayne that your uncanny eye pointed that out". Jake stood there smiling waiting for a response but there was dead silence until Romayne excused herself to go inside. P3 broke the silence, "I've been married to her for eight years and you stopped her cold, that was an amazing piece of work there chief" he said. Bernice's mouth was agape, "How did you do that, I missed it, how?" she inquired. Jake took her hand and simply said, "Didn't matter how I did it, what mattered was why I did it. No one will ever make you feel like a "less than"………ever". Bernice mouthed the words "thank you" once again this crazy night.

At that point, Bernice's other two sister in laws, Rosemarie and Roxanne emerged from the house. Similar in build to Romayne, these two were platinum blondes and a bit taller. "Do you guys want any food"? said Rosemarie. "Yeah, we'll get it for you, fix you both a nice plate" added Roxanne. P3 and Bernice looked at each other stunned once more. "No" said Jake, "we're fine but what I'd like to do is find out about you guys. Bernice here has told me how stunning her brother's wives look but I bet there's a lot of brains under that beauty. Tell me about yourselves". Both women smiled at the compliment. "Why don't you guys go in the hot tub and I'll help P3 here clean up some of these bottles" Bernice offered. "To the tub" said Roxanne. As Bernice watched them head toward the tub, once more she found herself grinning for what seemed like no reason at all.

Jake may have not been the top biller at the radio station but he certainly was the man most likely to flatter at the drop of a hat. Bernice was just getting to fully understand the extent of this and it worried her a bit. But she was also taken with the ease in which he traveled in his own skin and how he adapted to just about every situation. She first agreed to join him because he asked it as a favor but this guy, the way he defended her, the way he moved through life, truly connected with her. As she gathered the bottles with P3, she asked, "So what'dya think of Jake?" P3 said, "He's way different. He looks older than dirt, but he talks good. Doesn't matter what I think, though. All I know is your skin has no bruises on it and that's cool enough for me. He ain't no Richie which is great but you guys look like the number 10 walking together." Bernice looked thoughtfully at her brother, then glanced at the big, engaging man in the hot tub with her relatives and said, "That's okay, I always liked the number 10".

The conversation in the hot tub ranged from idle chit chat about inane things to probing questions by Jake about the family. He found out that the Vitales were in the demolition business and by all accounts were very well off. Roxanne offered the information that there was always money around and that the family never wanted for much. Neither could explain the logic behind the names the Vitales gave their off spring but it was agreed that P3's naming of his second son, (the first was of course named Primo IV) Shirley was a bit extreme. P3 said it would make the child tough, Rosemarie commented that it would make the kid crazy. Jake agreed. Utilizing his old reporter skills, Jake also found out that Bernice was in an abusive relationship with a guy by the name of Richie who had a Super Lube franchise. They knew each other in high school, dated and when she got accepted to Nursing School, Richie claimed he couldn't live without her. For the next 7 years, she hung out at the Super Lube fetching food for Richie and enduring his anger filled insults and physical outbursts. There were times she came home black and blue and the family tried to intervene. Danny, the most psycho of the three brothers even tried to plant an explosive under Richie's truck but Bernice herself unwittingly thwarted that plan by taking the truck to get washed on the very night Danny was set to do the deed. Finally Primo II talked to their priest and through the duo's intervention, Bernice slowly weaned herself from Richie. She began classes to pursue a degree in Physical Therapy and while not the best student, worked very hard to succeed. Jake was actually surprised to hear that Bernice was the first Vitale to go beyond high school. But the damage to her personality was done. The barbs of the family never helped. Roxanne told Jake that Richie was trying to stalk Bernice again and feared that he would never leave her alone. Jake just took the information in while he nursed his drink.

As Roxanne and Rosemarie excused themselves, they were replaced in the hot tub by a very large man (bigger than Jake and Bruno combined) and a petite blond with huge breasts. The big man set down a huge boom box CD/radio that was playing Power 108. Jake introduced himself to Crystal and Booker Wrobeleski. Crystal was a cousin of the Vitales and Booker whose real name was Warren sat in the tub toting 12 beers in a bucket. Crystal looked at Jake and said, "Are you here with my cousin?" Jake nodded yes. "She's a good girl, we grew up together and had tons of fun," she related. Jake found out that Crystal and Bernice haunted the same places he did as a kid, albeit twenty years later. After exchanging pleasantries Crystal started to ask about Jake's relationship to Bernice. He hesitated and that's when Booker jumped in. "She's trying to sell you something Jake, be careful" he said. "You know how to get in good with my cousin?" she asked. Jake nodded no. "Buy her this lipstick. It is a non stick, non smear lipstick. Watch", and at that point Crystal ducked her head under the water making a gurgling blowing sound as if she was slurping a soda with a straw. Coming up from the water, she proudly showed off the lipstick, which true to form, did not smear. "I think Bernice's lipstick looks fine" said Jake. "Oh she's a good girl but she needs to be a little more glamorous, "said Crystal. "How so?" asked Jake. "Well, I think she needs breasts, bigger ones and a landing strip wouldn't hurt her either, " she added. "A landing strip?" Jake asked. "Yeah, let me show you" and at that point Crystal lowered her bathing suit bottom to

display her pubic area that was neatly shaved into
what looked like an airport landing strip. Booker then
got up and started to yell, "Flasher, Flasher…..I'm
gonna go blind. Flasher, Flasher". Crystal then swatted
him down and he looked at Jake with a bemused look
on his face. Jake was tempted to scold Crystal for even
thinking Bernice needed work. But he stopped himself
when he realized her heart was in the right place.
Trying to quickly change the subject, he asked Booker
what he thought of Crystal's breast job. Booker took a
swig of beer, looked at Jake and said, "I like them. At
least now her tits are bigger than mine!" Crystal took
the bucket, filled it with water and dumped it on his
head. At that point, Bernice rejoined Jake and sat in
the tub. "What were you guys talking about?" she
asked. Jake said, "Breasts, lipstick, landing strips,
liquor, food, everything but football. By the way, what
is the score?" "Jeez, I don't know Jake" replied
Bernice, "I was so busy talking to P3, Eddie and
Danny that I didn't see. I'll go look if you want me
to". Jake, patting her on the shoulder said, "No, no,
you're just getting warm in here, let me get out and
see the game. I'll fill you in when I get back," he told
her climbing out of the tub. As he walked into the
house, crowded with revelers in their 20s and 30s,
Jake, out of the corner of his eye saw Crystal give
Bernice the thumbs up sign. He saw Bernice mouth
the words again this night "thank you."

Making his way into P3's house, this time Jake knew the drill. The kitchen and dining room were filled with tables of food and liquor while people paid passing attention to the game. Jake rarely went to these type of gatherings, especially when his team was playing. The last time the Packers played, he sat home in his boxers with his beloved dog Monty at his feet and his wife, heavily medicated from pain killing drugs from a head injury passed out on the couch. This party was certainly a departure from that domestic tranquility. Jake waited patiently in line to use the bathroom and could not help overhear a conversation between Bernice's two younger brothers Eddie and Danny. "How the hell did he get through the street?" Eddie whispered. "No clue man, all I know is he went into Gram's house looking for Bernice, then knocked over a plate of food on his way out. He was drunk and hammered. Bruno tried to intercept him but he cold-cocked him with a hammer he was carrying. Mom called the cops but they're tied up in Dixon at the Mall. The only guy here is Mikey and he's not even a real cop. He just borrowed a car and a uniform for tonight" said Danny. "Are you shitting me?" Eddie said. "If Dad ever found out we have nothing in the way of security he'll kill us both. Where the hell did he go?" "He's heading this way, I'm getting Mikey and my gun and if he tries anything, we'll plug him in the leg" said Danny pulling his cap further over his eyes. Eddie added, "While we're at it, let's give our lovely sister a shot for staying with that scum bag so long.". Jake closed the door behind him and could not believe his ears. The last thing he needed was to get shot in his bathing suit 30 miles away from home, especially on a Sunday night. What the hell was he doing out on a Sunday night anyway, his mother always told him to stay home on Sunday nights to prepare for the next day of school. But here he was, in the middle of God knows what. Leaning over the toilet, he felt slightly ill. Washing his hands, he looked out the window. He decided the bathroom was the safest place to be. After all, this Bernice person made her bed with this guy long before Jake ever heard of her. Jake had always had a history of saving women from bad situations and he reveled in playing the hero, but this was different. Age had given Jake a new perspective on pain and dying. While others craved excitement, like the Mecklenberg's where this night began, Jake was now willing to embrace dullness and boredom in his life. A good week was when everything stayed the same. He looked in the mirror and noticed some errant nose hairs and began to pull them.

Meanwhile outside, Danny positioned himself in P4's and Shirley's tree house overlooking the utility shed and pool area. Mikey, the diminutive rent a cop leaned near the shed. As Danny looked down from his perch, he saw that most people had gone into the house to see the rest of the game. There were a few stragglers in the pool and the hot tub was still occupied by Crystal, Booker and Bernice. There were a few employees of the family business starting to clean up near the hot tub. Booker had inserted a CD in the boom box and the strains of Junior Walker and the All Stars played. A few moments of solitude and then a loud racket ensued. It was Richie. Dressed in a wife beater tee shirt, painter pants and steel tipped shoes, he entered P3's yard. P3 walked right up to him to tell him to leave. Before he even opened his mouth, Richie kicked P3 directly in the groin. Her brother went down in a heap. Carrying a hammer Richie headed for the hot tub. "Well look at this" he sneered, "two bimbos and a blimp. Mr. & Mrs. Polock and Ms. Rich Bitch". Bernice said, "Richie, you're drunk, get out of here. You're violating your PFA by even coming here. Please leave". Richie, swinging the hammer laughed derisively. "I don't care about the PFA, you or anyone else. You'll be happy to know I'm coming here tonight to end our relationship. It's over clown girl. We are through" he crowed. "Richie, I'm glad to hear you talking some sense" chirped Crystal, "years from now both you and Bernice will remember the good times and will know you made the right decision". "Years, years, did you say years you stupid bitch? There ain't gonna be any years on this thing. This is ending tonight. I'm bashing this beanpole's ugly head in tonight. I don't care if I get life, she's dying here right in her pathetic mommy and daddy's compound. What a fitting way to go, her blood on their ground", the violent man said brandishing the hammer. All of a sudden, Danny's voice boomed throughout the yard, "Richie, I got a gun, I have you covered, one move, one tiny move and I'll shoot you dead. You know I could do it too, you went hunting with me and Eddie. The deer I killed were never drunk, you are". Richie looked toward Danny and at that instant, Mikey stepped out from the side of the shed.

Training a pistol on Richie, Mikey looked like the real thing. Richie, for the first time appeared scared. When Primo II appeared toting what looked like a semi automatic, he looked terrified. "Okay Rich" said Bernice's father, "let's just call it a night. You know you don't want any more trouble so just go away and I'll take care of everything". Richie, momentarily was mollified. From the window Jake saw Bernice sitting in the hot tub, shivering, eyes cast down, most likely dying of embarrassment. Jake could only imagine the ridicule she would suffer in the coming days over this incident. The situation looked pretty much under control. With danger out of the way Jake grabbed a 24 ounce can of beer and headed out side to be the comforting hero to Bernice. With women, Jake made his mark by contrasting his goodness against the evil of prior boyfriends. On a scale of 1 to 10, this was a 20. Donning a tee shirt from his gym bag, Jake grabbed a sweatshirt for Bernice. When he stepped outside, the stand off seemed to be winding down. Jake stood at the bottom of the steps watching. Junior Walker and the All Stars music still played on. Danny, Mikey and Primo II had their guns on Richie. Dropping the hammer, Richie looked around scanning the yard like a trapped animal. No one quite saw how he did it but in seconds, Richie had taken the boom box, jumped atop the edge of the hot tub and brandished it over the water. "Shoot me you bastards, give it your best aim. Your three babies will fry anyway when I drop this thing", he sneered. Everything stopped. Primo II looked at the boom box and saw the plug leading to the power outlet. He was sure it was live with voltage that would kill his youngest child. Danny raised his cap and looked to see where the cord led. Mikey relieved himself on the spot, a huge watermark covering the front of his khaki pants. Crystal took Booker's hand in hers to steel herself. Bernice shivered in the water, her once large frame now reduced to a bundle of shame, fear and loneliness. In a way, this event wasn't much different than what she felt in her every day life. Richie was baring his teeth saying, "Just look now who has the power now you big shot thugs. Me! And I'm gonna use it."

Bernice shot a look at Jake. In her face he saw a vulnerable victim who needed his help. Jake also saw terror, and embarrassment. In the midst of all this, Jake smiled at Bernice and started walking toward Richie. Barefoot, Jake padded over talking taking the assailant by surprise. "Richie, Richie, Richie, those people at Fitzgerald and Madigan are going to be very pissed when they hear about this" said Jake. "Who the fuck are you?" Richie bellowed. "Me, I'm Jake Yanick, sales rep at power 108. Ever listen to Thomas and Jefferson in the morning? I put the tags on those commercials the ad agency runs. I deal with those guys every week and while they are cool, they are not going to be happy you assaulted a body guard, kicked a poor bastard in the groin, held three hostages at bay, and made poor Danny Vitale up there bare his eyeballs. Now you want to electrocute these people in their own backyard!! Shit, after they put you away, they're not gonna be able to give the Super Lube franchise to a homeless guy in downtown Scranton!" said Jake with his arms folded over his chest. "I'll do whatever I want man, these people, I hate them. I hate that bitch in the tub, I'm gonna do her in because she doesn't want to see me anymore. Well, I'll fix it so she doesn't see anyone anymore" continued Richie hovering over the hot tub. Primo II made a move to get help but Richie stopped him cold by faking a toss of the appliance into the water. "How about this?" Jake continued. "How about if I put you on Thomas and Jefferson Monday morning to talk about your grievances. They won't make fun of you. Jefferson lives down the road from here, we can even tape it tonight". "What the hell am I gonna say on the radio? That I was in a stupid relationship with a frigid, Catholic slut who took marching orders from her family, who I gave the best years of my life to and who all of a sudden decided to become a whore college girl sleeping with her professors because she's too stupid to get grades on her own?" Richie exclaimed. Jake looked at him and said, "You can say all that, but you gotta know Richie this is show biz and no one likes a victim. Hell that speech alone will lose you your franchise." "You're full of shit, they'd never do that to me and my family. We're a big money maker for them no matter what I do" Richie countered. Shaking his head, Jake started to run his fingers through his thinning hair, "Richie, Richie, let me ask you a question. Does the name Joey Freskle mean anything to you?" Richie shook his head no. "Well Richie, Joey Freskle had 5 Super Lube stores in the greater Montgomery County area near Philly. This was in the early 80s when you and Bernice there were in grade school, so I guess you wouldn't know the name. But Freskle had a booming business, was a millionaire but he also had a side job. He managed the

New York Mets. They sucked. Freskle got fired. He
whined so much about getting fired in public that
within three years, they pulled his franchise. Now he
has a franchise called Doily Oily. Do you really want
to end up like that?" Jake asked inching further. "What
the hell are you babbling about, that's so much
bullshit! Listen Tubby, I've had enough of you, shut
the fuck up" Richie screamed. Something in Jake
snapped. Always overweight as a child, Jake had done
every diet known to man. No matter what he did, the
weight stayed. Two years ago he had started a
maniacal workout plan that got him up at 5AM and
had his legs aching when he got his day started for
work. Looking at Richie enraged him because even
though Richie was an abusive drunk who hurt his
friend Bernice, Richie also looked like the type of guy
who could down a pizza, 3 cheeseburgers and a six
pack and lose weight. All the years of snide putdowns
on his weight exploded into a cacophony of hate for
this one insignificant grease ball who had ruined Jake's
night. "Tubby? Tubby?" Jake snarled. "Listen you
piece of crap, I'll have you know I'm in the fucking
gym every morning at 5am, I eat fucking salads every
day for lunch while everybody else has hot dogs, I take
diet pills so bad I shake and sweat and you call me
Tubby?" Jake was screaming now and the rapt
attention of everyone was off Richie and on him.
Richie stared at Jake as if he had met someone crazier

than himself. Just then the moment was interrupted by a scream. Danny had made a leap off the tree house and was heading through the air for the pool in an attempt to either create a diversion or save the people in the tub. Jake, seeing Danny on the fly hit the ground and rolled toward the extension cord. Richie let the boom box go from his hands. Jake on the ground yanked the cord with all his strength. A second before the box hit the water Junior Walker and the All Stars stopped playing. Jake then grabbed Richie who swung hard and bloodied his nose. P3 and Primo II along with Mikey finally subdued Richie. Of greater concern to other people not involved with Richie was Danny. He had missed the pool by a foot and was sprawled out on the concrete motionless, baseball hat still attached to his head. Someone called for an ambulance that arrived with the real police since the emergency at the mall was over.

The short calm after the storm was broken when Booker said, "Shit, my boom box is flooded". Crystal hit him as they got out of the tub. Jake, rising to his feet with difficulty grabbed the sweatshirt and headed toward Bernice who was sobbing in the hot tub. He climbed in and sat on the edge and looked at her. "Boy, when you throw a party, you throw a party. This is better than Hollywood", Jake exclaimed. Bernice started to giggle, wiping away her tears. "See, and you were worried about your family" Jake continued, "It's not the family members you should be concerned about but the wanna be members. Come on, put this on, you're shivering". Bernice donned the heavy sweat shirt and looked at the front. The smiling face of Chief Wahoo of the Cleveland Indians looked back at her. "He looks like you screaming all red in the face at Richie", she said. "What you did took a lot of guts, you saved our lives. I can't imagine if you had missed that cord. We'd, oh God, we'd be dead by now, oh God, hold me please". Jake held her tight and patted her back in comfort. He wondered if he should tell the beautiful, 24 year old red head in his arms two vital truths of the night. Truths he withheld. Truth number one was that he was a married man, truth number two was that before he went into the house to check on the score of the game, he had unplugged the boom box because he was afraid Crystal would knock it over with her wild gyrations. Junior Walker and the All Stars ran, courtesy of the Energizer Bunny. Jake decided that silence would suffice for this evening. Bernice separated from him and looked up, smiling and said, "You remember those Super Bowl demons I told you about?" He nodded yes. "Well," she said pulling herself to eye level with him, "I think they're fading fast". "Good" said Jake, "I'm glad. I have to go to work tomorrow, I mean today, can I get dressed and go home?" Taking his hand and leading him toward the house, she said "Only if you come back. I promise, it'll be less crazy". "Are you kidding?" he said, "I wouldn't have it any other way."

Jake went into the bathroom and began to dress. He splashed some water on his face and looked at his watch. It read 245AM. He looked outside and some of the families were helping to clean up. Word came from the hospital that Danny did not break any bones. P3 was sitting outside with an ice pack on his crotch while Crystal and Booker tried to revive the boom box. When Jake got out of the bathroom, Primo II took his hand and thanked him for his fast thinking and his bravery. "We never forget a friend, you'll see that very soon" intoned the patriarch of the family. "By the way, Elway beat the Pack". Jake and the father shook hands and both gazed at Bernice sitting at the table warming herself with hot chocolate. "Is she trouble or what?" Primo II said. "Yeah" said Jake, "but a good kind of trouble". Blowing the steam from the hot cup, Bernice's eyes expressed thanks. "Hope to see you again" Primo II called to Jake on his way out the door. Jake nodded and smiled.

Both Bernice and Jake sat at the table in silence for what seemed like hours. Finally Jake got up to leave lugging his gym bag. Bernice walked him out the door of her brother's house. What followed next was something that totally blew Jake away. As they walked down the steps, their eyes were met by a blinding series of lights. Gathered on the street was the entire neighborhood. Old women dressed in overcoats over their pajamas, old men dressed in winter coats under their robes. Party goers who enjoyed the hospitality of the Vitales were also there, standing. The brothers wives, the kids all stood in the cold as if they were lined up for a mid afternoon parade. As Jake's feet hit the bottom step, the crowd cheered its approval. He was mobbed by pats on the back, kisses on the cheek and slaps on his fanny. He heard people say "Way to go", "You the man" and "God bless and keep him forever". Bernice led Jake to his car and as he got in, he thanked everyone for an enjoyable but eventful evening. Bernice gave him a chaste kiss and as the car pulled away he saw Mikey, the rent a cop driving the borrowed police car leading him back to the interstate. As he drove away to more cheers, Jake hoped that what had happened this evening would never see the light of day in the local media. He also knew that his life would be changed forever by the events of this night. As his car tooled down the highway, he put on a local sports station to get details of the big game, just in case his wife asked him about it.

When Jake got home he found Adrienne sound asleep. It was 4AM as he settled into bed. Jim Duncan's sales meetings started promptly every Monday morning at 8:30AM so Jake figured he'd take an hour cat nap, then head to the gym at 5:30. He drifted off to sleep but that internal clock he was blessed with woke him up and got him to the gym. The workout was going well until he fell asleep on the weight bench. Waking up one hour later, he realized this would be the first time ever he missed one of Duncan's meetings. Jake was upset that he had not stayed in bed for the extra rest and he became more upset that no one at the gym woke him up.

There are no true friendships between competing sales media reps especially in radio. But Jake had forged alliances with a few good people and topping that list was Jody Mecklenburgh. When Jody finally had her first child, Duncan gave her subtle suggestions to drop some lucrative accounts and concentrate on motherhood. She had worked too long and hard to do that so she devised a plan for Pete Cassidy and Jake to watch her baby at the end of the day while she returned to the radio outlet for the required recap meeting. For his part Jake was glad to help out because he knew he'd need a favor in return someday and had no doubt in Jody's reciprocity. The day after Super Bowl Sunday when he was going to be late was when he would cash in that chip. Calling Jody on her cell, Jake explained the situation. "Yanks" said Jody, "you aren't at the Blue Carpet shacked up with that WNBA player I saw you with last night, by the way thank her for the flowers". "No" said Jake, "just tell Duncan I'm going to be a little late because I had a problem at the gym with my eyes, I'll be in as soon as I can". Jody countered and said, "Yanks, Duncan chain smokes three packs of Camels a day, he eats hot dogs for lunch four times a week, that excuse, while true won't fly. Tell him Adrienne got sick". "I can't do that" he told her thinking how unseemly it would be to use his wife as an alibi for calling in late because of a liaison with another woman. It was a strange sense of morality but it was one he could call his own. "Tell him the dog is sick" said Jake after a long silence. "Great move" enthused Jody knowing that Duncan and his wife were big animal lovers.

The sales meeting started promptly at 830AM in the Power 108 auditorium. The combined staff of Power, Oldies and American Popular Standards took their seats. As usual Duncan sat at the head of the table but Jake's seat at his right hand was empty. Concerned, Duncan asked where Jake was. Jody was poised to answer with the concocted tall tale but before she could open her mouth Sal Basaligna, the Irish looking sales rep with the Italian name, beat her to the punch. "As you know Jim, because of the icy roads in the upper elevations there's a school delay today and Yanick had to get his girl friend to the bus stop!", said Sal with a hint of venom. The broadcast rumor mill was already in full gear and word had gotten on to the street already about Jake's statuesque "friend". The room exploded with laughter.

Any other person would have been categorized as an immoral person in this situation, but not Jake Yanick. His fellow workers found Jake charming, kind and generous with his knowledge and time. His assignations were not regarded as sleazy because Jake didn't portray them in that manner. Jim Duncan on the other hand loved this aspect of Jake's buoyant personality. Duncan was dominant in his milieu as well as his family circle but once outside that world, the intelligent sales executive became very shy and at times withdrawn. Penelope Hartz once told the story about a lunch she had with Duncan where for the first 50 minutes there was dead silence until she broached the subject of family. Duncan would be in awe of Jake's gift for gab, his willingness to put himself out there as well as his ability to connect with just about anyone. What impressed Duncan the most was Jake's ability to make any pretty girl smile. It seemed to Duncan that Jake zeroed in on a woman and his main mission was to make her smile with a quip, an action or even a faux pas that humanized him and put the woman at ease. Duncan, after hearing Sal's explanation simply said, "I'll bring Jake up to speed personally on what we cover when he gets in today". In the eyes of the staff, Jake Yanick, the person most likely to get canned by Duncan one year before, had arrived.

When Jake came to work, Duncan greeted him with open arms and after his usual 3 post-meeting cigarettes, invited the rep to his office. "So I hear you had a good time at the Mecklenburgh's last night" said Duncan. "Yup" was all Jake said. Duncan smiled and went over the meeting notes with Jake. At the end of their meeting Duncan gave Jake a slip of paper. It was a call in. In radio broadcasting, that was a lead that came in without prompting or provocation on the part of the station. Some other businesses term them as "bluebirds" where without effort a sale will fly through the window. Duncan husbanded these "gifts" for people who worked exceptionally hard or for people who he liked. Jake fit the bill on both counts but his bonding with Duncan helped too.

"This is a call that came in early this morning" Duncan told Jake. "The name of the company is 4 Emerald Group, they have a consortium of businesses and want to look at Power 108. They're right up the road right near the Tudor Inn, the place with the great wings. Can you meet with them today at 1PM?" Thankful for the lead and the confidence his boss showed in him Jake simply said, "I'll be there chief".

Tired as a dog, Jake drove his car onto a side street in the Hill section of Scranton. He pulled in a super market parking lot, shut the car off and reclined in his seat for a 25 minute power nap. This was a favorite place for reps to come to recharge their batteries, whether by weed, alcohol or simple sleep. Jake had the lot to himself and rested fitfully.

Rousting himself at 1230PM, Jake straightened his tie, drove to the restaurant and grabbed a yellow legal pad, a pen and some Power 108 business cards out of the Bill Blass briefcase Adrienne had given him for Christmas. When he entered the establishment he was met by a hostess who took him to a large table located by the kitchen door. Walking through the dimly lit bar Jake had his eyes downcast to carefully concentrate on his movements. When he looked up, seated at the table were Primo Vitale and his 3 sons. "We meet again" said Primo II, clasping Jake's hand in a firm shake, "I'd like you to tell us all you know about this advertising game". Jake, momentarily stunned, quickly remembered that these three men had seen him in a swimsuit not 12 hours before this meeting. He began his presentation for them with relish looking for another opportunity to show off how much he knew but wondering at the same time where this confab was going to lead.

Jake came away from the meeting with the Vitales with a suspicious and strange feeling. Jake left his meeting with them not to think that their interest in radio broadcasting was just a coincidence. No one had ever heard of their business or them in his informal survey among local business people. The men seemed affable enough and wanted to promote their business via radio. But the way they wanted to do it mystified Jake. Their business proposal was to use Public Service Announcements, image commercials that railed against drunk driving, teen age sex and marijuana use and then just end them with the tag line "This message brought to you by the 4 Emerald Corporation". Nothing more, nothing less. One of the failings Jake had as a sales rep was that he never had the ability to ask for more money than he thought was fair. With the Vitales he had no idea what to ask for because A). They didn't seem to be advertising anything but good will and B). He didn't want to ask for too much for fear the Vitales would think he was greedy. When he returned to the station for his recap meeting Duncan wanted details of his day. Jake eliminated the nap part but talked about his get together with the father and three brothers. Duncan told Jake he'd put together a budget for the Vitales and have the sales rep present it at their next meeting. Jake, relieved went back to his desk to plan his week, work on figures for his boss and then head home for a warm bath and a good night's sleep. Standing in the doorway of the sales office, Jake was taken aback by a huge object on his desk. Jody Mecklenburgh and Pete Cassidy sat upright in anticipation waiting for his reaction. As Jake moved slowly toward his desk he saw a vase with 31 red roses on it. "Someone has an admirer" cooed Jody. "Naw," said Cassidy, "he sent them to himself so we'd think he's a lady's man. Wait a minute, come to think of it, he is a lady's man". "Open the card will ya" said Jody, "I'm dying to know who sent them". Jake sat down in front of the fragrant bouquet and opened the small card. "Out of 31 Super Bowls played, none displayed more courage and finesse than you did last night. Always and forever, your "B" girl." Jake passed the card to Cassidy and Jody. "Oh Yanks this is well, this is, this is nice but............" Jody sputtered. Grabbing the card Cassidy simply said "This is what we term a sticky wicket. The girl really is impressed with you but I don't get the courage deal. Did it take so much bravery to stave off Poppy and Penelope?" Jake then recounted the entire saga of Super Bowl Sunday after he and Bernice left the Mecklenburghs. "Wow" said Cassidy. "You can write your own ticket with these people. It's pretty cold outside, do you think you can score some tickets off them so we can all go to

Aruba?" "Pete!!!" scolded Jody. "Yanks this girl obviously has some issues which I know you're into but she also has some muscle backing her up with this family of hers. I don't know if they're connected or not and I don't know what their story is as far as business is concerned. But I do know about family and if she is the apple of their eye, you have to be extremely careful given the Adrienne situation. You don't want to get in so deep that you won't have wiggle room you know?" Pete agreed with Jody and for a moment was serious. "Yeah Jody's right you don't want to jeopardize what you have with Adrienne but at the same time if you piss this girl off she's liable to arrange for you to become a speed bump in a mall parking lot," continued Pete. Jake took in the advice and then looked at the flowers. "They are beautiful though aren't they?" he said pointing to the elaborate display. "Did you hear a word I said?" asked Jody. "I did, I did" countered Jake. "Believe me all I wanted to do was show Penelope up last night. I had no designs on being a hero, the whole thing took on a life of its own. You guys know I love Adrienne. But this thing that happened was not really orchestrated. It started out as manipulation on my part but then it just exploded into all of this. I mean nothing like this has ever happened to me". Jody asked him, "How much younger is she than you?" "Well, I'd say about eighteen years between us", said Jake. "This is the first time I ever even entertained the thought of dating out of my demo." Pete exploded into laughter saying "Better brush up on that urban rap music, you're way out of the format". "You're telling me" said Jake, "when I told her I liked American Popular Standards better than Power FM" she says, "Cool, my gram likes that stuff too". "Why not date the grandmother?" asked Pete. "Pete!!!!" exclaimed an exasperated Jody. As the trio donned their overcoats and headed for the elevator they were joined by Jim Duncan for the ride down. Duncan, with a twinkle in his eye said to Jake, "Well well if it isn't the hero of the Mid Valley, how come you didn't tell me you were going to be front page news." "Jim, Yanks here is always front page news, you knew that when you kept him" said Jody joining in on what she thought was still another Duncan friendly shot of affection at Jake. "Hold on" said Jake. "Jim, what are you talking about?" Disembarking from the elevator Duncan pointed at the news box holding a latest edition of The Evening Record. The bold type headline read, "MAN SAVES 4 AT SUPERBOWL PARTY!!!!!" Underneath the headline was a file photo of Jake Yanick's smiling face for all the world, including his wife Adrienne to see with a vivid account of his heroics from the night before. Duncan offered to get him a paper, Jake smiled weakly, declined and drove home. Any hope of getting that warm bath and good night's sleep was now a remote impossibility.

As Jake drove home, he began to rehearse out loud how he got to a Super Bowl party an hour from his house and wound up saving 4 people clad only in bathing suits. Adrienne, though brain injured was far from stupid. Over and over he went through it in his mind. At long last he had the sequences in order that would make for a passable excuse. When he got home, his decrepit dog Monty met him at the door. There was a huge urine stain in the throw rug where the dying, diabetic dog had yet another accident. Jake cleaned the rug, put the dog outside and prepared the insulin injection for the pup. When the dog reentered the house, he held him and injected the life saving medicine into the animal. The dog sauntered to his bed and promptly fell asleep. Jake disposed of the needle and silently thanked the heavens Adrienne or for that matter any woman he knew had no access to a needle and truth serum. Walking up the darkened stairs, he entered the apartment and saw 10 messages lit up on his machine. The first 9 congratulated him on his heroism in Simpson the night before including 2 from TV stations that wanted to interview him for the next morning's news. The 10th was from Adrienne. He held his breath. For sure she had left him. Listening to the message Jake learned that his wife was calling from Philadelphia.

"Hey what in the world is going on?" asked Jake when he returned the call. Adrienne, seeming groggy answered in subdued tones. "I was walking home tonight and felt so bad, so depressed, so helpless that I decided I didn't want to feel this way anymore. So I called the number of this hospital that I saw online and asked if they'd take me immediately" she said. "Are you saying you committed yourself" asked Jake. "Well, not exactly, I just told them I was at the end of my rope and needed a support system of qualified people. So I got myself down here", she continued. "How?" asked Jake. "I took the bus. My God, there's a lot of drugs going back and forth from Philadelphia. You should have seen the bus station" she remarked. "You mean they took you without a referral?" he asked. She answered, "No, I got a referral from Dr. Lake". Jake was perplexed, "How in the world did you do that? I thought you two were at loggerheads in the way he was dealing with your treatment". "I persuaded him" giggled Adrienne. "Persuaded him how?" inquired Jake sternly.

"Oh you would have been proud of me. I happen to know that he has a support group meeting every Monday at 3pm. These are the crème de la crème of locals who think they have problems but really don't. They just need someone to hear their bitch sessions because they got the wrong color SUV or had too much bad sushi on their 23 day Alaskan cruise. So I came into the meeting and asked him for the referral. He said no".

"Then how did you get it?" wondered Jake. "I pulled out of my purse in a large clear plastic bag all the pills he's been prescribing for my brain injury," she said. "That's about 50 bottles, right?" said Jake. "Actually it's 53. So I pulled them out and started to catalogue how they didn't treat the illness, how he would give a pill to an alligator if it had a medical card and how if everyone in the room wanted real treatment, they should look elsewhere." "Oh my God" gasped Jake in response to his wife's tale. "So then he gets bent out of shape and wants to throw me out of his office but then a few of the patients start offering me money, right in front of a whole waiting room for the bag of pills. They were outbidding each other" she chuckled. "What happened then?" asked Jake. "He got pissed, called the nurse in, wrote out an emergency referral slip to McHugh rehab and here I am" she concluded. "Amazing" said Jake. Adrienne said, "Isn't it though? I was so sick and tired of people not believing me."

Complimenting his wife, Jake said, "Well you certainly took the bull by the horns". "I had to" admitted Adrienne. "I think you're feeling better because you took action. What's the treatment plan?" asked Jake. "I don't know yet. They are saying that it was an involuntary brain seizure. I'll keep you posted. These people down here really seem to know what they're doing so I'm pretty confident about whatever thing they want me to do" said Adrienne. "Well" joked Jake, "Just don't try to diagnose yourself. You always want to know more about these medical things. Why can't you be more like me, all I want to know is "Will it hurt?" Adrienne responded, "Well, if I were like that, I 'd be like you and there's only room in this big bad world for one Jake Yanick. "How true. But remember there's only one you too" he said tenderly. "Take care of yourself and listen to what the doctors say, don't try telling them what to do". Adrienne asked, "You think I'm still smart, even with my injured brain?" Jake responded, "Smarter than ever. And besides with me, at least it'll be a fair fight now", joked Jake.

Adrienne reassured him she was fine but very tired. Despite his fatigue, Jake offered to join her but she declined. After a few more minutes of mutual banter the two frequently shared via the phone, Adrienne asked Jake how the Super Bowl party was and how the day after it went for him. Jake, reclining back on the sofa simply said, "Oh same old, same old, ya know?"

The next few weeks would be a whirlwind for Jake Yanick. After initial interest about his heroics, that matter died down in the local news replaced by a story about a cross dressing judge who was apprehended shop lifting in an adult book store. Jake was in constant touch with Adrienne who decided to spend more time in the big city for her therapy. His presentation to the Vitales 4 Emerald Corporation went off without incident and Jake obtained a 5 figure advertising deal for the entire year. On purpose he had minimal contact with Bernice, working out in the mornings, doing his sales thing in mid-day and tending to his ailing pet in the evening.

One night while Jake was home alone with his pup, the doorbell rang. Wearing just boxers and an old tee shirt, Jake gingerly opened the door. Standing in leather suede coat, blue jeans, white blouse with a Blessed Virgin Mary medal around her neck was Bernice.

"Glad you dressed up for company, she said.

What are you doing here?, Jake asked.

Look, you've been avoiding me big time and I want to know why.

There are a lot of things going on in my life now and I have to deal with them.

I can help you deal with them, you know that, and besides I owe you my life.

No you don't, anyone could have done what I did that night.

Yeah but only you had the stones to pull it off. Look, it's cold out here, can I come in? If Adrienne finds us I'll tell her you were my teacher in high school.

How do you know about her? I didn't tell you about her!!

No shit Sherlock. I knew you were married the first time we spoke, the good ones always are. Look, my cousin Crystal is with me. Let us in and we'll have a three some.

Really?

No way you asshole! C'mon before your neighbors start talking more about you than I'm sure they do now.

Okay", said Jake.

Bernice motioned to Crystal and the two women came into the house. Jake offered them a drink, both took Coors Lites while Jake drank his signature Tab diet soda. Jake's dog was not having a great night. He was heaving and shaking. His tired old body was gasping for breath. Crystal approached the dog and began to pet him. Her usually gleeful expression turned to dismay.

"Jake" she said, "this dog is dying."

"I know" Jake said quietly. "I know".

Five years before Jake took the dog to the vet who diagnosed the pet with diabetes. The doctor instructed Jake in how to administer a shot and fully expected the pup to die within a year. By sheer force of will, Jake kept the dog alive since that initial visit. But this night, Jake and his dog were losing the battle. Crystal, Bernice and Jake crouched on the floor directly in front of the dog, petted and comforted him until his little life expired. Jake was numb. The two women helped him wrap the dog in his bed and took him to the backyard. Putting his body in the hole, and covering it, the three cried and held each other.

Jake got them a few more drinks and after two hours the women took their leave. Calling Adrienne, Jake told her of his pet's demise and both of them cried too. Hanging the phone up, Jake went to sleep in tears. The next day he went to work and was not himself. Duncan sensed it and asked what was wrong. Jake related the story of his dog and Duncan gave him the rest of the day off, called his wife Carol and asked her if it would be okay to send Jake's family a sympathy card on his loss. Knowing the pain of losing a pet, the Duncans sent their condolences to Jake and Adrienne.

Doing what he did in times of crisis and grief, Jake worked extremely hard at the radio station. He kept in touch with Adrienne every day and visited her on weekends. She was doing very well in her recovery, growing stronger every day. During the day Jake lunched with Bernice and met her in the evenings before he headed home to his empty house. Jake was burning the candle at many ends. It was a three tier flameout physically, emotionally and intellectually. He was juggling Jim Duncan's lofty career radio expectations, Adrienne's recovery aspirations and Bernice's on-coming affections with great aplomb but he was getting exhausted. It would not be uncommon for him to fall asleep at his desk doing his sales orders before he went home.

Perhaps the most troublesome to him was the situation with Bernice. Every morning he would wake up vowing to end it but at the end of the day could not. Bernice was becoming a fixture at Power 108 bringing Jake lunch or on his birthday a cake. On that day, Bernice went from office to office offering a piece of Jake's cake to the staff. Despite the respect and admiration all felt for Adrienne, Jake's wife, it was hard to hate Bernice with her winning smile and charming personality. While Jake used his personality to win women, Bernice targeted her own charm on people important to Jake. She, like Jake, innately knew it was about image. That image was not some bimbo trying to steal a wife away from a husband but a person who presented an intelligent and personable front who could only enhance Jake's life simply by being his friend. Their rendezvous usually was in the computer operated American Popular Standards control room. Sharing supper or just conversation the two would sit in the darkened control room and just talk about their lives. Sometimes they'd get up and slow dance to a Dean Martin or Perry Como tune

much to the amusement of the cleaning staff. For the
most part their talk was uneventful because even
though Bernice was pursuing a college education, she
was not a deep thinker. Nor did she want to rock any
boat, least of all a small cigarette boat carrying a
married couple and herself. But one night on her way
home from a night class Bernice stopped at Jake's
house. After a pasta dinner cooked by Jake that her
gram could only envy, Bernice made herself
comfortable on the love seat opposite Jake in his
living room. Taking her jeans off in another room,
Bernice donned a pair of Jake's neatly folded boxers
on the bed. Smiling to herself and thinking about
their chaste relationship, she thought it ironic that this
was the way she was getting into her "best guy's"
pants. Bernice loved the way he treated her, made her
feel, made her laugh. For all the money her family
had, she never felt safe or loved. Jake Yanick, of all
people accomplished that. She strode out of his
bedroom, got herself an iced tea and positioned herself
Indian style on the couch, school books opened in
front of her with her tortoise shell reading glasses
inching down her nose. After a brief interval of quiet
Bernice simply said, "You know it's all about the
hole, don't you?" Jake looked at her confused and
annoyed. No longer the object of a full blown pursuit,
Bernice would not be treated to the patented Yanick
"gaze". "What do you mean?" he asked. "The hole,
the reason I'm in love with you is the hole. You're

never gonna get rid of me because of that hole. The night the dog died, I thought we'd have to dig a grave but we didn't. The hole was there, that's not a big deal because people expect pets to die. But Crystal and I figured out that the hole in your back yard was there for five years. Five fucking years Jake. You had enough love in you to keep that mutt alive and fend off his death for five years. 60 months, 1826 days including leap year. To me that was amazing. If you could take care of him like that along with your job and Adrienne and me, then I know you're worth all the doubts I have of my success in winning you completely. I don't think anyone can ever have you entirely but I'm going to try, I'll try harder so be forewarned" she said nonplussed. Jake just stared at her vacantly secretly overjoyed but at the same time terrified.

Just then, the two heard a key in the front door opening it with a clang. A thump punctuated the silence. It was a piece of luggage landing on the front step. Adrienne yelled up from the bottom of the stairs, "Anybody home?"

Jake looked up in panic. Bernice whispered, "Adrienne?" Jake nodded yes. "Jake" Adrienne called up from the bottom of the stairs, "I have to get my briefcase out of the limo, I'll be right back, I thought I'd surprise you". Bernice said to herself, "Fuckin' A, you hit the bulls eye Mrs. Y" as she shed Jake's boxers which were cinched around her thin waist. She then started to throw on her jeans, gather her school books and clumsily put on her sneakers. "What are you doing?" asked Jake. "I'm booking you fool, you got a set of side steps don't you?" she asked adjusting her belt and tucking in her trademark white oxford into her jeans. "Yeah but I really think we should try to ride this through," said Jake. Secretly he was more than thrilled and relieved that she was taking off. He had his share of needy women who complicated his marriage before, it was quite refreshing to have a woman put him first for a change. Bernice's eyes got wide as saucers and she had to restrain herself from hitting Jake. "Are you crazy, ride this out?" she whispered. "I'm not that smart but consider this. I'm sitting here in your underwear on your couch. Your wife who has been under treatment for a brain injury and is on God knows how many meds is coming up the steps. Ride this out, sometimes I think you enjoy having your head up your ass. You, you........." Then she stopped dead in her tracks and dropped her purse. "You mean you'd not deny me, you'd not hide me like some back alley whore? Is this what you're saying

Jake?" His heart starting to beat furiously, sensing his escape hatch fluttering away, Jake nonetheless nodded yes. Grabbing his face, Bernice kissed Jake and with tears in her eyes said, "You are such a special man, I'll love you until I die, gotta go, call me" she said scampering down the hall into the dining room, opening the door and running down the side steps.

Straightening the living room up Jake heard a succession of three thuds. The first was the car trunk closing, the second was Adrienne closing the front door and the third was Bernice landing on the bottom of the steps in a heap after tripping on her untied sneakers en route from Jake's house. A searing pain enveloped her lower back as she tried to move. Gathering herself up she whimpered in pain as she pawed her way to her car arching against the side of the house for support. She crawled in the cold dirt and pavement sweating profusely. Opening her car door from the passenger side she barely lifted her long legs over the console and drove herself to the nearest hospital. When the attending transport people saw her after she pulled her car half way up the sidewalk, she looked at them and said, "My legs and feet are numb".

Meanwhile not more than 6 blocks away Jake and Adrienne caught up on what went on while she was away.

"How in the world did you get here in a limo?" Jake asked his wife as she slipped out of her clothes and sorted through Jake's laundry bag for a used shirt he recently wore. Pulling the buttoned shirt over her head, his wife inhaled Jake's smell. "You could get a clean one you know?" offered Jake. "Are you kidding? I know better, you'd have a fit if I took a freshly pressed one. It would be grounds for annulment," she said. "Yeah, I guess you're right. It looks good on you, so tell me about the limo ride" he said. "Oh, the limo, well you know I got myself down there by bus so when I told them that when I checked in, the hospital said they'd arrange transportation from their building to the bus stop. So they send this cab with a guy driving who was obviously high on something. And as he started to load my bags in the trunk, he puked on them. All my stuff. So I freaked. I started screaming bloody murder and the security guard came and saw what was happening. Here I was being treated for a brain injury, I was pretty good at coping but then this happens. So they decide to get another cab. And I point out the matter of my puke stained clothes. The hospital was sympathetic but the cab company was not. So I start to scream" said his wife who positioned herself on the couch in a dainty fashion. "Screamed?' Jake asked, "what did you scream?" "I think it was something strange and lewd like "mother fuckers or something like that" she added. "You did that in public? You?" he said incredulously. "Yes I did" replied Adrienne, I mean I screamed it until my voice was hoarse, I think blood was coming out of my vocal chords". Jake just shook his head in amazement as his wife continued. "Finally, the cab owner got so spooked because I kept on reciting the phone number from the side of the taxi, that he arranged to have a limo take me home, have my clothes and bags dry cleaned and provided me with a box lunch to snack on for the drive home," said his obviously proud wife. "Adrienne, you never used to get set off like that before the injury, you just kind of let things flow and were easy going to a fault" observed Jake. "Oh how true that was but I found out that insanity can be a powerful weapon" she said coldly looking her husband straight in the eyes. This momentarily spooked Jake because when his infidelities were rampant, they were all with crazy women. Now the calm woman he went back to had the potential to be crazier than all of them put together. While those women used their craziness for pity, Adrienne was quite capable of using her own brand of insanity for power. The irony of it all was not lost on Jake.

Jake had to use his skills to pull Adrienne back to some home based reality. Sitting on the recently vacated love seat, Adrienne and Jake cuddled, kissed and held each other between conversation about her new physicians and her upcoming treatments. "I cannot believe how much better I'm doing" said Adrienne, "I feel as if I have a doctor who knows what I'm feeling, who understands me. They don't look at me like I'm crazy or imagining things. I actually went to class down there and they taught me compensatory strategies. This is kind of like cheating but not really, you know?" Jake nodded. "And despite my ability to now just go crazy on people like I did to get the limo, I also recognize that I am a different person and you will be too because of this. The big thing is that I'm going to desperately need your help. The therapist in the support group said that most married spouses leave when someone gets brain injured. I told them I thought you'd be around, will you?" Jake stroked her cheek and looked into her eyes and said, "Absolutely". Kissing her she laid her head on his shoulder and said, "You have to be my brain. You have to remind me of basic things I used to do so I won't get derailed. I'm going to need a huge checklist but more importantly I'm going to need a big magic marker to check off what needs to be done or what can be expendable. I know you're busy with your job and all but I'm counting on you more than anyone I ever did in my life. Are you up to the challenge? Can you help me?" Looking at her intently Jake smiled and said, "I'm going to make you the smartest woman in America". She giggled and whatever concerns she had about her future melted away. Jake always had that calming effect on her. The man was a lunatic if his favorite tie was lost or if a kitchen knife he liked was out of its place. He could explode if his sock drawer spilled out onto the floor but in a crisis, when the chips were down, Jake was there lending support, being the cheerleader and offering innovative solutions to what seemed to be very insurmountable problems. On this night as the two walked arm in arm to their bed, Jake had no idea that someone other than Adrienne would need his rock solid commitment and support to heal.

Jake's cell phone rang when he was on his way to work at Power 108. "Hi" said the voice on the other end. "It's me, I'm in the hospital, I fell down your steps last night and now I can't move my legs" said Bernice in a matter of fact manner. "Oh my God" said Jake, "where are you, who's with you?'

"My mom, can you come here now?" she asked plaintively. "I'm on the way" said Jake. Jake called Jim Duncan's voice mail and told him Adrienne came home from the hospital and he needed time to spend with her. Jake sped down the highway to the hospital. Entering the room, Jake was not prepared for what he saw. Bernice was in a casket like contraption with her head anchored by what appeared to be two bricks. Bars surrounded her bed and she was stationary. She could not move her head back or forth. Bernadine took his hand and sobbed. "Look at our girl Jake, how can this happen, how can this happen?" Jake consoled her and wondered how much Bernice told her mother. "What did the doctor's say?" asked Jake. "X rays, they are waiting for the reports now. There's still a lot of swelling though". Jake nodded. Both hovered over Bernice, Bernice stared at both of them and began to cry. Her mother got a tissue but Bernice asked for Jake's necktie. It was a navy blue poly blend. "This is his pasta tie mom, my tears aren't going to ruin this" she said. The three sat and waited. Primo II stormed into the room and glared, "What the hell happened?" No one was telling him anything until Jake finally spoke up, "She was over my house, she fell down the side steps, and drove herself to the hospital." Primo looked at Jake and said, "Were the steps up to code? Cause if they weren't I know a guy, ya know?" Jake nodded. The day passed and the three waited until someone came in to give them the news. "I have good news and bad news" said the doctor, Troy Barnett. "The good news is that there was no damage to the spinal column, the bad news is that there is nerve abrasions to the spine. You have a ton of bruises surrounding the lumbar region. Treatment for this will be long and tedious. I foresee at least 8 months in therapy. With luck, you will walk again, but this is going to be a long haul. Any questions?" said the lanky physician. The group had none. Bernice's parents were relived. "Daddy, I know this is going to sound stupid but could you just tell me a funny story about grandpa, please?" asked his prone daughter. "Sure hon, I'll tell you the kind I used to tell all the time when you were a little girl, could you excuse us here?" Primo asked his wife and Jake.

The two walked out of the room and into the hallway. Bernadine looked in Jake's eyes and said, "I never thought my daughter would want anything to do with a married man. But you are something special. I see that. She sees that. You have no obligation to us, even to her. But in the next few months she is going to need you to be her legs, her spirit, her desire. I don't think you'll cut and run, but if you do, do it now. Don't go back into that room unless you are willing to stand with her, by her and for her. You need to be her footsteps, her backbone but mostly her heart. I'm going to go to my car right now. If you walk with me, I won't think any less of you. Do you understand?" said the woman roughly a year younger than Jake. She reached the long hallway and Jake was still standing in front of her daughter's hospital room. From across the way, Bernadine blew Jake a kiss and as the elevator door closed, she bade him goodbye. By this time Primo came out of the room and prepared to leave. Jake feeling guilty told him, "I'm staying". Her father kept walking and simply said, "I knew you would, my daughter didn't, my wife wasn't sure but I knew. By the way, Danny wants to kill you. Come to think of it he wants to kill everybody, but I'll handle it. Go in there and make my little girl happy." Jake waved and went back inside to join Bernice. The sedatives had finally taken their effect and she was out. Still, Jake stayed.

Calling Duncan, Adrienne, his mother and his clients, Jake was covered for the next 14 hours with lies, alibis, exaggerations and half-truths. At 10PM Bernice woke up. Jake was still in his signature blue double breasted suit but his navy shirt was missing his stylish monochromatic tie. Giggling, she said, "You still here? What a glutton for punishment you must be." Jake smiled and said, "I'm here for the duration, you're going to be fine and I'm going to stand by you. You had to know that right?" Able to sit up now without her prior restraints, Bernice answered, "No Jake I didn't know that. I fully expected you to run. Like everyone else has in my life. Or worse yet, blame me and say I was stupid". Jake replied, "Well you know in hindsight you should've tied your shoes". Giggling she said, "In hindsight, you should just kiss my ass!!!!" Fingering his tie, she continued, "You look so stupid without this tie, standing there all in blue, you look like that guy on TV, the repair guy who's pissed that no one needs him or wants him anymore. All you need is a little hat." Jake chuckled, "Between you, Adrienne, my job, I have my hands full don't I?? I kind of envy the Maytag man right about now". A wide smile crossing her face, Bernice said, "That's it, the Maytag guy. Jake, you are the Maytag man, that's my new nickname for you, MAYTAG. You're big and dependable. MAYTAG. Oh baby, I got you now, that name is gonna stick to you like stink on poop". Jake looked at her and said, "You mean stink on shit right?" Bernice feigning disgust said, "Us Catholic girls don't say gross stuff like that". "You don't say that stuff but you keep a married man around?" asked Jake. "Well, I never told you I was perfect now did I?" she retorted. Smiling, she told Jake to head home knowing full well that he'd return every day to help her recover. As he left the room, he said goodnight. In a little girl voice she said, "Good night Maytag!!" and then drifted off to sleep.

For the next few months Jake's life resembled a major airport. There were take offs and arrivals, departures and deliveries. The entire common thread throughout it all was scheduling. Once squandered idle minutes now became precious commodities to Jake. The regimentation was a way of life for the sales rep with the many commitments. Adrienne found the strict adherence to a format quite helpful in her quest to regain her occupational skills. The minute by minute regimen gave her insight first hand into how to plan her shattered life. Her husband became the master of the plan. She proclaimed Jake to her friends as "the man with the plan!!!!" God forbid if that well schemed orchestration failed. Jake could then be short, irritable, livid and irrational. At first Adrienne thought it just her maniacal husband being an idiot. But then she began to worry about the high stress load Jake seemed to be carrying around him constantly.

For her part, Bernice was amused by his storm trooper tactics but fully understood why he needed to be the way he appeared. If both women could compare notes on his behavior, they'd come up with the same things. If anything, Jake was consistent. It is ironic that both women used the same tactics of sarcasm and humor to calm him down. It worked every time because Jake was in dire need of amusement.

Power 108's place in the market was well assured but now the new management wanted to grow the station. Duncan's new GM wanted to make a name for himself and Jim Duncan wanted to just maintain the success he brought to Power 108. The only way to do that was to keep his boss and owner Big Bob Little at bay. Jake continued to do well at the station but a nagging concern was the unpaid bills left by the 4 Emerald Corporation. Despite the assurances by Primo that Jake would not be held responsible for Bernice's accident, his three sons who controlled the stock felt they should punish Jake for their sister's disability. Despite Primo II's protestations or perhaps because of them, the corporation reneged on their bills. Attempts to take them to court were stymied because after taking one look at the associations, the bean counters at Power 108 found that a non payment law suit was small potatoes to some of the people under the umbrella of 4 Emerald.

Adding insult to injury was the behavior of Bernice's youngest brother Danny. Maladjusted from birth, Primo's youngest son loved to blow things up. He spent his spare time in the woods behind the company headquarters experimenting with explosives. Large booms would be heard through the Mid Valley. After a while, the sounds were ignored since it was a given that Danny Vitale was just blowing something up for sport.

So here he was, Jake Yanick. Mid 40s, married to a wife with a brain injury, overweight, hair falling out and limited prospects in his career. Add to that a mistress who was crippled, had a "connected" family, most of which respected him but at least one plotting to kill him, and virtually no time for himself. This was not the life Jake had envisioned. Growing up he had seen first hand the relish his father took in taking care of his family. Being responsible was a virtue in the Yanick household. But Jake was taking this to a brand new level altogether. Jake had thought about getting out of either draining circumstance. But dumping Adrienne was not even a consideration. Every day he grew to love her more. He was so proud of her progress and the way she fought back from her injury. Plus she provided him with his core comfort. No matter how bad things went, how tired he became, Adrienne's arms were his shelter.

While Jake viewed Adrienne as permanent, he thought of Bernice as temporary. First there was the age difference and secondly it surprised him that he even lasted this long with her. He felt an obligation to stay with her when he was out of her sight. But when he was with her, he was more thankful for her time than she was for his. It was an odd pull she had on him. There was no intellectual stimulation to speak of and Jake certainly wasn't in it for the sex given his B girl's condition. But he dutifully made time for her and definitely did what he did best with beautiful women, made himself indispensable. His heavily-scripted week gave him only Sunday nights to decompress and have time for himself. This relaxation usually manifested itself in a hot bath that put him to sleep in an instant.

One day Jake was leaving work. Walking to his car, he sensed someone following him. Turning he saw Bernice's cousin, Crystal. Jake enjoyed Bernice's relative immensely. Both of them had a lot in common. Both grew up in households where fashion was not very affordable. The two constantly battled a weight problem and had to work very hard to look attractive. Jake resorting to strenuous morning work outs, Crystal to plastic surgery. She had no inhibitions and no illusions about her IQ. Crystal made Bernice seem like Churchill. Still, Jake found her pleasant, engaging, fun to be with and totally devoid of any guile. "What brings you to the Electric City?" said Jake. Looking confused Crystal said, "I thought I was in Scranton." "You are, it's a nickname" noted Jake. Crystal gave him a blank look and asked him if he wanted to have a drink. Telling her he didn't drink when driving, they settled for a Coke from the deserted Power 108 break room. Taking their drinks to the Oldies studio now dark and running by computer, the two made themselves comfortable in the broadcast booth. Crystal shook her blond tresses, puffed her chest out in a way that would make Penelope Hartz look like a nun and smiled at Jake in an extremely sultry manner.

"I have a proposition for you Jake," she announced sipping her Coke.

"I'm listening" said Jake.
"I want to replace Bernice.
You want to what?
I want to replace her, fill in for her, kind of like a
stand in at a Broadway show. Like a pinch hitter.
Where the hell did you get this idea?
I thought it up all by myself. Look, it's perfect.
I don't want to replace Bernice, I doubt if she'd want
to be replaced or substituted for," countered Jake.
        Looking dejected, Crystal went on anyway.
"Jake, look, Bernice is crippled. Your wife has
problems with her brain. You are serving them both
like a slave, who's serving you?
I'm fine Crystal. I'm doing well. I cherish both of
them and I'm getting by.
Oh yeah, when was the last time you just let loose and
had some fun?
I have fun all the time. Adrienne and I cook, we go to
shows, we go for rides, we have a great life. Plus I
help her with her therapy.
And my cousin?
We talk, we listen to music, I teach her about politics,
opera, I help her with her therapy.
Who helps you with your therapy Jake?
I don't need help, thank you very much.
Huh, you're lying. You might lie to your wife and my
cousin, but I'm too dumb to be lied to.
What?

You heard me. You just love being mister fixit, Saint Fucking Jake. You're like the Christopher Columbus statue.

The what?

You know, the statue in New York, give me your poor, your masses, put them in a huddle, you know the one where he's holding the torch.

Uh, that's the Statue of Liberty, not Columbus and unlike you, she's a lady!

Who gives a shit Jake? All I know is you love being this saint dispensing little bits of Jake to good little girls but you wouldn't know what to do with a bad girl if she came up and bit you on your dick!!!" she screamed.

The oldies music blared loud as the two fought. Otto Mattic, aka Dale McMichaels, the part time traffic reporter for the stations and full time engineer looked in to see if everything was okay. Jake waived him off pointing to Crystal and his long time friend just nodded his head and let them be.

After he left, Jake said to Crystal, "I really resent you talking to me that way. You are way out of line. I'm right on target Jake. You love being a good guy but in reality you are two timing your wife, my cousin and even yourself. You just cloak yourself in this mantle of goodness to cover up your ugly and vile lies.

Fuck you Crystal.

No asshole, Fuck you."

Crystal lifted her arm to hit Jake but he blocked it. Angry he pulled her close until the two were inches from one another. Both stared, both waited for the other to blink. It wasn't the Cuban missile crisis but it was damn close. Crystal spoke first provoking Jake's responses.

"Jerk off!"

Dummy

Asshole.

Bitch.

Liar.

Fake.

Slut.

Whore.

Fraud.

Fool.

FuckYou"

Within seconds of the cacophonous insults, both were locked in an embrace, their tongues probing inside their heads. All the pent up anger, passion and resentments of their past came to a boil in one huge explosive encounter that left them both spent when it was over. As Lou Christie's "Rhapsody In the Rain" played on Crystal asked again if she could replace her cousin.

"No" said Jake.

"You're smart. You're probably right. Where's the bathroom?" Jake pointed her in the direction of the ladies room and waited for her to come out. They both walked silently toward the elevator and McMichaels cheerily yelled after them, "You guys going to dinner now?" In unison both of them replied, "Screw you" to the bespectacled, confused engineer and left the building to go their separate ways.

Crystal arrived home after her encounter with Jake looking a bit harried and unkempt. Waiting for her was her husband Booker who was royally pissed. "I thought you told me you were going to be in the work shed until 7pm tonight. I checked and they said you left at 4pm. Where the hell were you until then, it's 8:05 now?" said the mountain of a man she'd been married to for 15 years. "Are you a time keeper now Booker? Oh gee, let's have a parade because my husband can tell time! Look I'm getting real tired of you following my every move. I was where I was and there's no doubt about where I was and when I was where I was, got it???" Booker was totally confounded, "Huh? What the fuck are you talking about?" Leaning against the huge meat locker that held various assortments of game and venison steaks, she folded her arms defiantly and stared at her mate. "If you must know I had a meeting with Jake to see if he'd want me to replace Bernice. With Bernice crippled and Jake's wife's brain problem the guy needs a pal. A bud. Someone he can go to lunch with and do stuff with" said his blond wife. "Oh I see, you want to replace your cousin, look hon, I paid Dr. Frapini $6500.00 for your new set of tits, I don't want no other man pawing them especially that fucking Jake Yanick" her husband retorted. "You don't like Jake? Why?" asked Crystal. "He's too smooth for his own good. Walking around in his suits, smelling like a queer with his Halo cologne" bellowed Booker. "It's Polo, Polo" said his wife. "Who the hell cares?" screamed Booker, "the guy loves more than your cousin, he loves every woman on the face of this earth and he ain't laying a hand on you. Replace my ass!" Crystal placed her hands on her hips and said, "Look Booker, all I wanted to do was keep the guy company. Do you know what it means to replace my cousin? It means we say the rosary once a day, we go to church every week, we exchange recipes, we compare outfits, that's it. Did you ever know my cousin to have a wild bone in her big tall body?" Booker sat down on the wicker chair in the breezeway of their home. Taking off his Bears hat, he scratched his beard thoughtfully and replied, "You know come to think of it, she's pretty straight laced. You mean that's all they do, him and Bernice?" "Booker, they study together and if they swap spit once a year, she's in the confessional the next morning wearing black!" exclaimed Crystal. The two looked at each other for what seemed to be a very long time. Crystal broke the impasse by saying, "And besides, Jake rejected me. He told me that his number one love of his life was Adrienne and that Bernice was his priority right now too because of how she got hurt at his house." Booker was incredulous. "You have to be kidding me, that piece of shit rejected you, what kind of ass hole is this guy? Who wouldn't want you as a lover? Is he stupid? He'd rather be with a bookseller or a skinny beanpole than you? I'm gonna fix his wagon for insulting my beautiful wife. You'll see" said her spouse with a wild and crazy look in his eyes.

Crystal was not the smartest girl God ever created. But being married to Booker gave her uncanny survival skills. The very fact that she shifted the focus from Jake the pursuer to Jake the rejecter was victory enough to stave off her husband's inquisition and end the matter right there. If Booker came after Jake, he'd do so thinking he was defending his wife's honor instead of punishing her lover. In a marriage like hers, small victories were usually the only ones available.

"Do you want me to make you some supper Booker?" Crystal asked sweetly. "Yeah, I guess, why don't you throw on some steaks and I'll open up two cold forties of Colt 45. We'll eat like we did when we were first married" said her now calm husband. While Booker got the beers, Crystal opened the freezer, slipped in a sealed zip loc bag which contained the remnants of her passionate encounter with Jake and got the steaks for their dinner.

PART THREE

Fortress Broadcasting stormed into the radio market with fanfare. The radio group, founded by two Oregon attorneys was in an acquisition frenzy for three years. Neither knew radio but knew how to acquire struggling AM/FM businesses. When the broadcast industry was deregulated, it became possible for stations to be bought and then totally programmed en masse. In radio markets that were small, Fortress's buying of the majority of properties guaranteed dominance in both rating points and sales. Having had great success with this methodology, Fortress figured that a foray into the economically depressed Pennsylvania market would be easy pickings. On one hand, they were right about acquisition issues. Owners who were on the bubble, squeezing out tiny profits were only too happy to sell to Fortress. Wanting to make a huge impression, Fortress officials over paid for some properties. In the world of Fortress Broadcasting, more meant better. There was no doubt in their minds that within a year their radio group would dominate the "coal cracker" market. There was an air of confidence that bordered on arrogance that intimidated most radio executives into giving Fortress free reign as they stormed into what used to be a very competitive but gentlemanly business.

The only person not scared of Fortress was Jim Duncan. The only human who was said to have intimidated Duncan was his wife Carol in their early courtship days. But other than her, Duncan was steadfast in his core beliefs of the radio business. Analyzing the situation in his office one day, Duncan came to the realization that Fortress was doomed to fail from the start. Others, upon hearing his theory acted with ridicule, laughter and disbelief. After all, this was America and bigger was better. A few whispered that Duncan's red and orange sales binders were passé and that the market was passing him by. Radio reps at Power 108 at long last tasting a bit of success were demoralized by the talk coming out of the Fortress facility. Mega bucks coming from corporate for promotion, Friday afternoon champagne parties for sales and programming staff alike as well as huge monetary bonuses for grabbing a percentage of one client's advertising budget were all hot topics of discussion.

Duncan called a special staff meeting to address the Fortress acquisitions head on. In the conference room Duncan stood before a flip chart that had the number 37 on the top and the number 32 on the bottom. No one at Power 108 had ever seen Duncan stand at a meeting. He told the staff the meeting would last no more than 5 minutes. They were out in less than three minutes. "A lot has been said about the entrance of Fortress Broadcasting into our market" said Duncan. "There will be talk from our competitors down the road about how great it is to work down there. Some of you will be asked to join their staff.

Keep in mind you are bound by a non compete clause in your contract. I don't think Fortress will think any of you special enough to pay you 6 months not to sell. The real issue here though is this. Fortress paid 37 million dollars for all of their radio properties. The entire radio market in this region produces only 32 million dollars in advertising revenue. With three radio groups splitting the 32 million, there is no way Fortress can recoup what they invested for at least twenty years, if ever. Keep those two numbers in mind, they paid 37 million. Even if they had each and every dollar of the market, if we handed them our profits and growth in a sack and said "Here take it", they'd still be 5 million dollars short. Any questions?"
The staff looked at each other, then at Duncan, "Okay then, have a great day" said the sales director as he watched his people get up and leave the auditorium. He knew he had hit a home run with them and defused any revolt that might have been coming. One thing sales people always understood were numbers. The type they didn't have, the ones that were out there and the kind that it cost to do business. Duncan had given his sales staff two huge gifts that day. Logic to fight back the emotional tide Fortress rode in on, and a very clear delineated business equation that everyone could understand. On the day Fortress flexed its muscle, Jim Duncan's staff from Power 108 had a record breaking sales day.

Jake continued on with his career at Power 108 and its AM station. He was named Salesman of the month three times and had the respect and admiration of his clients. His reputation as a dependable radio rep was becoming very clear to the competition at Fortress Broadcasting. Jake of course did nothing to discourage the talk of how wonderful he was. He had mastered the art of the unobtrusive invasion. Perhaps this was Jake's greatest people skill. Jake would approach his target seemingly preoccupied with something else. Out of the corner of his eye he would scan the perimeter of the room until he saw someone. When that particular someone asked Jake if he needed any help, Jake looked surprised, feigned helplessness and then began to gently invade that particular person's intellectual space. Since Jake was controlling the agenda, he came out looking like a star. On his visits to Fortress Broadcasting, Jake employed this technique with great success enabling him to meet the Fortress Sales manager Queenie Foxx.

Queenie Foxx was a radio lifer. An average sized woman, with curly brown hair and a ruddy complexion. Foxx had made her bones in Miami radio before moving to Pennsylvania and becoming top sales rep at Star Time Communications. Males did not necessarily regard her as sexy or beautiful but she had that certain something that made men want to be with her. The sales records she set at Star Time were legendary and she was on the fast track to being the

General Manager of the property until her ascent was derailed by a fellow female sales manager Sarah Jones. In a huge corporate catfight that would have been worthy of a mini series, Foxx came out on the short end when it was rumored Jones tipped off the existing managers of the impending coup. Queenie had set up a meeting with major sponsors of the station in an attempt to get them to drop their revenues for a few months when Sarah was at the sales helm. This drop in income would provide corporate management with a reason to make a change. The plan was fool proof until one of the advertisers mentioned the plan to Jones' husband on the golf course. Foxx and her plan were found out. After unceremoniously being escorted from the property, Foxx for the first time since high school was without work.

When radio reps get fired or quit, they do one of two things. Usually they go on to other fields but the real hard core types decide to open up their own ad agency. Queenie did the latter with one client, the gigantic family owned clothing outlet Bugsley's Bargain Bin. The opportunity for this came when Suzanne Bugsley fired the ailing Red Rose who for years did the family's advertising buys. After Rose's death, Queenie began to fill the void. Queenie quickly moved most of the store's business to Fortress Broadcasting. Within weeks she obtained a position as a sales rep at its jazz FM outlets. Three months into her stint she became the Sales Manager and one month after that she was named the General Sales Manager of the entire operation. After just a few weeks in this position, she ascended to the General Manager's position of the Fortress group. Her rise was staggering to many radio observers. Usually, it took years for a radio professional to move through the ranks of sales rep, Sales Manager and then reaching the top rung, General Manager. She cut her ties with Bugsley's and concentrated on building the Fortress sales staff. That would be a tall order since Fortress had few veteran reps left, most of them having been raided by Power 108's Jim Duncan.

Fortress had its old pros like Penelope Hartz, Jim Poppinaro, Dash Drozdeck and Little Johnny Walker. New comers like Tom Patrick and Bill Timmons showed promise but the sales staff was too small to handle the recently acquired 11 radio stations. Fortress began a hiring blitz in the market, advertising heavily and recruiting people from all walks of life. Fortress put on the front that they believed in training but in reality when they hired an individual, he or she was given a 12 week window to see whether they could stick or not. In a way this was survival of the fittest. The facility was selling the glamorous dream of radio. People in factories, restaurants and menial labor jobs saw it as their ticket to a better life, a professional avocation. Broadcast majors who wanted an entrée into the world of radio also hopped on the Fortress bandwagon. The radio giant processed hundreds of applications and began hiring at a dizzying pace. The problem was that not every new hire understood sales, radio or even current events. For every rep the new owners hired, they lost 3 in the training process. The problem was two fold and identified by Jim "Poppy" Poppinaro. The first concern was that there were not enough veteran reps in the market to go around. The second problem was that the new people who were trained had no idea what they were supposed to do and rather than be nurtured and developed, they were simply let go. Fortress had an endless supply of applicants that they could rely on. Complicating this problem was the fact that the corporate heads in Oregon began to take off their peacock suits and their true colors began to show. Budgets for promotion were cut, health care benefits were slashed and programming salaries were frozen. This occurred when their unrealistic dreams of profitability were not realized immediately. Jim Duncan's prediction was coming true sooner than anticipated. The suits at Fortress saw that they grossly over paid for the properties and now were in a panic to recoup their losses. The once stress free work environment was now filled with uncertainty. Champagne Fridays gave way to Beer Thirties with old cases of beer brought out of the prize closet as a reward for a well worked week. Each week, at 5:30 on a Friday, the staff mingled and then went on their way for the weekend. As time went on, attendance at the Beer Thirties began to dwindle. Foxx saw the sagging morale as a way to boost herself corporately. Her strategy was to surround herself with a team that would be loyal to her. She would take the few vets she had and use them as mentors in order to build a new, stronger staff. She asked Jim Poppinaro to begin the under-ground recruitment effort promising him a $500.00 bonus for each new rep he brought in. Poppinaro's first target was going to be his old friend Jake Yanick.

Jake's career at Power 108 was stalled because of the billing problems with the 4 Emerald Group. After Bernice's accident, the commitment to radio and Jake was not a top priority anymore. It didn't count that Jake was the only one who visited her in the rehab facility everyday. Even though she made no secret of the fact that she still adored Jake, the family never quite forgave him for her accident. Jim Duncan was doing his best to calm the waters around Jake but there was pressure from Big Bob Little to get the huge bills paid. Efforts to obtain legal remedies resulted in two station vehicles exploding one dark Saturday night. Poppinaro, ear always to the ground, sensed that Jake would be ripe for the picking and began his pursuit.

While Jake was the master of the pursuit of women, Jim Poppinaro excelled in chasing down the sale. Using lawyer's logic and humor, Poppinaro cajoled, harassed and brow beat clients into submission. Poppinaro was only too willing to use those same strategic tools with Jake but in reality it would have been overkill. Jake Yanick was ready for a change. His once bright star now dimming at Power 108, Jake's only two advocates were Duncan and Jody Mecklenburgh. His life was a mess. Adrienne had reoccurring bouts of depression that at times incapacitated her, and his girl friend was working to regain the use of her legs. Booker, upon hearing of his wife Crystal's plans for Jake showed up regularly and ambushed either Jake, his car or his house. Every time Jake heard Nazerath's song "Love Hurts" he had to laugh.

Poppinaro lunched with Jake and gave him the reasons why he should join Fortress. Poppy told Jake that as a seasoned rep he would be a valuable commodity. He told Jake the established accounts would be his for the taking and that Queenie Foxx would regard him as a true asset for her team. When Jake asked about his non compete clause which prohibited him from working for another company, Poppy said he was sure the company would either go to court to fight it or give Jake a 6 month "job" while he burned out his contract. Poppinaro stressed the fact that no one in the history of the market had the opportunity to get rid of his contract that way. Jake would be the very first. After various meetings Poppy furiously pushed for Jake to make a decision. The truth was Jake's only stumbling block was Jim Duncan. Duncan's professional friendship and respect were something Jake cherished. He did not want to be

portrayed as disloyal. It would take Jake six weeks to
make up his mind. The rep consulted with all of his
friends. Most said he should make the move but Wally
Peterson comfortable in his perch in New Jersey
cautioned against it. At a summertime weekend
gathering at the Mecklenburgh's lake home, Peterson
weighed in. "Queenie Foxx and Poppinaro are first
and foremost sales people, they are selling you the
idea of "them", their company. They are going to do
and say anything to get you to buy them, their deal.
You are their customer, they'll tell you anything to get
you to buy "them" " said his first sales manager. "Do
what you want man" said Wally, "but I think you
should stay put". Peterson's words would be prescient.
Jake himself had real doubts when he heard Fortress
wanted to dump Little Johnny Walker from their sales
staff. Walker was an institution in the local radio
market and did everything the new company told him
to do. This recurring development was unsettling to
Jake but Poppinaro glossed it over as part of the
business and pointed out the strength of the new
format Jake would be selling on a rumored talk
station. Queenie Foxx took Jake out to lunch and
advocated her cause eloquently. For any doubts he
had, the fact was Jake wanted to be wanted. His ego
needed that, both professionally and emotionally. The
delicate balance between his two patients, Adrienne
and Bernice were taking its toll on Jake. The least of
his problems was choosing a new job. If he could, for

the first time ever in his life, he wished he could pick a new existence. His final decision would of course hinge on his personal life. Adrienne thought he should move on because she felt his efforts were always under appreciated. She of course did not know about the 4 Emerald debacle. Bernice wanted him to quit altogether and take a job with her family business enabling Jake the time to visit her often at the hospital. Jake nearly considered the offer until he was tipped off that B's brother Danny was still unhappy with him over his sister's situation.

Jake's final decision was based on the fact that both women needed him closer to them. The money, the newfound prestige, the added accounts, did not matter as much as the fact that both Adrienne and Bernice wanted him nearby. When Jim Duncan made the announcement of Jake's defection to Fortress broadcasting and the reason why at a general staff meeting, Fontana spit his tobacco chew in a paper cup and mumbled once more to no one in particular "Anything for a chick!"

At the same when Jake Yanick was going through his negotiations with Fortress broadcasting, Craig Storm was preparing to leave his job at the company's Scottsdale, Arizona stations. Storm and Yanick's path would cross in the grand sales plan engineered by Queenie Foxx. Against conventional wisdom, Foxx staffed each of the 11 radio stations with a Sales Manager and a stable of reps. Storm, a relative star in Arizona had taken a floundering sports station and brought its revenues up by 213%. Coupled with the arrival of the Arizona Cardinals, the invention of the baseball Diamondbacks and his hard work ethic, it was easy to see why Storm would be the most logical candidate to oversee the Pennsylvania AM operation. Schooled in the retail business, Storm took to the radio business with a serious resolve that made others sit up and notice. Over 6 foot 2 and looking like the late singer Richie Valens, Storm was an engaging man who valued his family, his faith and his sense of honor and fair play. Jim Poppinaro thought the teaming of Yanick and Storm would be beneficial to the company. So did Queenie Fox

Foxx had to persuade Storm to leave an established account list as well as half of his family in the west. His teen age son would start his senior year in the fall. The sacrifice was tough for the family but as Wally Peterson predicted to Jake, when Queenie Foxx sold something she rarely missed her target. Storm first lived in a superb 4 star hotel at the company's expense. Within a few weeks, he was moved to a lower class hotel in an inferior neighborhood. Any reservations he might have had were eliminated by his sunny optimism, the fact that the deed was already done and for that matter, he had no way to turn back the decision clock. Meeting before his first day at Fortress, Storm and Yanick felt good about the upcoming working relationship. Both had come from similar working class backgrounds and educations. Each loved the Green Bay Packers and took their radio careers seriously. Both held their wives in great esteem and Jake was grateful when Storm made no judgments about Bernice. Each man was reminded by Queenie Foxx that they both had their work cut out for them. Storm came to radio as an outsider and developed a passion for the medium, Jake was literally born to it and made no secret of his love for radio. Little did the two realize that this new venture and their ultimate treatment would change their long held perceptions of what broadcasting meant.

Storm anchored his staff with Jake and Tom Patrick. Patrick was a 6 foot 3 handsome ex baseball player who had a quick wit and an even quicker temper. Like Storm, he was a dedicated father and husband who enjoyed the antics of Jake's double life. One of the things both Storm and Yanick loved about Patrick was his inventive way of selling radio. If he had to bring in 20 advertisers at $2.00 a piece to get something on the air, he'd do it. Jake, while burning out his non compete acted as a promotion liaison and mentor to the new staff. Storm hired a former FedEx driver, a topless taproom bouncer and a part time computer salesperson. This would be a 5 person sales staff for a station that barely billed under $100,000.00 a month. Storm worked with each of his new recruits but it got discouraging when each day none of the three brought in any business. Part of the key to good sales was building a good relationship with the client. A radio client who trusted their sales rep would give the person, that rep carte blanche, to do right by them. Jake had a few clients like that because he built them through his years. Tom Patrick's clients were more personally based but nonetheless just as critical. Both Yanick and Patrick could walk into any of their clients and get them to buy just on the rep's say so. The newer team members did not have that tool in their arsenal and Fortress was too impatient to give them the time to develop. Storm was fond of saying, "Sales is like shaving, if you don't do it once a day, you look like a bum!" When Queenie saw no numbers coming from the new guys, she went on a tear against Storm.

Another thing going wrong for Fortress was that with each station having a sales staff along with a sales manager, the Fortress sales staff was in a war with itself rather than Star Time Communications and the folks at Power 108. Cannibalization of accounts was so common among the warring parties that prospective advertisers shut out any new Fortress reps because they didn't have the time to see all of them. It got to the point where Patrick and Yanick used Bernice's hospital room to make phone calls to clients to set up meeting times because the Fortress cubicles were not sound proof. Since every rep was desperate to make their goal, stealing of client information was commonplace.

Queenie Foxx thought that every sales rep should exceed their goal. In a normal situation, that would be a reasonable expectation. But at Fortress, this flew in the face of clear logic. There was only so much money to go around, advertisers had commitments other than radio and people would buy something not when a Fortress broadcasting rep told them to but when they were ready to buy. Foxx began to get corporate missives from Oregon that weren't pleasant. Her solution to lagging sales was to abolish all the cubicles for the sales reps and put in desks that were lower in construction so that she could keep her eye on everyone. When this didn't work, she jettisoned her management team. Sandra Roth went back to automobile sales, Will Walkens was demoted to promotions and three imports she hired were escorted out of the building one afternoon without warning. Two of the 3 transplants had just closed deals on new houses. The managers were replaced with cronies of Foxx. Two of them essentially became staff informants. Foxx, holed up in her bunker, relied on people who possessed a pigmy factory mentality. But in the corporate world where the bottom line was new dollars, she needed visionary thinkers. Many were dismayed when she shunned the old pros's advice and took the word of her less than sophisticated minions.

Storm and his staff found the navigating very tough in the radio market. The old "Nifty 1050" was going through an identity crisis. Once the premier station in the area, now it was a dormant shell of itself. The reason was brought to Jake's attention one night when he ran into an old high school friend. The friend advertised on the station because of his loyalty to Jake and his perception of what the station once was. "The problem with your station Jake, is that no one knows what it is anymore. The format has changed so many times that I keep on trying to focus a message but the changes prevent continuity. There is no consistent message but more importantly I have no idea if the program I am sponsoring will be around next month!" said his friend Terry Wurst. Jake thought long and hard about the conversation he had and decided to share it with Craig Storm. His sales manager was a reasonable man who put a positive spin on everything. When Storm agreed with Jake it surprised and delighted him.

The two men decided to request a meeting with Queenie Foxx to voice their concerns. Both men prepared their presentations and felt they were armed with a logical argument about radio 1050's prospects.

After the duo ended their remarks, Queenie Foxx seemed annoyed and simply said, "The two of you are not the same people you once were". Jake was confused and said so. "I don't understand what you mean, that we aren't the same people. What does that mean?" he asked. "It means that you aren't the same people I knew" replied Foxx. "Do you mean we changed as human beings, we got dumber, smarter? What do you mean by that?" Jake asked getting more exasperated by the minute. "It means you are not the same two guys anymore, you're looking for excuses instead of getting results" she said. "Look", countered Jake. "We are doing more billing with good quality clients than this station deserves. These people aren't buying rating points, they are buying us. The relationship. It's the only consistent thing they can rely on. To say that we are making excuses is ludicrous". Storm looked over at Jake and decided to jump into the fray. "I think what Jake is trying to say is that things need to build. "The Nifty 1050" was a glorious institution for over 5 decades and now you want us to rebuild the loyalty that has broken down over the years. It's like a team that has to rebuild itself" said Craig. "I never played any sports myself but I do know one thing, you aren't the same people you used to be. I have another meeting, go and sell. Find the old you" Queenie barked.

Dejected, both men walked back to their desks trying to make sense of what they just heard. As they made their way through the building, they passed Penelope Hartz who was sashaying toward the production studios. "Gee guys" she said to them, "you guys don't look like yourselves today!" Jake turned to Storm and said, "Jesus, another one!!" Storm smiled and said, "I don't know about you but I'm going to check out myself in a mirror!" From that meeting on, Craig Storm's job was fraught with peril while Jake's standing as the carpet bagging genius was all but a dim memory. As time went on, Jake and his fellow sales staff were not at all happy with the way Queenie Foxx was running the operation. Apparently the suits at Fortress felt the same way but for different reasons. Jake and his boss, Storm, wished there could be more humanity in her methods while the higher ups wanted a better bottom line to make up for all that money they had spent on the properties. Queenie Foxx's next move in the company chain of command was not at all voluntary.

Jim Poppinaro arrived early at the radio station on most Mondays, Wednesdays and Fridays. He showed up at 700am on those days because he went to sleep at 8pm the night before. He lived like the perpetual college student. He had the minimum amount of furniture in the Victorian house he'd bought. There was a sofa, refrigerator, bed and a few chairs. Poppy went to bed early on those nights he was not on the town or when he could not play on the maternal instincts of Jody and Jerry Mecklenburgh to wrangle a dinner invitation. He wandered around the building that morning waiting for the support and sales staff to come in. He disdained talking to the "on air" staff because he wasn't sure they had taken baths in recent time. He felt long hair was unkempt and any type of piercing was an affront to the body. Poppy went to the men's room and washed his hands for the fourth time that day. As he exited, he caught sight of a figure familiar to him, but one he had never met.

A supreme gossipmonger, he rushed toward a phone and called his former partner in crime at Shawnee Broadcasting, Donald Albright Norris. Norris was a sales rep with Poppy until Fortress bought the radio stations. Norris was nicknamed "Cronkite" because he always had some news.

He was a jovial man who had a penchant for stealing client's data, rifling through co-workers desks and basically stabbing anyone he could in the back. But when he was called on it, he began to cry telling the affronted and offended how pathetic and needy he was, then wrapped himself around the victim in a big bear hug asking for ultimate forgiveness. It always worked. Fellow workers addressed him to his face as "scuzzball", "sleazebag" and "slug". But he was always the first guy to go to a family's wake, or comfort anyone in jeopardy of losing their job. He had a direct pipeline to Jim Duncan, the General Sales Manager at Power 108. When you told Norris something, you told Duncan too.

"Don, Poppy. You wouldn't believe who is sitting in the lobby" said Poppy in a conspiratorial tone. "Who?" said Norris ears perking up. "A talk show host that's who" Poppy said. "Pop, is it Larry King, Rush Limbaugh, who the hell is it?" Norris knew full well the drill, employees seeking a job in the early morning hours were either jumping ship at one place or if it was a talent, there was going to be a format change. "It's the girl, the girl newscaster who got fired 4 times when you were here, you know",

Poppy explained. "You mean Coral Rock, is she back?" asked Norris. "Yeah she's in the lobby waiting to see Hammerstock the Fortress veep, Poppy related. "Oh doctor, this means "The Nifty 1050" is going all news and talk. This is huge!!!" said Norris. "Now Don, you don't say a word about any of this to anyone, not even Duncan!!", Poppy implored. "Hey" Norris said, "my lips are sealed, and besides Duncan doesn't go in for any gossip. I never tell him anything, you know that. I'll talk to you later, okay?" "Okay" Poppy said as he hung up the phone, reached for his bottle of 409 and furiously began to disinfect the just used phone. Norris looked out of his office and saw Duncan ambling down the hall with a 24 ounce coffee and a fresh pack of Camels. "Hey Jim, need a light?" he called after him following him to the designated smoking area of the radio complex.

Coral Rock was born Cora Lillian Rockefeller. Her father was one of the second generation Rockefeller cousins who had met her mother at Ohio State when he was a senior and she was a freshman. After a three month courtship, they married. Cora's mother quit school, and after three years of law school and 2 little girls, Mr. Rockefeller decided to move on.

Cora's mother got a settlement of $850,000 which was a fortune in the 1950s. She remarried a man who ran through her money with abandon spending on alcohol, unusual business schemes and more alcohol. He was cruel to Cora and her sister Hannah. Cora, who took advantage of tennis lessons provided by her mother had a way out. She left home at 16 and became a tennis protégé traveling to Europe and South America, essentially never looking back. Her game was played with an angry intensity. She was rated 15th in the world at one point but traded the rankings to finish her education. After graduation, she went on the tour again, this time ranking in the mid 40s. Shortly after turning 30, she became a tutor and tennis instructor to rich European children. This stint in her career gave her a worldliness she missed by being the daughter of a divorced mother. But seeing those pampered kids made her seethe with anger knowing that she could've been one of those "fortunate" kids. At the age of 38 she longed to return to the U.S. but had no place to go. Fate then stepped in. Cora took a vacation to Ireland because of an interest

in the Irish culture. On a tour she met a middle
aged gentleman by the name of Darren Syracuse
who was also in the country because of his
interest in the culture. The white haired man was
engaging, elegant, and handsome. Both visiting
Americans struck up a conversation about her
career in tennis. He then invited her to dinner and
she accepted, fully expecting to have a fling with
the jaunty gent. When she arrived at the
restaurant, the man introduced her to a woman
sitting next to him. She was 25 years younger
than he and was introduced as Mrs. Beth
Syracuse. The three had a great time with
Syracuse offering Cora a job as a personal tennis
trainer for Beth and their children. She was
stunned at the generosity of the offer but shocked
at her own cynicism. How bitter had she become
she wondered. In Syracuse, she first saw a
predator instead of who he was, just a nice man
trying to provide for his family, albeit a rich
family. She was angry, confused and ashamed.
She felt the hills of Pennsylvania would be a
welcome change for her spirit, and maybe life.
When she arrived in Pennsylvania, she found the
Syracuse family had interests in both radio and
TV. A voracious follower of the news, she was

intrigued but set about to teach the young Syracuse kids tennis. As a byproduct of her job, she was invited to many social functions and made quite an impression with her beauty, intellect and biting sense of humor. There were various liaisons with men but they were tightly controlled and no hint of scandal ever surfaced.

One stormy November Saturday morning, a former mailman, Don Jackson went on a shooting rampage killing 27 people. 19 of them were his kids from 6 different women. Jackson, a dour man was unpleasant but not known to be violent. In her bed, oblivious to the terror, she received a phone call from Darren Syracuse who asked her to go to his TV station and answer phone calls on the situation. She threw on clothes and went to the facility. The phones were ringing off the hook with a killer on the loose in a small town of 50,000 with a police force of 48. She recognized the anchor, an elderly World War II vet by the name of Harry S. Buckley. Buckley did not look well. In fact he had a case of vertigo and could barely stand. The station had gone to live coverage and Buckley's words began to slur.

His face was sweating. During a break, he keeled over and passed out. There was the cameraman, Cora and a frantic intern named Hollie Evans. The station I.D. slide of the laughing Indian with the NBC peacock sticking out of his rear end stayed on camera. Darren Syracuse from his fourth floor office called down to see what was going on. Cora explained the situation. Darren told Cora to call an ambulance, then take Buckley's copy and read the news. He instructed her to be natural and just ask questions. He would get a replacement to the studio as soon as possible. Cora did as she was told, fixed her hair and went on camera asking questions to police authorities any sane person would ask in this insane situation. The manhunt lasted 4 hours until the shooter was caught. A half-hour into her commentary, Syracuse had a reporter on hand to relieve her. But he never did. That was how impressive Cora Rock was on that fateful day.

For the next 11 years, Cora, now Coral Rock would report for the NBC owned TV station in Northeastern Pennsylvania, move to Chicago to anchor a morning news show, and wind up on a Fox station in New York. Ultimately she returned to the city where her broadcast career began to be with the ailing Mr. Syracuse who had become a sort of father figure to her. After his death, his widow sold the station. Coral hooked on with a talk radio station and became more popular in that medium than in TV. She was fired 4 times in the conservative area for being pro-choice, anti marriage and against the death penalty. Whenever she was terminated, it was front page news and upon her return the ratings doubled. Out of work for 4 months, she accepted an interview with Fortress Broadcasting to do a live call in talk show.

The time started to drag on and she looked at herself in a mirror that was part of the front desk scenery. Her milk white skin had few wrinkles and her auburn hair had no hints of gray. She wondered to herself if, at the age of 48 she could still turn a head. Just then she heard a loud commotion and saw a short man with a large pompadour hairdo entering the front office lugging a watermelon and being trailed by a chimp dressed as a soda jerk. She silently thanked God she never took drugs because if she had, she might see things like this every day." Well hello there" said the man bouncing back and forth on his heels to make himself appear taller to her. "I'm Johnny Walker, the greatest radio sales rep in the country. I used to be Little Johnny Walker, the greatest nighttime personality in the history of radio. Perhaps you've heard of me", he continued. "No" she simply said. "Oh come on, I had Little Jonathan's House of Music, the Johnny Walker fifth of great liquefying and electrifying music" he proudly told her. "I'm sorry, I didn't grow up here.........I came from" Before she could finish, Little Johnny Walker had an epiphany. "Hold it, you're Coral Rock, how can I miss that. You were here for four tours and we never met?" he asked. "I worked nights "she told him. "Well. If there is anything I can do to help you, after all, I've been here 36 years, I know where all the bodies are buried and can be of immeasurable help" he said in a low, sexy, radio voice that she imagined drove the teenyboppers wild in a bygone day. In a former time and place, she would have crushed someone like Little Johnny Walker but she found him oddly charming and somewhat sincere in a clumsy sort of way.

"I do have a question Johnny, what's with the watermelon and the chimp?" she asked. "It's Wednesday and on Wednesday, Tommy McMurtry passes the watermelon around the studio for the guests. He cuts the watermelon in half and has each person in the studio pull out a piece with an ice cream scoop. It lasts about 5 minutes, a lot of local dignitaries come and go to be on the Watermelon feature", said Johnny. "Where are they?" she wanted to know. "Oh, they're here" he intoned seriously. "And the chimp?" she asked. "The chimp is part of a sponsor promotion we're doing with Goodness Golden Ice Cream. We are going to have the chimp pass out ice cream and the flavor is unique. This is a heavily Polish area and the sponsor is calling the new pieroagie ice cream, HUNKY MONKEY ice cream and Tommy is going to interview the chimp" Johnny said with excitement.

"I'm thinking there are all kinds of health issues, ethnic slurs and animal rights questions all wrapped up into this promotion, don't you think?"Coral said voicing her concern. "Nah," said Johnny, "This will be smooth as glass......
......with class".

Just then Tommy McMurtry stepped out of the studio belting out the opening lines to musical "West Side Story." The booming singing voice did not fit with the slight, handsome older man with red hair and a mustache. "Hello" he said and beckoned Little Johnny into the studio. Coral walked over to the speaker and tuned in 1050 Radio to hear this deal. Whether she got the job or not, at least she'd have a story to dine out on.

A Salsa version of "Tea for Two" began to play as the distinctive voice of Tommy McMurtry began to boom through the speaker. A much respected radio newsman in his day, McMurtry's reputation in the business was solid. He had been the first radio voice to report on the death of John Kennedy in this part of the world and was offered a position as a network night time newscaster but turned it down to be with his wife and kids. For the last 10 years he hosted the morning show, a show she would most likely follow if she were hired. Losing herself in thought, she didn't notice Hugh Hammerstock, the tall, handsome Kevin Costner look-a-like Nebraska transplant who oversaw the Fortress stations on the east coast. . "Coral, hi, I see

you're tuning in to Tommy's show, great stuff.
Hey are we keeping a lid on this or what,
sneaking you in early in the AM, getting a jump
on the competition. If you accept our terms, we'll
surprise the crap out of everyone in the market
bringing you back" he said with a smile that
reeked of insincerity. "Well, let's hear what you
have to say to me", she replied. "Cool, but let's
finish listening to McMurtry, this is a gas" he
said as he turned up the speaker.

McMurtry was going through the
watermelon distribution, naming state senators, a
hot dog vendor, a judge and a local Mayor. It was
a typical McMurtry bit. Then it happened. "Oh
yes folksie wolksies, here we are passing the
watermelon and going in for a big piece of the
red stuff without the pits, putting her hand around
the watermelon rind is none other than the former
tennis pro, former newscaster, who was taking a
load off in our lobby this morning, Ms. Coral
Rock. Go ahead Coral, grab that piece without
the pits and just let that cool fruit touch that
beautiful mouth" McMurtry broadcast. "Those
fucking idiots" yelled Hammerstock loping down
the hall. "They blew your cover, all my secrecy,
all my hard work" he continued. Just then Little

Johnny Walker was exiting the men's room with the chimp in tow. "You, it was you, you little shit ass, get the fuck out of here with that chimp, you and McMutry blew our cover" yelled Hugh, veins popping in his neck. "We didn't blow anyone yet" said JohnnyWalker "but the day is still new and we are after all in sales!" Hammerstock then reared back and began chasing radio legend Little Johnny Walker and the chimp down the hall around the "u" shaped offices.

Dressed in her signature white tee shirt that accentuated her still perky breasts, light blue jeans weathered boots and navy blazer she wondered aloud what other interesting characters there would be. Looking up, she saw Jake Yanick's broad shoulders as he entered the radio station. "How's it going?" nodded Jake who smiled and winked. "Okay, and you?" she asked. Walking down the hall, Jake called after her, "My father used to say that when your feet hit the floor in the morning, then there's absolutely nothing to complain about, do you agree?" Coral laughing out loud said, "Uh huh, I agree". Jake stopped in his tracks, turned around and said, "From what I heard about you, this is going to be the last time that will happen". Coral Rock responded to him by doing something she hadn't done in years, giggle like a schoolgirl.

Jake thought the outing of the Coral Rock situation on McMurtry's show was hysterical. Both he and Tom Patrick were excited about the fact that the dynamic talk show host would be available to sell to the entire market. Patrick, always the brain trust came up with an idea called "Rock On the Road". His plan was to sell the Coral Rock show at various dining and lunch establishments in the area. The live remote broadcast would showcase Coral to the public and give the station much needed exposure. Patrick worked out a plan that had each rep sell a "Rock On the Road". It was a "win win" for everybody. Coral got exposure and a talent fee, the sales rep got a huge one time billing bump and the station made money. Like many projects at Fortress, this great idea was almost derailed by management.

While Coral Rock got the job at Fortress Broadcasting, management had no idea where to put her. All Hugh Hammerstock wanted to do was acquire her in the market, so no one else could have her. The broadcast conventional thinking was that because she was a "chick", teaming her up with a morning D.J. might work. She tried a very brief and unsuccessful week stint with the morning man for the urban FM station. It was not only a generational clash but one of culture too. Coral, while hip had no use for some of the raunchy lyrics and gross behavior of her young counterpart. Not that she was a prude by any means, but she remembered her stint as a serious journalist and felt demeaned by the position. Her next stop was at Lion 103 the country station. She alienated the hardcore C&W audience by ridiculing the rural areas of the region, their dental work or lack thereof and their accents. Management then moved her to 10pm to 2AM where she did a 4 hour sex talk show. This ended badly because the opinionated Ms. Rock railed against teens having babies, advocated mandatory sterilization for welfare mothers with more than 3 kids, maintained that women who had children from different fathers multiple times be branded as "serial fornicators" and felt that gay bashers should spend time in jail with "bubba" for even uttering a hate crime idea. She was either talking over the heads of the people listening or there was nobody out there. Either way, it was just Coral railing on a 50,000 watt channel for 4 straight hours with no listener/caller interaction. Coral was a true talent but she needed the right medium.

"The Nifty 1050" was gradually moving away from entertainment and going into a news format. Tommy McMutry, an old news hand did very well in this new genre. Teaming Coral up with Tommy was out of the question since two salaries in one time period didn't quite match up to the billing. Coral herself approached management with the idea of doing an afternoon talk show. After thinking a while, they agreed and the Coral Rock program was born.

Unlike the typical local show, Coral eschewed guests and preferred to have the callers be the stars. Dubbing it "caller driven radio" Coral scored huge successes with her first forays into the local market. Many of her fans from TV listened. She was establishing herself as a force and one of the gems of the Fortress operation. Coral was fearless in her presentation and commentary. One of the reasons was being fired to her was old hat.

For her part, Coral decided that this time she would not be the flaming diva. Her goal was to work well with the money men of Fortress in order to preserve her career. She was more than willing to go out on calls with the sales reps and help them sell the "Rock On the Road" concept. Craig Storm even invited her to a few sales meetings. As time went on, the roster for the remote shows began to fill up. Patrick sold the majority of them but Jake got a few booked too. Up until the remote at his old friend Terry Wurst's sticky bun shop, Jake's contact with Coral was minimal.

Terry Wurst was pleased with the progress "The Nifty 1050" was making. He was more than eager to have a "Rock On The Road" at his business. Terry's wife, Dorthea ran the store while he tended to his other business ventures. Both agreed that the broadcast would help them sell gift baskets for Christmas. The day was Dec. 12th, 1998 and as luck would have it, the date was historical.

As was his custom, Jake got to the broadcast early overseeing the technical setup. He was always careful not to appear to know more than the engineers did but made subtle suggestions to improve the quality of the broadcast. The store, clean, well lit, scrubbed to the max smelled like an old time bakery where just breathing could add calories to your diet.

"Well, here we go Terry. This is going to be some day we picked," said Jake.

"You bet" added Terry. "They going to impeach him today?"

"Right in your store today my man, before thousands of listeners. We're carrying it live but then Coral is going to be giving her commentary and taking calls. Who would ever think that when we were in high school, we'd be at the same place when such a momentous occasion was happening!" said Jake.

"Yep, life sure is funny Jake. She's going to sell my gift baskets in the middle of all that yammering, right?" asked the store owner his back to the door. "Damn straight my man" said the strong familiar female voice. "I'll sell those sticky bun baskets even if I have to peddle them with fish nets and a mini skirt". Terry turned around, smiled and said, "You're everything I thought you'd be" taking her hand to shake it. Jake smiled and commented, "I've never seen you in a skirt, I find your last comment intriguing". By this time, Terry's wife Dorthea came from the back work area and said, "Only you would find that intriguing". Terry laughed and said, "I'd agree with Jake but I'd be a dead man by sundown".

After the banter, the quartet got down to work outlining points they wanted to make and when the commercial breaks would occur. Jake, like Patrick believed in getting the maximum bang for his clients buck. He always felt that more was better when it was for his client's business. Coral watched him intently as he zeroed in on the couple's requests for their business and wrote out the points on a legal pad. What impressed the talk show host more was the way he included her in the discussion. As the group worked, Thomas Patrick entered the building with Craig Storm. "We just wanted to stop in and say hello" said Storm, "do you mind if I sit in and talk with your wife and

Jake?" Terry said, "Jeez, I get the boss and Jake, I must be an important guy". "Naw, he's just hungry for some sticky buns" joked Jake. While Storm, Jake and the Wursts sat down to chat, Coral excused herself and got a cup of coffee. Thomas Patrick busied himself looking at the broadcast set up.

"Looks pretty good, huh?" said Patrick, "our boy Jakey does nice work". Coral walked over with the steaming coffee in her hand. "I hate to use this word, but he's an intriguing guy". "Oh yeah, he's really something, he'd give Clinton a run for his money" said Patrick. "That bad huh?" said Coral. "No, not really. He's an equal opportunity womanizer. The secret of his success is that he treats everyone the same. He gives a lot of himself to a woman. Jake lays it on the line right from the start. He tells them who he is and what he is and despite that, they love him," added Patrick adjusting the wires connecting the speakers. "Well, a dog is a dog I guess" said Coral with disgust, "I guess pigs go to pigs in this case, huh?" "Shit no, Jake's a real class guy and the women are freaking spectacular. He has the most beautiful women in his life. The wife." Interrupting him, Coral asked, "There's a wife?" "Oh yeah", continued Patrick, "Looks like Meryl Streep. Then there's this tall redhead, looks like a model, Bernice is her name, man is she a head turner! Big bucks in that family too. No, Jake attracts class acts which is kind of strange for a funny looking guy like him. I mean we all can't be as good looking as I am, ya know?" Coral smirked and said, "You think you're good looking?" "My wife does. She also says if Jake looked like me, he'd be dead from all the women hanging on him" added Patrick. "Your wife sounds like a very kind woman", said Coral with a hint of sarcasm. "Oh yeah and she's a good cook too" noted Patrick as he went for a coffee.

The meeting between Jake, Craig Storm and the Wursts broke up and Jake passed Coral's way as he headed out the door to visit another client. "I'll be back for your show" he said to Coral. Coral, arms folded defiantly responded, "I'll be here but I'll be damned if I'm changing into a skirt for you". Jake stopped dead in his tracks and said,
"It's radio, no one cares what you wear". "Smart ass" muttered Coral as he headed toward his car.

The event went extremely well. Congress impeached Bill Clinton, customers streamed into the store and ordered gift baskets for the holidays and Coral received a record number of phone calls. Since it was a Friday afternoon, Jake and Coral did not have to return to the office. As Jake helped the engineer pack up, he saw Coral lingering in the background. "Did you get your check?" Jake asked referring to the talent fee the Wursts had to pay as part of the agreement. "Oh yeah, I got it, thank you for making it so smooth. Sometimes I have to beg people to pay me" she told Jake. "Well, I'll

have you know you are a very special case. The last time I had talent here, Terry paid them off in cappuccino and cookies but because of your wealth of talent, you got the cash" smiled Jake. "Don't you ever get tired of it?" she inquired. "Tired of what, this crazy business?" he asked. "No" she said, one hand on her hip, the other in her right jeans pocket, "Of all the bullshit you spew. I mean you are so full of crap, and the thing that pisses me off is that you do it with this little boy "Oh jeez I got caught with my hand in the cookie jar" smile! It's maddening." Jake was momentarily taken aback. "Hold it, hold it" he said defending himself. "What was the bullshit part, about your talent? I think not. The cookies and cappuccino part, well that was what I call a double E". Coral, despite herself was now curious. "A what? What the hell is a double E?" "Jake speak", for the phrase Entertainment Enhancement. It gave weight to the story, gave it a lift, made it interesting, witty, more responsive to you as a listener. I always mean what I say when it comes to three things, my women, my family and my clients. But a little embellishment is not a bad thing as long as it entertains. And you

have to admit I interest you because you're still here having this silly argument with me. In a way, I now matter in your cosmos" said Jake leaning against the wall of the shop. "You are nuts, my cosmos is my business and you aren't going to be in it" said Coral.

The give and take was broken by Dorthea Wurst who asked the duo if she could get them a coffee. Both demurred and the woman continued her work behind the counter. "See," continued Jake, "We belong in each other's cosmos. I'll prove it to you".
Incredulously Coral said, "Oh I gotta see this".
"Okay," said Jake, "I'll ask a series of questions.
"Do you buy brand names rather than generics?
Generics.
Are you monogamous in your relationships?
Always.
Do you believe in God?
Hell no.
Do you think masturbation counts as sex or just intercourse?
Just the old in and out.
Do you smoke?
Yes.
Do you like the smell of smoke?
Hate it.
Do you put salt on watermelon?
Yes.
Do you like hotdogs?
No.

Can men and women be buddies and not have sexual yearnings?

Absolutely not.

What about baseball?

Boring.

Do you still hate Nixon?

More than ever.

Well, that proves my point!" concluded Jake. "That proves nothing!!!!" shrieked Coral, "we have absolutely nothing in common". "Very true" agreed Jake, "which is why we belong in each other's life. We balance each other, shit, we cancel each other out!!!"

"There it is, the bullshit quotient again" countered Coral. "It's not bull, it's true and I challenge you to accept it and me in your life. It'll be the best thing that ever happened to you not to say the most entertaining" said Jake. Coral looked straight into his eyes and said, "I'm going to do this, but I'm going to prove you dead wrong. We are going to be a fucking disaster as friends, you'll see." "Prove me wrong, go ahead but it's going to be quite a ride, I'm warning you". "I consider myself warned, how do I begin? Want to go for a drink?" asked Coral.

"No, not right now, I have commitments tonight but I'll see you next week and we'll talk about scheduling", said Jake. "Scheduling, scheduling" her voice shrieking, "You're gonna schedule me, put me in a time slot?" "Yeah, that's right, in due course you'll come to appreciate my penchant for time and efficiency. It will make our meetings seem more worthwhile" assured Jake. Both eyed each other until Coral said, "Okay, how do we seal this silly ass deal? With a kiss I bet?" "We're friends, we're not going to do a Hyeland", replied Jake. "A Hyeland?" Coral asked looking confused. "Sealed With A Kiss, Brian Highland, 1962, remember it?" Jake inquired. "Yeah I do, is this more Jake speak?" asked Coral. "Yep, part of the program. I'll get together with you next week. Okay?" said Jake. "Sure, that's fine".

The two said goodnight to Dorthea Wurst and as they walked out the door, Jake said to Coral, "You know even though we're friends, as a woman I regard you as a 5B!". "A 5B, what the hell is that?" she asked. "Well if I was driving in my car and saw you walking down the street in a mini skirt, I'd roll down my car window and yell, BABY-BABY-BABY-BABY-BABY" laughed Jake emphasizing the word BABY in an extremely lascivious manner. Despite herself, Coral laughed and grabbed his arm as the two walked out the door.

Terry Wurst walked to his wife from the back of the shop and asked, "Anything interesting happen while I was away?" "Oh nothing much" replied Dorthea, "just watching a train wreck start in front of my eyes".

True to his word, Jake forged a genuine friendship with Coral that was both entertaining and eye opening. Coral was impressed by Jake's dexterity in multi tasking his personal life while the sales rep was only too glad to be seen in the company of a local media icon. Both served each other well as sounding boards for the craziness that was Fortress Broadcasting. The programming department was under constant assault by the corporate bean counters that cut money at will, while the sales department was like a revolving door with numerous hires and fires.

Jake was big on reality checks and when something didn't sit right, he confided in Coral. The stations were not making their budgets, plain and simple. Clients were stretched to the limit but Queenie Foxx always thought they could be squeezed for more. This put enormous pressure on Jake's end of the operation. Coral, on the other hand, was being told to be more controversial to increase ratings. The more caustic she became in the conservative area, the less people listened. Since both Jake and Coral were experts at putting on a perfect front and not sharing their feelings in the workplace, it was only natural they gravitated toward each other. They generally met at Daniel Langan's House of Clams, a small seafood eatery that was off the beaten path. The last thing the two co-workers needed was even a hint of an affair between them.

"You know what really bothers me about this job, what really eats at me is that I am very good at what I do. And if they just left me alone, things would be good" lamented Coral. "I agree with you but these people are incapable of doing that. I think modern broadcast management runs like that; if they slow down that means they have to think. They say change is good but in some cases, you don't fix what isn't broke" added Jake. "Change! Huh, you look like a guy that is so afraid of change yet you deal with it very well" noted Coral. "I hate change, I enjoy boredom, change stinks generally. But I tell myself that life is change. But these guys, when they change something, they ruin lives" said Jake shucking open one of the large chowder clams Langan's was famous for. "Don't eat that one" cautioned Coral. Jake nonetheless smelled it and feigned eating it. "Let me eat thy poisonous venom and die in peace!" he joked dramatically. "You eat that one, you won't have to worry about change anymore", smirked Coral. Jake put aside the unhealthy clam and dug into the other good ones. It was odd, that Jake, a risk taker in his personal life, embraced the safety of a boring existence. It was just one of the bundle of contradictions that made him who he was. "Please understand this Coral" said Jake. "I am the most empathetic person in the world and I respect managers and what they need to do. But in this day and age, they are like shooting stars that burn out quickly. And with their ignition comes great upheaval. In the last couple of months four managers have come and gone, Storm is on the bubble and miserable, people who have relied on community oriented stations for years now find the only thing they enjoyed as entertainment is gone. Why? Because certain managers inflicted change where there was no need. And you know what? Those implementers of change will be gone and off to another town leaving a lot of pain and misery in their wake". Coral was taken aback by Jake's passion on this issue. "This is all about Tommy McMurtry and Little Johnny Walker, right?" she asked. "Damn right, "said Jake trying in vain to open up the saltines with his fingers, "It is all about them. People bond with them, the widow who is lonely, the poor sick guy whose family is out of state, these are McMurtry's people. And they are being abandoned for a slick homogeneous out of town format that means nothing to them. Don't even get me started on Little Johnny Walker either. The guy is an institution and they treat him like crap. You revere the pioneers, not toss them out. Coral nodded in agreement. "Jesus Christ, who the hell can open these things up" he said in frustration using a ballpoint pen to break the seal of the uncooperative crackers. "Am I glad we're not gonna have sex" said Coral looking at Jake trying to manipulate the cracker packaging. "Oh, I'm a real disaster in the bedroom" added Jake, "you'd hate it, take my word on that". Coral laughed out loud at both the absurdity and blatant honesty of the comment. "A womanizer who is awful in bed, that's a new one" she commented. "It isn't about the bedding my friend, it's about the final tally, the end game. When it's all said and done, the important thing is how I touched their lives. Did I make them better people. Make them smile. Give them memories, that's what the rush is for me" countered Jake. "So you mean if I gathered your women up and one by one interviewed them, without failing everyone would be happy, "commented Coral. "What woman is ever happy" replied Jake, "But I think if you probed they'd say I'm better than most men they came in contact with. I can almost guarantee that". Coral smiled at Jake and told him, "I know I'm very happy with the way this friendship is going, I'm pleasantly surprised". Jake shot back, "As well you should be". At that point, Coral threw a bunch of used shells at Jake in jest. The moment was interrupted by a loud siren that rocked the restaurant with its blaring.

"What the hell is that?" shouted Coral as she got up to stride to the window. Jake in the meantime slumped and hid himself under the table. Coral was concerned because she at first lost sight of Jake. "Jake, get up from under the table, what the hell is wrong with you? Don't be such a pussy!!! Get up!" she commanded. "Okay, okay, " said a resigned Jake.

Jake's theory on loud noises or other interruptions was that if it didn't concern him, he just got out of its way or wasn't interested in it at all.

Coral grabbed Jake's hand and forged out the doorway with him in tow. She headed for the source of the noise and felt a searing heat envelope the front of her body. A huge blaze burned brightly in the night sky. Jake instantly knew the fire scene, it was the old Joanna Fashions dress factory building. Coral knew the history of the property too remembering that it was to be turned into a small business incubator by the Chamber of Commerce. Within minutes the media was on the scene and Coral Rock gave the TV cameras a blow by blow account of the fire as well as a history of the facility. As the cameras rolled, the inferno crackled in the background as the attractive Coral Rock succinctly summed up the structure's place in local lore. Standing behind her, oblivious to how it would appear to his employers, his wife and girlfriend was Jake Yanick caught on film. There was going to be some explaining to do but on this night, Coral relived her past TV glory days and Jake stood, unconscious to the world, in that reflected light.

Jake got home late that night and settled into bed next to Adrienne. They both talked about routine household items before Jake, exhausted started to drift off to sleep. It was the type of twilight slumber where you were most vulnerable to saying anything to anybody. "So what were you doing tonight?" asked his wife. "Oh, a little bit of this, a little bit of that", he sleepily replied. Jake hated when his wife employed this technique. She would wait until he was drifting off to sleep and then hit him with a question about his whereabouts. He mostly had a knee jerk reaction of panic and almost always she caught him in a lie. Jake's ploy was to give his wife elements of the story so that he could at least say he was partially correct, partly truthful. "I had a bite to eat with Coral Rock tonight", he said lazily. "So that's why you two got on TV?" asked Adrienne. "Yeah, I just happened to be in the camera cross fire" said Jake. "So, what did you and Coral talk about?" asked Adrienne. "Work, life in general, you, a few things" said Jake fighting to keep his eyes open. "Uh uh" was all Adrienne said letting her husband finally sleep. The next day at the gym Jake caught himself on the morning news program with Coral. To his relief no one at the gym said anything. It was a different story however at Fortress. When Jake walked into the morning meeting, Thomas Patrick yelled across the room, "Hey handsome, you looked real good on TV last night". Jake just nodded. Queenie Foxx shot a glance at Jake and he accurately read that the gossip machine was in full operation regarding his appearance. After the morning forecasts and assignments, Jake walked back to his desk with Jim Poppinaro. "What the hell are we forecasting? What are we trying to predict? You know I think projections are so dumb. How can I possibly give an accurate estimate on what money I am going to bring in, it's crazy!" commented Poppy as he ate a large glazed donut. "Do you lie sometimes?" asked Jake. "Everybody lies, but me. I remember the one time everyone had Hooper Trucking on their prospect sheet, every last sales rep in the building and Queenie went nuts" noted Poppy. Jake blankly nodded thinking he had to call Bernice up and touch base with her. "Hey Jake" whispered Poppy conspiratorially, "are you tagging Coral Rock? That's the big buzz around the station. Is she really that hot?" "Of course not" said Jake, "where do you get this stuff?" Poppy responded by saying, "Hey it's all over town, it was on TV for Christ sakes, your big rag doll better not find out or you'll be in the soup". Jake thought long and hard about Poppy's latest observations. He felt bad that there was this perception for Adrienne, Bernice and for Coral. He rushed to the phone to call Bernice. Determining that she had not seen the video, he made a date to see her in the rehab facility in the afternoon. On the way out the door, Jake was confronted by still another sales rep, this time Bill Timmons. "So," said the smirking Timmons, "you got something going on with Coral there Jakey?" "No" Jake said flatly. "Can you pick me up a dub at Power 108?" asked Timmons. "Yes" said Jake without emotion as he headed out the door.

Jake's various client meetings that day were non eventful. He bought two box lunches, picked up some flowers and went on his way to see Bernice. As he entered her room, he caught sight of her lifting weights with her legs and doing curls with her arms in a continuous motion that seemed so fluid it belied her actual condition. Shooting him that glorious smile, she sat down for lunch after she finished her required regimen. Jake regaled Bernice with stories of Poppy and his clients while she shared with him information about the latest doings of her family. It was a relaxed, easy meeting the two thoroughly enjoyed. "You look very tired" said Bernice to Jake. "I worry about my Maytag breaking down, don't know if I can ever find those quality parts to fix him up again". Jake smiled and answered, "I'm fine, I'm just a little worn out today. Lot of stress at work, ya know?" Bernice leaned forward and said, "You don't have to stay there, Daddy would love to have you work for us. That would fix everything". "Oh Bernice, please, your brothers would throw me in the explosives machine when no one was looking," he said. "I'd fish you out Maytagger, and pull you to safety" she smiled. "Yeah?" asked Jake. "Uh huh, but since you're not giving up on this silly broadcast business, which is long term stress, let me deal with your short term needs, " she said sensually. "Oh wow, is this the special treatment option your so famous for?" asked Jake hopefully. "Oh yeah sweet cakes. Let's get down and dirty" cooed Bernice. Jake leaned back in the chair and waited as Bernice took a pillow and sat on the floor directly in front of him. Looking up at him, she took off his designer shoes and sexily slid his socks down his feet. The couple had done this before. This was pretty much as sensual as the two got but Jake thought it was better than contact sport sex. Jake leaned back and closed his eyes while Bernice took his bare feet in her long tapered fingers and began to massage them. For one brief moment in Jake's crowded, busy life (one of his own choosing) he achieved nirvana.

Smiling, he thought about how truly lucky he was and began to drift off to sleep for a quick catnap. Just as he was in that twilight stage of blissful drowsiness, something both familiar and surreal happened. "So, I was watching the TV news last night and I swear I saw a guy who looked a lot like you standing right beside a very attractive older lady. At first I thought it was you because he was well dressed, very well groomed and ever so gallant standing beside her", she said softly. Putting more pressure on his heel, she continued "But then I thought my Maytag is way too tired after his hard day of wife loving and girl friend caring and managing all those clients to even pop the top on his little itty bitty ice cold can of Tab to let even try to fight a big bad old hot fire with an attractive, hot older lady by his side" sneered the tall muscular woman at his feet. Jake was in a strange state, he had heard everything she was saying but was unable to think or move. Plus, he couldn't formulate the words for a plausible denial. Bernice continued massaging softly and then abruptly pulled back the ball of his foot toward him squeezing it as if she were trying to twist it off like a bottle cap. "Ouch!!!", whined Jake, "what the heck are you doing? Stop that!!" Bernice persisted. "We have to make something very clear here" she told him holding his left foot hostage in a hold any wrestler would envy, "I don't mind you spending time with Adrienne, she was already in place when I came along but under no circumstances do you start another project. I'm your ultimate alternative, I accept that but I'm not going to play third fiddle in your orchestra, understand?" She released his feet, threw his socks at him, picked up the pillow and crawled back in bed with her back toward him. It was a side he had not seen of Bernice. This one time meek girl was now a woman of steel. Jake thought about her similarities with Adrienne in this situation. Both women seemed to be stronger after spending time with Jake. He thought it uncanny how his two women struck him for the truth when he was most vulnerable. He wondered if somehow they were comparing notes. After a few moments of self serving thought, his focus shifted back to his B girl lying on the bed. "Hey" he called out. "Go away" she said. "Oh come on, nothing is going on with her, she's a friend, she's an ally at work. We were just eating and then that fire broke out. I thought Danny had moved his hobby south of here and wanted to congratulate him on his work" continued Jake. "Danny's not a fire bug, he blows things up stupid", she replied. A few silent moments ensued. Then she turned over and looked at him, "I'm mad at you and only two things can fix it, you know what they are. So if you want to make this right, be on your way sir!!!" Jake got up, put on his shoes, left the room and went down to his car. He went to his trunk, pulled out a small package and carried it back to her room. and stood in the doorway. Bernice looked up and smiled. Jake drew the curtains, darkened the room further by turning out the lights and took a scented candle out of the small bag. He placed it on the table in front of her along with a Godiva Dark Chocolate Raspberry filled bar. Lighting the candle, he stepped back and began to sing, "She's a rag doll, such a rag doll, such a pretty face, should be wrapped in lace...ooooo, oooo, ooooo, rag doll, I love you just the way you are". Bernice looked at him with tears forming in her eyes. "Thank you so much, I knew you'd do it again for me. It's our little ritual. Remember the first time you did that for me?" she asked. "The first night you were in the hospital, but I didn't think you heard me or remembered anything about it" replied Jake. "Believe me Maytag, " countered Bernice. "I remember everything about every moment, good and bad I spend with you". Their quiet moment was interrupted by an aide who thought someone was smoking because of the candle. "Hey, I have to get back to work" said Jake. "Call me later my little Maytag, okay?" Bernice said. "You got it my little rag doll" called Jake. The aide looked at both of them, shook her head and said, "Love makes normal people crazy, that's all I gotta say". Bernice shot her a look and said, "We aren't in love, if we were, it would be all over for that fella" pointing toward a retreating Jake.

Jake went to his afternoon meetings and got back to the station late. As he was walking to his desk, Coral called out to him from down the dark hallway. "We've got to put a stop to this!" she said. Jake turned around and said, "A statement like that gets people like us in trouble". Walking to meet him, she countered, "I'm serious, we have to nip this in the bud. Think we should call a press conference?" Jake was now both angry and confused. He didn't know whether he was angry because Coral didn't want people to know they were having an affair or wanted them to know they weren't. "Why do you of all people care what people think?" asked Jake. "Oh jeez, there you go, you fucking prima donna, you think it's all about you. This has nothing to do with me and you but

everything to do with your perception. I don't want to
be known as the programming side of the Queenie
Foxx equation here. That's first and foremost. The
second thing here is that you have your hands full
already and I'd kill you, physically and mentally.
We just have to demonstrate that we are good friends,
and that's it" said Coral. "I think we should just go
about our business and let them wonder. We need to
become more than good friends though, we need to be
allies. It occurs to me that you are the only person here
with a moral core. I want to use you as my reality
check. Unless you just want to haul off and slug me in
public sometime" offered Jake. "There is some crazy
shit going down here, isn't there" said Coral, "it seems
like people are just dragged down every day. Not only
on your side but on our side too. Okay, I'll be your
ally. Do you want me to square everything with the
bookworm and the beanpole?" she asked flirtatiously.
"Don't call them that, Adrienne and Bernice"
corrected Jake. "The wife and the girl friend" added
Coral. "I'm fine with them, I explained it all like I
always do," said Jake. Coral told him, "One of these
nights, one or even both of them is gonna cut you up
in pieces when you are just drifting off to sleep, you
know that twilight time when you are just drifting off
and you hear sounds but can't move but you hear
everything and you……….." Jake, getting alarmed at
how well the radio host knew him, cut off the
discussion on his sleeping habits. "Gotta go" he said to

Coral. Coral smirked and chuckled, "Touched a nerve, huh?" and walked back into her studio to talk to her audience.

Portia Dion worked for Frankie Pannini for 10 years. She met Frankie at a racetrack where the gambler became fascinated with the young woman's dexterity in picking long shots. A conversation ensued and that night Portia received a job offer to run the Pannini finances. She would be paid a huge sum to oversee the burgeoning family empire but also to pick races on the side. Pannini was a good employer and there was little friction between the two. Coming from two different worlds did present some problems. Once Portia introduced her partner Jill to Pannini and his response was a blank stare. "You got a partner, jeez I got partners too. What do you need partners for when I pay you that good? Aren't my partners sufficient for your needs that you gotta go into business with another partner?", said the businessman. Once Portia explained what the association was all about, Pannini was mollified but nonetheless still confused.

Portia ruled the finances with a firm hand. Being primarily a cash business, the business manager made certain that accounts were earning dividends, the money was clean and the payouts to vendors and "associates" went out on time. She was also a skilled investigator who could glean information from a casual conversation. Portia was a Pannini favorite and could count on her boss to do her any favor.

Like Portia, Pamela Devane was a competent business manager. Unlike Portia her people skills were ugly. Pamela was in her job for 16 years and had seen GMs and various owners come and go. Her arrogance and abuse of her staff were breathtaking in their cruelty and unkindness. Despite this she was kept on because of her business acumen. When Fortress took over they relied on her expertise to keep the ship afloat. Fortress funneled a great deal of money into the new acquisition. Just as quickly, the faucet went to a drip when the reality of the station's billing came to the fore. Fortress execs were surprised to see three guinea pigs dressed in formal wear waddling around her office. The critters were bigger than most and emanated a foul smell. This was tolerated until the day Little Johnny Walker brought the chimp in for McMurtry's promotion and the riled monkey nearly shredded the guinea pigs. The consternation this event caused gave Fortress the opportunity to jettison Pamela and begin a new search for a new business manager.

Portia wanted to return to school to finish her Masters degree. Her partner Jill, had an apartment near the University and she asked Pannini if she would mind if she took a leave of absence plus a letter of recommendation to work somewhere part time. Her boss said yes and dutifully wrote out a letter to a few places. One of those places was Fortress who was in dire need of a steady financial hand. Portia answered an ad that ran on one of the Fortress stations. Armed with the glowing letter from Panini, and after an initial interview, Portia was hired outright. She was given the task of unraveling the puzzle that was called the Fortress business office. Taking morning classes, Portia worked from 12noon until 9pm. This gave her the opportunity to become friends with Coral Rock. Both women hit it off immediately for many reasons. Roughly the same age, they had shared numerous historical experiences. The two had libertarian views on personal conduct but conservative views on social mores. Both were atheists but displayed Christian like qualities to people in their industry who deserved much less than that. But the defining bond was the way the Fortress female management structure seemed to operate. They were appalled at the petty, spying, catty "chickocracy" that dominated the office world they lived in. At first Coral was reluctant to say anything at all because she felt she stood alone in this belief. But the two did a reality check one day on the issue and after that they became inseparable.

Portia was a tall blonde with a nice build and very flippant personality. Jim Poppinaro was instantly attracted to her. For her part, she enjoyed Poppy's wit, his commitment to his job, his zero tolerance for dead beat clients and his silly quirks. She also knew of Poppy's abhorrence of gays. Recognizing Poppy's beliefs were not prejudicial but merely cultural in nature, Portia hoped to maintain a friendship with the rep. Portia felt that Poppy was an intelligent rep who never had any problems getting money for clients. She hoped his on surface prejudices would not prohibit them from being friends. In the cutthroat world of radio, it was an act of faith on her part and one that her friend Coral respected. One day Portia confided to Poppy about her concerns she found at the company and much to her delight his reaction was even handed. This was important because Fortress was becoming a divided camp between people who were trying to do the right thing while doing their jobs and those that were trying to prevent that for deluded reasons. The alliance between Coral, Poppy, and Portia in time would have a new member, Jake Yanick.

Very rarely do people from various backgrounds click, but this quartet did. Coral saw the double standards used for programming decisions, the company preached quality but wanted cheap. Jake, once a beneficiary of Jim Duncan's favoritism was now stung by Queenie Foxx's harsh expectations of him. A hard worker, Jake had no problem with his efforts but was royally pissed when she and her minions would purposely derail him and "The Nifty 1050" staff. The AM side was treated like the ugly stepchildren of the group. For every step Jake and his gang took forward, Queenie pushed them back two. Poppy tried to navigate the stormy seas but was stuck training new sales people who had no clue about the business or customer relations. Portia rounded out the group with her inner knowledge of the finances. More importantly though she believed that there was a good way to handle people and that was with honesty and dignity. The four Fortress employees met on the fly throughout the business day. There was no gossip, just quiet reality checks, body language and secret signs whenever something bizarre was happening. Portia heard rumors that Queenie Foxx was going to fire both Jake and Coral because of their alleged affair. The deed was going to be done on a Friday afternoon after one of the beer thirties and Coral's show. Queenie was going to fire Coral because of low ratings and dispatch Jake with a sexual harassment charge. Portia huddled with her friends and came up with a plan. It was a dandy and only the strength, character and confidence of a Coral Rock and the guile, smarts and innovation of a Portia Dionne could have pulled it off.

The courtyard below the station offices was filled with employees sampling the beer and donated donuts. Jake and Coral carefully avoided the gaze of Queenie Foxx. As the party started in earnest, Jim Poppinaro asked for everyone's attention. "Attention, attention, uncle Poppy has an announcement to make gang. Actually it's two announcements, no wait, it's three announcements" he said as the crowd groaned. "No, no, I'll be quick, the first one deals with our own Jake Yanick, I am pleased to announce that Jake has won the Pocono Prides award for his creative work in radio advertising for his series of commercials for the "Pub and Rub" massage parlor and for his non profit contribution of radio commercial expertise to "The Little Lost Souls of NEPA". Jake come on up for the award" yelled Poppy. Jake bounded up for the award, looked around and said, "I'm accepting this award on behalf of all of us because you make me shine every day professionally. Also, to my boss and mentor, Queenie Foxx, I say thank you for the way you inspire me every single day here at Fortress, you are a true treasure". Thomas Patrick mumbled to Storm, "She's a treasure all right, somebody should bury her!".

Poppy stood proudly, reveling in his master of ceremony duties. "My next announcement has to do with ratings. I have in my hands here the inside trends, now this is not the official ratings but just an idea of where the ratings are going, up or down. Going up, Coral Rock with adults 25 to 54, number 4 in the time slot, up from number 8" yelled Poppy. The group went crazy, Queenie Foxx shot a look over to the program director of the urban rap station wondering if he leaked the info. He shook his head in a negative manner and then shrugged. Jim Poppinaro's reputation was based on his total knowledge on just about every aspect of the market and this announcement proved it. Coral stood up to accept her award. "I just want to thank all of you, especially the sales staff who go out there every day and bust their asses to get the revenue for my show. You are the soldiers of truth. You are my inspiration" she enthused. Half of the eyes were on Coral, the other half were on Jake watching for his reaction. Surely with this setting, the emotionally charged duo of Rock and Yanick would dissolve into a love fest outing the affair everyone was sure they were having. "And I'd also like to recognize someone truly special, a man who has become a part of my life and soul..........." This was sure to be it, a public declaration of love for Jake. The ratings and awards be damned, Queenie would have them both where she wanted them on moral turpitude. Coral continued, "This man changed my life by introducing me to someone I love now, I will love in the future and forever. Jake Yanick, thank you for introducing me to the great Portia Dionne." The crowd went silent and then Dash Drozdeck began the applause. Political correctness, fear of retribution and just plain shock prevented any other questions from being asked. The group partied on for a while until people left muttering to themselves.

That night, Jake sat in Bernice's rehab room. Her family's money allowed her the luxury of a terrace. While she sat next to Jake, Portia Dion and her real life girl friend Jill Monroe drank wine while Coral Rock opened up a Havana cigar puffed it and passed it to Jim Poppinaro as the nighttime air caressed them all. This was a silent victory celebration of co-conspirators who all dodged the ammunition of

Queenie Foxx. Bernice, knowing what a conspiracy was felt that Adrienne Yanick should be sitting right next to her. Her father's business friends might be dubious at best, but since knowing Jake she had never seen or heard about the lack of honor in one given profession such as broadcasting. She gazed out at the setting sun and hoped Jake would soon find another line of work. While Jake's B girl day dreamed, on the other side of town Jake's wife was acting. Adrienne sat down at her computer in her office and was doing a career search to see what was available for her husband to do employment wise the rest of his life. Adrienne had no idea what went down at Fortress this day, she didn't have to. Her search results were her own labor of love for this character they called Jake Yanick.

Little Johnny Walker had been a mainstay of the broadcasting business for over 35 years. Walker was regarded as the go to guy when it came to big sales projects. He knew everybody in the market and had the ability to do a deal without compromising his integrity and conscience.

One day Jake had lunch with Walker and the two took a drive in the veteran's Porsche. Jake could hardly fit in the tight vehicle but went along for the ride. Walker was a renaissance man of sorts teaching swing dancing, Japanese language, as well as owning every electronic gadget known to man. "Jake, Jake, I have this new device which can pick up cell signals. If I wanted to, through my radio I could pick up cellular signals and have them blaring in stereo. Check this out" said Johnny as he began adjusting the tuning knobs on the car radio. Jake was essentially bored by the technical end of the broadcasting game but humored his old friend by feigning interest. The two sat in silence waiting for a sound. Suddenly after what seemed an eternity, a crackling sound emanated from the speakers. It was a woman's voice. "You know I love the way you do it, don't you, you are so strong and filled with passion, oh you make me so hot all the time" cooed the woman's throaty voice. Both men looked at each other thinking the same thing. Before they could say a word, a man's voice responded, "Oh yeah, I think about you all the time, you instill something in me that I thought was long dead, oh

please, please come up into my office…now!!!!" Just
then, the spying duo saw Queenie Foxx's car speed by
them on her way to the broadcast studios. "Holy Shit,
that was Queenie talking to Hugh Hammerstock." Said
Walker. " Hugh Hammerstock?" asked Jake. "Yeah,
the regional vice president of Broadcast Relations.
"They are sleeping together" responded Walker. "So"
said Jake. "This is huge! Now I don't care who sleeps
with who but this explains the fast track she's been on,
oh man I can't believe this!!" added Johnny. "What
use will this be to you though?" asked Jake. "How in
the world would you present it to anyone and why
would they care? It's personal stuff". Little Johnny
looked away and said, "Yeah I guess you're right, but
she was breathing pretty heavy, don't you think?" Jake
replied, "If you like that kind of stuff." Both sat in
silence for a while until Jake started to giggle. "You
know what would be hysterical?" asked Jake. "If we
put this on tape and gave it to Big Boy Leroy Brown at
the urban station. Can you imagine what he'd do with
that?" Walker stared ahead blankly and did not say a
word while Jake kept on cackling. Jake eased himself
out of the car gingerly and bade goodbye to Little
Johnny. He had a brief meeting to attend and began to
walk to his car when his pager went off. It was
Queenie Foxx. He returned the call. "Jake, can you go
to a meeting with Johnnie Walker and Hugh
Hammerstock? I want you in on this to see how it goes
down but more importantly I want you to see a true

professional in action. Nothing against Johnny but you can learn a lot from Hugh," said his now non-panting manager. "Sure" said Jake. "I'll be happy to attend, where is the meeting?" "I need you to be at Big Winners Ford at 3pm. Little Johnny and Hugh will meet you there for the meeting with Walt Franko", she replied. "I'm there" said Jake as he walked back to Walker's humming sports car. "Hey" called out Jake, "Queenie wants me to go to that meeting with you at Walt Franko's, are you okay with that?" Walker turned and said, "Wonderful. You are finally going to see me in action. I am going to knock your socks off, as a matter of fact, I'm going to knock everyone's off when they see the deal I made for a contest on the FM stations." Jake stood in front of Walker and said, "I'm impressed, did you get a huge buy out of him?" "Better than that, I got this guy, Walt Franko who has a reputation of being very cheap to give us not one, not two but three vehicles for each FM station to give away. It's a multi season promotion Jakey! You watch and see how I'm going to reel him in" said Johnny. "You know Hugh's going to be at that meeting with us, right?" said Jake. "Fantastic!!!!!!" said Walker, "I can really show him a thing or two about sales. See you there kiddo". Jake watched as the buoyant veteran rep pulled out of his view. Jake was pleased for Walker given the fact that the Fortress people made it clear they were not happy with little Johnny Walker.

Jake killed time by going back into the station to do some paper work. When he walked by Queenie's office he noticed the door was shut. Walking down the hall, he passed the small, crowded conference room where he saw the team of traffic goddesses watching their afternoon soaps. Unlike other sales people, Jake had no problem with their lunch time diversion given the fact that it was these women who scheduled a rep's commercials. To get on the bad side of them would not be a good idea for a salesperson. Jake continued on toward the back row of studios and stopped to see a commercial being cut. While he looked in, he noticed Big Boy Leroy Brown doing the voice over. Looking at Jake, Leroy motioned to Jake to come in. "Hey man" intoned Leroy, "want to help me with a commercial? I need an extra voice." Jake, always the ham complied readily. "Okay man" said Leroy, "this is what you need to do. At the top of your voice yell Vack To Be Ya, got it, Vack To Be Ya". "What the hell does that mean?" Jake asked. "It means nothing man, not a thing but I need you to say it loud and I need you to say it proud. Right when I cue you, just scream it but do it with feeling."said Leroy. "How the heck am I gonna get feeling when I don't even know what the hell it means" countered Jake. Leroy calmly said, "Just listen to the beat of the music, it'll take you there". Jake heard the beat of the music, started to rock back and forth and all of a sudden began to pronounce the words in a low guttural voice, "Vac To Be Ya".

Then he began to laugh at the stupid phrase but still kept with the beat. "Vac To Be Ya" he said again. Finally with the music at a crescendo, Jake screamed from a place he thought never existed, letting the words flow deeply, "Vac To Be Ya". Big Boy Leroy was ecstatic. "That's it man, that's it, the white boy's got some serious soul. You're on fire dude!" said BBL complimenting the rep. "Mind if I use it?" asked Leroy. "Nope, go ahead, enjoy, just let me know when it's going to air". Jake walked out of the studio and ran into Coral Rock. "What the hell was that all about?" asked the female radio talent. "Just doing my part for radio history" remarked Jake adjusting his suit and tie in the control room glass. "You sounded like a complete idiot" said Coral. "Glad you were impressed" smiled Jake. "Where you off to?" asked Coral. "Big meeting, I'm a very important man you know," said Jake rolling his eyes. "That's why I like you" said Coral, "you don't take this place or yourself too seriously". "It's how I survive every day" said Jake as he walked down the hall. "You look real nice for your meeting" Coral called after him. "Thanks", Jake said calling after her, "I know".

Jake got in his car and drove to the meeting thinking about the curvaceous Coral complimenting him on his clothes. Momentarily distracted, Jake had to bring himself back to the issue at hand which was the meeting with Little Johnny Walker and Walt Franko. As he drove he thought about Johnny

Walker's career and how long he had lasted in this crazy business. He started to tune around the radio dial and wound up listening to the urban station Fortress owned in hopes of hearing himself on Leroy's commercial. Jake had no clue on the type of music that played on the station, did not like it, did not understand it. Just as he was ready to change the channel he heard Leroy's voice intone, "Join us tomorrow morning at 6am for the sounds of monkey love only on your urban rap authority". The promo was clever with an animated version of the old Captain and Tenille hit "Muskrat Love" which Jake found amusing. But then he heard something very familiar, something he had just heard a few hours before. "Oh my God!!!!" Jake said out loud. "It's the cell phone transmission little Johnny Walker picked up on his receiver, how in the hell did that happen?". Jake hastily switched the station as if doing so would erase the commercial. Pulling into the car dealership, he saw little Johnny Walker doing a little two step as he approached him. Walker, smiling said, "You hear Leroy's promo on the urban station? Wasn't it fantastic???" Jake looked at his fellow rep uneasily and simply said, "I guess", and followed him into the building for the meeting.

The Walt Franko Ford dealership was an institution for many years in northeastern Pennsylvania. Walt was the son of a coal miner who parlayed a GI bill education into a multi million dollar auto operation. Walt worked 7 days a week at his trade and did everything by the book. His relationship with little Johnny Walker came about when he sold Walker his first car. Virtually ever man and woman over the age of 30 bought their first car from Walt Franko. Franko's office looked like the inside of a brothel with bright red velvet walls and huge leopard print covered couches and chairs. As Jake plunged into an easy chair he prayed he'd be able to lift himself out. Franko was an imposing man with a shock of white hair, wearing a not very stylish short sleeve shirt a size too small for him and a clip on tie that ended mid chest at his breast bone instead of the customary belt buckle.

Little Johnny Walker regaled Franko with stories of successful clients. Jake could tell the two had an easy going relationship that was built on years of trust and experience. "Want some milk there Johnny?" asked Walt, "it might make you taller." "No, I'm fine" responded Walker, "but I would like to know where you get that wonderful neckwear, lucky day in the Cracker Jack box?" And on it went as the trio waited for Hugh Hammerstock to show up. Finally, the banter ended and Walt asked Johnny, "Where the hell is this jimbroni we're waiting for?" "He'll be here in a minute" said Johnny trying to buy some more time. An uncomfortable silenced permeated the room until there was a tap on the door. It was finally Hugh Hammerstock who strode in and introduced himself.

Franko and Walker tried to hide their annoyance with the late arriving District Sales Manager.

"Hey guys" said Hammerstock. "I hear we're doing a deal today, right?" Walker, Franko and Jake all nodded in agreement. Jake thought it was both strange and rude that Hammerstock did not even offer an apology or even an excuse for his tardiness. Walker, taking his cue from Hammerstock simply said, "Let's put this thing together because Walt I know you're a busy guy". "Hey" interjected Hammerstock, "we're all busy guys". At that point, Jake was intrigued. Hammerstock was doing the exact opposite of what Duncan had taught him at Power 108. He was not at all mannerly in his remarks and demeanor and if anything appeared to be arrogant and antagonistic. Walker was frantic in his attempts to ignore Hammerstock's behavior.

"Walt, I think we are going to make history here today with this type of multi station deal we are doing now" began Walker. "First of all, I am personally grateful for your time and your interest in this project". The auto dealer smiled and replied, "Well Johnny, I've known you for years, ever since you were a teenager wearing satin jackets to your high school hops. I trust you when you tell me this is gonna be a good deal for both me and you". "That's so kind of you to say" said Walker, "a compliment like that coming from a guy like you means a great deal." Jake thought things were going extremely well. Little Johnny Walker had Walt Franko in the palm of his hand. "So Walt, to recap, you are going to give us three Ford Sables loaded, for the multi station giveaway. We are in turn going to do a 24 hour a day promotion, 2 60 second commercials an hour, billboard sharing on 52 placements as well as sponsorships of news, sports and weather on all morning drive shows and a features sponsorship for the Coral Rock news program. How does that sound to you?" asked Walker. "Sounds like I'm part owner of your station. This is a fantastic deal Johnny that's going to work out very well for all of us" replied the jovial owner. Walker asked, as a courtesy what Jake and Hugh thought. Jake nodded his head and simply said, "This is a great deal!". Then Hugh weighed in. "This is the deal of all time, and for a few measly Sables. When I did a promotion similar to this in Kansas City, I got the dealer to give me three SUV s, but we'll kindly bend over and say thanks to you Walt" smirked Hammerstock. Jake could not believe his ears. Little Johnny Walker's mouth got dry. Walt Franko's once jubilant face now exhibited a tight smile when he said, "Well Hugh, this isn't Kansas City". Walker now reeling shifted gears and pulled out the contracts. Franko took them and said he would have his Finance Manager sign and deliver them to Fortress at 5pm that afternoon. Johnny Walker was relieved because this was the way Walt had done business with him for years. The three reps exited the building and went their separate ways, Hugh Hammerstock totally oblivious to the chaos he nearly caused. "See ya men" he called out as he drove away. Johnny Walker looked at Jake and shook his head. Jake said, "He could've said thanks, don't you think?" "But he didn't" said Walker in a singsong voice.

After the appointment, Jake made a quick pit stop at the demolition business to have his oil changed. One of the perks about knowing Bernice was that his car never wanted for anything in the way of repairs. The family business had a full service garage to take care of its fleet. Danny worked under the hood and also fixed his windshield wipers. Jake waited in the office watching the three overhead TVs that showed horse racing from Philadelphia Park and Monticello raceway. In the corner was the omnipresent Silvio whom he had last seen at the Super Bowl party with an adding machine and phone at the ready. Jake was fascinated but not especially curious about this end of the business. Finally Danny came out and called Jake throwing him his car keys. "How much do I owe you?" Jake asked. "Nothing bro, it's on the house". "Thank you" said Jake. "You know" Danny said, "you play your cards right with my sister and all of that will be yours!" pointing to a huge warehouse, a fleet of trucks and a red silo that was designed as a stick of dynamite. "Gee, thanks" said Jake who stood looking at Danny. Jake stood and looked at Danny, Danny staring, gazing back at Jake. The men eyeballed each other for 2 minutes until Danny broke the silence. "What are you waiting for?" Danny asked. "Well since I'm going to be part of the family business, I'm just waiting for your mom or sister to come out and start my car, isn't that how it works?" Danny erupted in laughter at the crack and retreated to the garage cackling and howling all the way. Jake was pleased he had reached a chord in Danny and got in the car to return to the station.

Jake returned to Fortress and began to do his paperwork. Little Johnny Walker's desk was right across from his. You couldn't help but overhear any conversations. At 5pm, Walker got a phone call from Walt Franko. The usually loquacious Walker simply responded to the auto dealer in one word answers, then ended the very one sided conversation with "I understand completely", then hung up. Jake did not have a good feeling about this call but sat in silence doing his orders. After a few minutes Johnny Walker leaned across his cubicle and said to Jake, "Walt Franko just called and told me there was a mistake in his inventory department and that those three Sables were already sold." Jake looked at Johnny and said, "Gee, I'm so sorry".

As the two looked silently at each other, Hammerstock exited Queenie Foxx's office with suitcase in hand, overcoat donned for his flight out of town. Jake glanced over at the departing manager, looked over at Johnny and shook his head in disgust. He had never seen Johnny Walker quite so sad and defeated as he was this afternoon.

Jake was having lunch with Adrienne when his pager went off. It was Jim Poppinaro. After his mid afternoon snack with his wife Jake called Poppy who asked to meet him at Billy's Pizza Corner. Jake drove to the establishment and went inside finding Poppy in front of the salad bar. Poppy was examining the lettuce for dirt when Jake arrived. Poppy turned around, put his arm on Jake's shoulder and said, "We're doomed!" Despite the rigors of his life, Jake still possessed that eternal optimism that was not to be denied. "What happen, Herbert Hoover resurrect himself from the tomb?" Jake said making sport of Poppy's Republican leanings. "No, sit down and I'll tell you. This is on me", said Poppy waving a waitress over. Jake noticed that the server was a young girl of average build with bad skin that she easily camouflaged with a foundation base. He ascertained that she had her wisdom teeth pulled, had size 32B breasts and stood 5 feet 6 and a half inches tall. Poppy slapped the table hard to get Jake's attention and put in his order. "12 cuts of the square pizza, double pepperoni and triple cheese on all of them and a bucketful of Coors Lite. I want double enforced paper plates as well as real silver spoons and four chilled mugs brought out at 15 minute intervals. That okay with you Jake?" Poppy asked. Looking up at the

young girl, Jake smiled and said, "Fine". The
waitress taking the menus looked first in Poppy's
direction, then in Jake's saying, "My name is
Nancy in case you need anything else" winking at
Jake on her way to call in their food.

Poppy adjusted his huge frame in the booth
and repeated himself, "We're doomed". "Why?"
asked Jake. "I hear it on good authority that Dash
Drozdik is going to be the new GM and that
Queenie Foxx is going to be demoted to General
Sales Manager. This is terrible, just terrible. She
is going to be on us like white on rice, stink on
shit, like, like…." Said Poppy. "I get it, I get it"
Jake said. "Jesus she is going to micro manage us
to death and the damn thing is we can't do
nothing about it either," continued Jake. "Wait it
gets worse, do you know who her second in
command is going to be?" asked Poppy. Before
Jake could answer, Poppy shifting in his seat
yelled out loud, "Fucking Bill Timmons, Bill
Fucking Timmons, he's a little nazi, you know
that Jake???!!!!!!!!!!!" Everything stopped in the
restaurant when Poppy yelled, heads turned in
silent shock. The great secret between Poppy and
Jake was no longer that after the outburst. The
thing was though it meant virtually nothing to the
people eating their lunch.

Bill Timmons applied for a sales position at
Fortress when he heard an ad on the radio.

Timmons wore black rim glasses, had a perpetually sincere look on his face coupled with a smile that he could control at will. He joined the AM sales staff then after closing a few big deals transferred over to The Squirrel, Fortress's alternative rock station that was supposed to knock Power 108 off their pedestal. Timmons was formerly a manager at a Hardees fast food restaurant. His success particularly irked Poppy given Poppy's mistaken perception that he needed a Masters Degree to sell radio time. Timmons worked his way up by outworking everyone in the building but also by forwarding personal info on all the reps to his boss. This terrified everyone in the building except Jake who made no secret or no apologies for his life.

The ramifications of the new switch were going to be felt. There was no doubt. Drozdek was going to be a figurehead. Drozdek went from being a manager to a rep more times than Poppy changed his underwear in a day. He acquired the nickname "U Haul" because of the number of moves he made in the office. Drozdek would do what Foxx told him, which was going to be the Program Department's problem. But Queenie's control over the reps was going to be a challenge to anyone who enjoyed the business. Poppy and Jake, along with a few other reps took their jobs seriously. At the same time they had enormous amounts of fun. Radio afforded engaging people an opportunity to make money, meet interesting people and provide a service to those businesses that wanted to grow. A rep knew when a business was at its spending limit. That was why they were regarded as good sales people. The corporate philosophy of Fortress was to get all the money you could on any given day, no matter if it was good for the advertiser or not. Most times, Fortress looked like a hungry buzzard eyeing the next fat corpse in the road. Because of the large nut the parent company had to crack, it made good people do bad things. And those who fought the company paid the price by demotion or elimination.

After talking over the latest developments, Poppy waved for the check. Both men agreed that new challenges were ahead. Poppy paid the bill while Jake chatted up the waitress and got her e mail address. "You don't even know how e mail works Jake!!!!" Poppy scolded him. "I have never seen anyone who was so good with introducing themselves to women, they all love ya". "Yeah", snorted Jake, "everybody except Queenie Foxx! All of a sudden Poppy got a look of disgust on his face. "Shit, here comes Tom Patrick, what a pain in the ass, he's always trying to sell me a candy bar or tee shirt for one of his damn kids at that school. Did you tell him to come here?" asked Poppy. "Yeah, I did" admitted Jake. "I'm buying life insurance from him. He sells it on the side, I'm going to chunk myself up so that if I die the women in my life will be able to live a good life and not think I'm such a shit." Poppy just shook his head and motioned at the young waitress cleaning the tables, "Gonna put her on a policy?" "Don't be silly" Jake countered, "I hardly know her but I can always add on".

The regime of Drozdek and Foxx began with a great flourish. At a general staff meeting it was announced that there would be few changes in personnel at the company. That afternoon Little Johnny Walker was fired after 34 years of service. In addition, Craig Storm was made Director of New Business. Both moves sent shock waves to the veteran reps on board. The new management duo might pull one over on the new sales people but the old pros knew this move sucked. Being made Director of New Business meant getting kicked out of your office, moving to a cubicle, being stripped of your billing accounts and getting two shiny new phone books to develop as a list of cold calls. The treatment of Storm, one of Fortress's imports was not lost on anyone in the building. Tom Patrick commented, "Jeez if they treat one of their stars like that, what chance do I have here?" For his part, Storm took the move with typical grace and class. He looked people in the eye, held his head high and reported to work on time every day.

The exit of Little Johnny Walker did not go well. Walker was one of the last holdovers from Shawnee Broadcasting. Queenie Foxx tried to take away his client base many times but was met with a slew of cancellations at every attempt. His customers were loyal to Walker. Little Johnny used to say to tell his clients that "They were getting the number one radio rep in the market" and despite that bravado from the diminutive man, usually over delivered on what he promised. Foxx said that Walker was let go because of his negative attitude. But the truth was Walker was fired because he essentially told the new reps the truth about their prospects at Fortress. He explained to them that there was only so much business to go around and that the promise of $100,000 a year after 6 months was bullshit.

Later on in the day, it was announced that Tommy McMurtry was also given the heave ho by management. While Walker was the last vestige of sales, McMurtry was the last surviving link to the glory days of WSUN. An original member of "The Nifty 1050", McMurtry endured management changes year in and year out. His popularity with the public was evident at parades and remote broadcasts. But McMurtry did not fit into the bottom line plans of Fortress and was escorted from the building too.

The next day Foxx called a meeting and did not mention the departures. She did however announce a new round of additions to the sales staff. Looking at her existing staff she said, "I'm stuck with the staff I have but don't necessarily want. I'm hoping these four new people will inspire you to do better. Let me introduce to you Bertha Black who was a clerk at Goose Road convenience stores, Jack Richards from the Blue Bird restaurant where he worked as a dish washer, Melanie Hazleteen from the Pub and Rub company which I believe is a combination bar and massage parlor and Ed Shishlaw who recently finished a tour with the Ringling Brothers Circus." Standing in her blue pin stripe suit, she looked at the room, gauging the reaction of her staff. Everyone, including Jake sat in stunned silence. "I am going to prove to all of you under performing phonies that I can take anyone off the street and make them better reps than all of you put together. I will mold them, shape them into what a Fortress rep should and can be. After I do that, then maybe you can learn from their example".

Normally when a bombshell like this is dropped on a staff by managers, all sales reps exit the building and congregate in diners to discuss the changes over eggs and coffee. These are "bitch" sessions that are very therapeutic and let one rail and vent against the boss. Foxx deprived the reps of this luxury, telling them that they would be in a lock down all day long in the building to re-evaluate their accounts and update their files. It was ironic that with the biggest bombshell in the market was dropped sales people, who talk for a living, were being held incommunicado.

Despite the efforts to quell gossip Poppinaro called Don Norris at Power 108 and got the goods on the new reps. Bertha worked for 21 years in the store and had the dubious ability to annoy anyone at will. The story went that when one of the mini marts was being robbed, Bertha terrified the would be gunman by her violent screaming. The robber, who had an empty pistol fled the store. Richards had 5 children and was married 5 times and seemed like an amiable sort. Shishlaw had been with the circus 9 years and reportedly was on the lam from the law. The most normal of the bunch seemed to be Melanie Hazleteen who formerly worked as a dancer and massage therapist at the Pub and Rub. Poppy found out that Melaine actually grew up and went to high school with Crystal, Bernice's cousin. Excited, he relayed this information to Jake who was intrigued but very cautious about meeting this new woman on campus. Jake had seen way too much in this facility to trust anyone. His few bastions of trust like Little Johnny Walker and Craig Storm were being eliminated one by one. His relationship with Tom Patrick while strong, bordered on the comical. Foxx would call Jake into her office and rail about Patrick's temper, his sidelines and his general attitude and how she wished he would resign. Jake would never react to her rants only saying he'd speak with Tom about her concerns. Then Patrick would follow Jake into a meeting with their boss and Queenie would castigate Jake for his womanizing, his love of designer clothes and good wine and the rumors she heard about Jake's supposed sexual activities. Patrick laughed it off but told Queenie he'd have a word with Jake about her concerns. It got to the point where when the men passed each other on their way to meet Queenie, they'd give each other a one word warning about the subject she'd be covering. "Temper" Jake would say to Patrick passing him in the hall, Patrick would counter with "babes" as he walked past Jake. Trust was a valuable premium at Fortress Broadcasting. Any false move, any perceived misstep could get you fired or demoted. On one hand Jake didn't care, doing things like keeping a scorecard noting the number of reps who exited who exited the company since he started. Among his array of photos of Adrienne and Bernice, and his Green Bay Packer and Cleveland Indian keepsakes, Jake had an 8 inch paper with a huge number printed on it. The number varied whenever a memo came out bidding the rep God speed and wishing them well in their future endeavors. Jake's posting of the daily scorecard did not escape Queenie Foxx's spies. Then there were the issues of love for the business and pride in what he did. Despite the obstacles in his way, Jake still loved radio and wanted to make a mark with News 1050. He had great affection for the station's mainstay Coral Rock. The sexual attraction didn't even enter into the equation anymore. Coral was his sanity check in the madness he faced in his professional life.

The very fact that Coral was female did not help her with the new management team. Like McMurtry's position before, everything hinged on the bottom line. Coral was holding on by her fingertips and was inches away from cancellation. Her ratings were strong but her billing was poor. Queenie Foxx and her minions never really embraced her as a woman because Coral regularly pointed out the hypocrisy of the modern woman's sisterhood. She looked to the sales reps to maintain her program. It was on a slippery slide lately because of all the changes made at the station, the shabby treatment of McMurtry and the wholesale defection of Little Johnny Walker's client base. Even the consistency of one show like Coral's could not withstand the many changes inflicted on the once proud "Nifty 1050". Jake was at his wit's end knowing that Patrick's and his piecemeal efforts were only a band-aid on the problem. As he sat at his desk he focused in on a picture of him and Bernice taken by Don Norris's wife at the Mecklenburgh's Super Bowl party. He looked at the perfect hair and the smile. He wondered if she was still smiling about him in her rehab room trying to regain use of her legs. Jake felt responsible for her accident and was ashamed at his deception and cowardice. His daydream was shattered by the ringing of his phone. "Maytag honey, it's me", said the voice on the other end. Jody Mecklenburgh and Jake always talked about conjuring people up. It happened again to Jake and he made a mental note to tell Jody about it. "Bernice I was just thinking about you" said Jake. "Conjured me up eh, you'll have to tell Jody, listen Jake, daddy wants to meet with you. Can you come up the hospital tomorrow afternoon? asked Bernice. "What's he going to do kill me in front of you?" Jake joked. "The thought has crossed his mind but there'd be too much blood. I mean you are a big man and all. But we've been talking. Talking a lot. For the first time, like a father and daughter. If I don't blame you, why should he?" Said Bernice. "Hey" said Jake, "I still blame myself." Feeling the gnawing at the pit in his stomach every time he thought about her injury was a daily occurrence for Jake. "Well" said Bernice in a feigned dramatic sultry voice, "you ought to blame yourself you big dope, it's all your fault I'm here. I knew you'd be trouble from the first moment I laid my eyes on you but I'm a woman who likes trouble, who courts it like a gang banger sniffing out a virgin, like a dog scooping out a bone, like a........." Jake interrupted her, "Are you done?" "Yup, I got it out of my system, so you gonna come up and see me Maytagger?" she asked. "Wouldn't miss it for the world kiddo, want me to bring you something?" said Jake. "Just your smiling face" she giggled hanging up the phone. Jake hung the phone up and felt a pang of real excitement. He was always glad to hear from his B girl but wondered exactly what this meeting with her father was all about too. Looking at his watch, he realized it was time to go home. He called Adrienne and asked her whether she wanted him to cook tonight or bring Chinese home. She chose the Chinese option so Jake called the restaurant and made his order. Getting up from his cubicle Jake caught Tom Patrick staring at him and grinning, "Amazing, absolutely fucking amazing" said his fellow rep in awe of Jake's dexterity in managing his life. Putting his suit coat on, Jake gathered his briefcase and simply said to Patrick,

"It ain't easy being this sexy" and walked out of the building on a day that was difficult for everyone at Fortress broadcasting.

Jake woke up at 5am the morning he was to visit Bernice and her father. He went to a local supermarket and bought huge Hershey Bars, red apples and the largest oranges he could find. Taking the items to his car, he arranged all of them in a basket he had in his trunk. Carefully fastening it with a royal blue ribbon, he placed it back in the car so it wouldn't tip over. After a brief stint at the gym, he selected a starched white shirt, blue double breasted suit with matching socks, shoes and braces and looked for his royal blue silk DKNY tie. Alarmed at not finding it, he began to panic because royal blue was Bernice's favorite color. Much to his relief the tie was tucked away behind his hundred other cravats. Jake went to his job and left the building early after his daily morning harangue from Queenie Foxx. On the elevator he ran into Penelope Hartz. His relationship with her was now completely repaired and they became the best of friends once more. Penelope looked awful. Jake told her so. "It's this job Jake, they are grinding us into a pulp. I can't live like this anymore but I'm making too much money to leave" she sighed. There was no hustle in Penelope's bustle anymore. She seemed forlorn and that made Jake sad.

Jake got to the rehab center early. He carefully placed the basket on the patient's desk, sat down and waited. Since he was early he took a quick 5 minute nap. His head slumping over his chest, he was

awakened by a strong hand on his shoulder. It was
Primo II. Startled, Jake looked at Bernice's father who
extended his hand for Jake to shake. Jake was pulled
up from the chair and motioned to follow him down
the hall. The two men walked to the therapy center.
The room was a bit crowded and both Jake and Primo
stood against a back wall. Across the room, about 60
feet away from them were a bank of small offices.
Bernice dressed in a white tee shirt and royal blue
shorts appeared in the doorway with her walker.
"There's my two favorite guys" she cheerily yelled
out. Just then she shoved the walker aside and
screamed "Are you ready for some football?" and on
cue, a huge boom box started playing Hank William's
ode to Monday Night mayhem. Bernice carefully
balanced herself and put one foot in front of another.
Carefully she plotted one step at a time until she stood
in front of the two men with her hands on her hips.
The music kept on blaring until she raised her arms
and it stopped at her direction. "Well, are you
impressed?" she grinned. "My God, My God, my little
angel" said her father tears welling up inside him. Jake
momentarily distracted by the buxom nurse's aide
operating the boom box for Bernice quickly refocused
his attention and simply said, "This is wonderful,
wonderful, the best news I've had in months". Bernice
hugged them both and with their aid walked into the
rec facility's meeting room. Primo, showing great
sensitivity to the couple offered to get Jake's gift

basket for his daughter. Alone in the room the two
giggled and began small talk.

"How's my Maytag doing today?, she asked.

Good, quite a display in there.

Hey, I know you love my long legs so I thought I'd
give you a thrill.

Consider me thrilled.

Cool.

How's Adrienne doing?

Still tired but getting there. She did an author's tour
and book singing promotion by herself the other day.

Super. I'd trade some of her muscle strength for a bit
of my brain.

You have no brain anyone would want.

Hey my brain is fine. Now my heart, well that's
another matter!!

Who has that?

Not gonna tell ya big boy.

Then don't complicate things and keep it to yourself.

Suit yourself. But I am not responsible, you started it.

How?

By digging that hole in his backyard" she said
grinning.

    Primo appeared in the conference room carrying
the basket. Bernice looked at Jake and thanked him.
"Hey" said Primo, "what if I got that for you, you'd be
thanking the wrong guy!" Bernice shot a look at her
father and said "Oh come now Daddy!! Don't start
exaggerating again". She carefully looked through the

contents of the basket and pulled an orange out. "Daddy, do you remember gram telling me that in the old days if a man was in love with his woman he'd bring her the most perfect orange he could find to show his devotion? In Italy the orange represents the sunlight and Jake was thoughtful enough to pick me out the most beautiful orange I've ever seen" said Bernice. Primo looking annoyed simply said, "Uh huh". It was one thing to visit his daughter and see her walk for the first time since her fall at Jake's house but Primo was on a tight schedule and the last thing he needed to hear was his daughter waxing poetic over a Sunkist. Bernice offered the men a piece of candy and then began to slowly fold the royal blue ribbon that was attached to the basket. Exasperated her father said, "What in the world are you doing now?" Looking at him, she put the ribbon in her huge Fendi purse and said, "Believe me I save everything, and I do mean everything Jake gives me".

Sensing her father's impatience Bernice gave the floor to her father. Primo moved forward and began to talk to Jake.

"Jake, first of all know I have no ill will toward you because of my angel's accident. That's all it was, a freak accident.

So Danny's not gonna kill me? asked Jake.

No, he's fine. I never hold a grudge against a good man. And Jake, I dare say I think you're a great man and I'm proud to be associated with you. I want to do two things. The first is I want to reinstate all my advertising with you and your new company. In return I want you to keep an eye on one of my relatives who recently took a job at Fortress. His name is Jack Richards. Jack has had some hard knocks. He's been married a number of times, has kids from different mothers, his life is a mess. You look after him and I'll take care of your sales goals. But you keep me informed of how he's doing? Understand?" said the family patriarch.

Jake nodded his head in agreement but Bernice had a worried look on her face. Jake and her father agreed that since 4 Emerald defaulted on the Power 108 deal Fortress would require all the money in advance in cash. Jake agreed to put together a budget and asked Primo how much he wanted to spend. Without blinking an eye, Primo said, "Quarter of a million for the first 3 months, a million a year". Jake swallowed hard and said he'd get right on it. Bidding Primo goodbye Jake continued his visit with Bernice. He asked her why she was worried about a simple task like looking after Jack Richards. "Jack Richards daddy's half brother, he's Lorraine's child. He is a decent sort but has had bad luck follow him from birth. I believe this because my mom told me Jack was conceived in passion, not love. Passion is bad, love is good. You know that Jake, right? You and me, we never had passion, I bet you and Adrienne have great passion. Passion bad, love good. I'm telling you Jake,

you're gonna have your hands full with this. And let's
not forget the terrible people you work for, I'm going
to pray hard for you on this Maytag. I will my love"
she said reaching into her purse and pulling out a
tattered case with rosary beads in them. Jake thanked
her for the warning, kissed her goodbye and walked to
his car thinking about everything that just happened.
One thought dominated Jake's mind though, it was the
turn of the century and he had the love of a woman 20
years his junior who still prayed the rosary. He smiled
and shook his head in disbelief. She wasn't his wife,
but hey, nothing was perfect. He went back to Fortress
to draw up the contracts that he knew would change
his life and career.

Queenie Foxx was in a battle of her own making. Fueled by ambition, she wanted to put huge numbers on the Fortress scorecard and look good to corporate. Unlike Duncan's philosophy of consistency, Foxx felt that constant upheaval kept her reps competitive. Sales reps were called off the road at will for "coaching meetings", accounts went ignored for weeks or sometimes were bombarded by 7 reps in one day and surprise confabs were inflicted on sales people who already had the day planned. Penelope Hartz labeled it "kindergarten cop" tactics. One day Penelope, Poppy and Jake were having lunch with Jody Mecklenburgh. That afternoon Foxx called the three in separately and grilled them about their day and asked them not to fraternize with the competition. Poppy told Foxx that he was friends with Jody long before Fortress was on the scene and most likely long after they left. Poppy was the only rep who seemed to have the balls to take on Queenie because of his incisive legal mind. In another time and place, both could have been lovers. Queenie for her part respected Poppy's billing prowess and on the surface didn't seem to hold the truth against him. The other reps were another matter and were subject to Queenie's distrust and paranoia.

One day Jake was told to cut his day short and come in to the office. Queenie announced that she was going to ride with Jake to show him how to obtain new business. Jake drove her around in his car and the two visited tiny businesses that most likely had paltry amounts of money to spend on the huge ad budget Queenie Foxx was proposing. One of the places was a stationery store called LaBowe's. Jake was quite familiar with the store. As a child his mother bought him his "back to school" items there. He remembered fondly the neat rows of pens, papers and colorful greeting cards neatly displayed in the elegant store. Queenie looked at Jake and said, "They should be on our air". Jake, taking a page out of Poppy's book said, "There's no way they are going to advertise. I can tell you that right now". "See Jake, you've changed since I recruited you. You're not the same person I hired. You're very negative" she said. Jake asked her to explain why she felt that way. "I don't understand what that means that you think I'm not the same person, what does that mean?" he asked knowing the question would annoy her mightily. She just glared at him and they went in the store.

The silent hum of the ceiling fan was the only noise in the store. Jake and Queenie were the only two there. Jake rang the service bell on the counter as he did so many times as a child. An elderly, well-groomed woman came out.

"Good morning" said the clerk.

"Hello, I'm Queenie Foxx and this is Jake Yanick. You have a beautiful store here. We're from Fortress broadcasting and we'd like to talk to you about

advertising today" said Jake's boss determined to
show him up. The woman took Queenie's card, looked
at it and then handed it back to the dismayed sales
manager.

"Oh, we don't advertise" said the woman.

"That's funny" countered Queenie, "everybody has to
advertise".

"We don't" said the lady, "and we've been here for 75
years, same location, same goods, and we don't
advertise".

Confused and slightly exasperated, Queenie said,
"How do you get people to come in the store and buy
if you don't advertise?"

The woman looked at the two, raising her left hand
with eyes looking upward pointed to the ceiling with
her index finger simply said, "Him".

"Him who?" asked Queenie.

"God" said the woman. Jake was ready to burst out
laughing but thought he'd be fired on the spot.
Queenie was momentarily stunned but recovered quite
nicely by saying "Well, thanks for your time" and
turned to walk out of the store. When Jake and
Queenie turned to leave, the store was packed with at
least 12 shoppers looking at greeting cards, stationery
and expensive pens. Jake opened the passenger side of
his car for Queenie who asked him to take her back to
the radio station since she had numerous meetings to
attend that day. Jake asked if she wanted to continue
on with him to find new business and she seethed

silently before saying "I'm sure you'll find some on your own".

Jake along with Poppy, Penelope, Craig Storm, Tom Patrick and other veterans were good reps. Like seasoned athletes they knew how much energy needed to be exerted on an account but more importantly how far they could go in their pursuit of the dollar. Each had relationships with foes in print, TV, and specialty advertising. They recognized that there was a pie and only a few got a piece of it. Queenie's superiors felt that Fortress should have the entire meal instead of the pie. She instilled that idea into the heads of the new reps along with her main sales second-in-command Bill Timmons. Timmons and Queenie truly believed they could be a dominant force mainly because the bosses at corporate showed them model communities across the country that achieved that goal. Both felt they could transplant that success to the Fortress headquarters in Pennsylvania. This logic contradicted Jim Duncan's longstanding belief that this radio market was unlike any in the country. The region had over 45 radio stations with various niche formats whereas the markets Fortress was successful in were vastly under populated by media. Jim Duncan's success was recognizing this diverse array of communication outlets and dealing with them as partners instead of competitors. Fortress wanted to prove Duncan wrong and the only way to do that was with new empty headed reps who would believe what they were told, not with the vets who were influenced by Duncan.

Perhaps the most empty headed of these reps was Bertha Black. Black was an extremely gruff woman who bore an uncanny resemblance to Marjorie Main, the 1930's actress who made her fame as Ma Kettle. Loud, rude and ignorant she was relentless in her pursuit of an account, anyone's account. With the way Fortress was set up, no account was safe from Bertha who stormed in and virtually tried to sell anything at any price on an appointment. Besides having the annoying habit of picking and eating her own skin in sales meetings, Bertha eavesdropped on calls. In a lot of ways Jake thought she was brain injured because of her emotionality and crying outbursts but that is where the comparison to his wife's illness ended. Tom Patrick regarded her as retarded and told Jake if school records could be unearthed he'd be right. Others reps complained about her to Foxx but Queenie saw her as the perfect project to mold in her efforts to show up the vets whom she thought were against her. After the stationery store debacle with Jake, Queenie decided to concentrate her efforts on Bertha and let Bill Timmons ride Shishlaw, Hazleteen and Richards. Timmons was like a dictator with his three reps, holding meetings at 7am, keeping them at night until 8pm and making them listen to motivation tapes on his car stereo. Ed

Shishlaw left to go to the men's room one day and never returned leaving his briefcase, and madras sport coat behind. No one ever heard from him again. Hazleteen took a terrible dislike to her treatment, smiling and flirting in front of Timmons but making no secret of how much she despised him. Timmons felt that the voluptuous young woman should lead with her looks and made that point to her daily. She resented it because she was told radio sales was a honorable entertainment profession, unlike her last job at the Pub and Rub. She thought her days of selling sex were over when she joined the radio team but was dismayed when Timmons said she should wear more revealing outfits on sales calls. Jack Richards took the brunt of the propoganda Timmons inflicted. A good soul, Richards was grateful for his "last chance" to make a success out of himself for the sake of his family. He took to heart every critical thing Timmons and Foxx inflicted on him but also had a ton of other issues outside Fortress that seemed to wear him down. He presented a funny quip and smiling face but deep down he was a man in pain. But Fortress was too busy to deal with anyone's pain and this new plan touting the "new blood" was going to change everything. What one could not predict was how these decisions would ultimately cause a series of events that would not only change Fortress broadcasting but all of the people associated with it.

Primo II met with his sons about the advertising proposals for Jake. Joining him was Frankie Pannini, who laid down the law to the sons that Jake was a friend of the family and should be treated with respect. Pannini felt very comfortable in the fact that Portia was the business manager and would look out for their interests. The group wanted to advertise a new product for home recycling that was similar to a kitchen garbage disposal. Pannini's factory would make them while Primo's company provided the blasting power to refine the raw materials needed for the unit. It was agreed that both Portia and Jake would meet with Primo who would give Portia the $250,000.00 in return for Jake's scheduling of the broadcast time.

When Jake got the news he was elated. It would be his opportunity to shine in many ways. First, he could become a true economic partner with his wife Adrienne and take financial pressure off his family, second, it would redeem him with Queenie Foxx, third, it would help him with his standing with the Vitales, and fourth, this windfall would provide Jake with the clout to give other reps at Fortress a leg up on their billing. Not a selfish man, Jake would spread out the money among different stations. The benefit for the client would be they would get maximum coverage, the plus to the reps would be that this added money would keep Queenie Foxx's wrath away from their door.

Jake called a meeting of Craig Storm, Jim Poppinaro, Penelope Hartz, Tom Patrick and Jack Richards. In his hands were ARFs, or Account Request Forms. Whenever a rep wanted a new account, they had to fill out an ARF. A sales manager would sign off on it and the account became protected. Jake handed them out and suggested they all hand the form into Queenie Foxx. Poppy disagreed. "Jake, if she sees all of us with these forms, she'll know something is up. We've got to distract her from these things here" said Poppy. "How about when we did the spec tapes?" asked Tom Patrick. They all laughed remembering the incident. Spec tapes are simulated commercials that tell an advertiser how they might sound. Queenie had railed that there was no new business because there weren't enough spec cassettes going out to prospective businesses. She decreed that each rep had to write and hand in 2 spec tapes a day. The silliness of that idea manifested itself when more than 40 reps inundated the production studio with 400 requests. Jake at the time said, "The best way to kill a bad idea is to agree with it". The group debated their dilemma over and over with no solution in mind. Finally Penelope Hartz said, "Let's just hand the order in with the payment. She can't take that away or claim it was someone else's unless someone in this room tells her". "That's it" said Poppy. When all the reps came to an agreement, it was decided that they would all meet with Jake and Portia to write their orders, and then present them to Queenie signed, sealed and delivered at the Monday morning sales meeting.

That weekend the reps met with Jake and Portia, furiously working against the deadline of Monday morning. The veteran reps came to hate the Monday meeting. It was a dog and pony show where Queenie asked each rep what their biggest sale was. Lately because of the natural cycle of business and the allocation of newer accounts, a.k.a. bluebirds to the new reps the vets did not have much to show in the meeting. There also was a new trend developing, the new salespeople like Hazleteen and Richards had small orders compared to the ones handed in by Bertha Black. It had become abundantly clear to Melaine Hazleteen and Jack Richards that they were being tossed aside in favor of Queenie's project. Richards took it with resignation while the feisty ex go go dancer did nothing to hide her contempt. Bertha Black usually had the biggest sale that was usually engineered by Queenie. When Bertha announced her deal, Queenie would gaze at the rotund rep like Nancy Reagan looked at the President when he was giving a speech. All of these were motivations to get the ducks in line by Monday morning.

The big day arrived and as usual the meeting started on time with Queenie Foxx and the ever smiling assistant Bill Timmons in tow. Bill Timmons said that he had a huge surprise for everyone. Strutting around the room, he handed out copies of the children's classic story "The Little Engine That Could". Each rep was given the task of reading a line and then waiting for the next one to finish it. This took roughly 15 minutes until the room exploded in a chant, "I think I can I think I can". Penelope Hartz rolled her eyes and shook her head. Bertha Black started to cry uncontrollably telling the group she always liked the little choo choo as a girl and now felt like a big choo choo. Patrick whispered to Jake, "Now she's a fucking caboose or pre rail, horses ass!". Jake almost exploded in laughter but held it back.

When Queenie asked for the big sale from each rep, she started with Bertha Black. Bertha announced her sale of $3200.00 from Nursegetters, a health care recruiter. After the rest of the reps announced their deals, Queenie zeroed in on her veterans.

Poppy was the first to stand, "4 Emerald Corporation, $41,666.00 paid in full to Urban 102. Stunned silence, then tepid applause. Penelope followed, "To Stardust 94, 4 Emerald Corporation, $41,666.00." More applause. Craig Storm then announced, "Fortress new business development, all stations, $41,666.00," then raised a defiant fist in the direction of Bill Timmons. Tom Patrick rose and said, "This is getting redundant, to Sports 790 and our country stations, from 4 Emerald Group, $41,666.00. paid in full. Jack Richards stood up and sheepishly smiled said, "The Squirrel, 4 Emerald Corporation, $44,666.00, paid in full." Rooting for the underdog, the room exploded for Jack. Jake Yanick then stood up and smiled. Everyone in the room suspected Jake had engineered the deal. Most were secretly thrilled that he had accomplished this huge and monumental feat. Jake, looking at the sales reps, gave his total. If each rep had over $40,000.00, what would Jake have, the amount had to be staggering. Jake stood up and said, "Nifty 1050 News, targeted to Coral Rock show, $38,670.00, 4 Emerald Corporation." The room was silent, then there was the sudden realization that Jake had given more of his share to the struggling Jack Richards. The room erupted in a sea of applause and appreciation for his gesture. Queenie Foxx and Bill Timmons had no choice but to join in. Timmons couldn't resist a jab though, "Why so little Jake? Richards beat you on this?" Appalled the group waited for Jake to deck the smiling fake. Jake smiled and said, "Sometimes the best man beats you" looking over at Jack Richards. At that moment, Jake could have owned them all in that room. Portia gave the report on the financials and Jake announced that the commercial was already loaded and ready to go. It was not lost on anyone in the room that the voices on the commercial were those of little Johnny Walker and Tommy McMurtry. Jake and the veterans had won a victory over the forces of Fortress Broadcasting. It was a sweet moment, but Jake, knowing this business and the people who made it up, knew it was just that, a moment.

The older reps had prevailed at least for now and they went out to celebrate. There were warring factions in Fortress Broadcasting and no one could ever determine who would finally win out given their corporate policies. But for now a few of the victors would celebrate. Portia and Coral were invited from the non sales side. Jim Poppinaro, Penelope Hartz, Craig Storm, Tom Patrick, and Jack Richards joined Jake at Sirens Sports bar. Jody Mecklenburgh, Pete Cassidy and Don Norris were invited from Power 108. A few felt Norris should not be invited because of his direct line to Duncan but the majority felt that Duncan deserved to get some good gossip. There was still a never ending reservoir of affection for their old boss. The group gathered and unlike other times the talk centered on personal and moral issues rather than radio. With Coral Rock acting as a type of de facto moderator, the conversation steered to modern day relationships. Penelope complained that men could never take no for an answer, Storm worried about his children growing up in the modern climate of free wheeling sexuality, Patrick showed off pictures of his wife and kids and Portia talked about being gay and being taken seriously in business once she made her preferences known. The issue went around to fidelity and Cassidy told the story about Jake and the waitress from the popular Brussel's restaurant. "So here we are

and Jake here is making excellent time with Gloria
this stunning waitress who works there. He's giving
her the Yanick look, you know the elbows on the
table, the gaze and she's intrigued. So then he asks her
what she likes and doesn't like about men. She tells
him she loves everything about men, they can be dirty,
poor, ignorant, ugly, and on and on. So Jake's thinking
he's doing pretty good you know until she says the
"one thing I demand in a man is fidelity." Jake looks
up at her, stands up, extends his hand, says "nice
meeting you" and bolts from the place never to be
seen again" explains Pete. The entire table cracks up
because knowing Jake the way they do, it has to be a
true story. Penelope wonders how Jake has the energy,
Poppy is amazed at how Jake will get someone to spill
their guts the minute they meet him and Storm says to
the group it is the strangest type of philandering he's
ever seen. Coral Rock said, "Yeah, it's almost like he
parcels out a little bit of himself at a time and just
knows how much to measure and give to everyone.
You never offered me a spoonful of sugar" Coral
complained. "You'd drink me whole and spit me out
in a New York minute" said Jake and the group
heartily agreed. Norris remarked drinking his
O'Doul's that his wife was struck by how beautiful the
women were for such a funny looking guy. He pointed
to Patrick's good looks and wondered why Patrick
didn't get the attention Jake got. Patrick, having a few
beers too many whipped out his false teeth and said,

"Because Jake's choppers are real". A collective groan went up from the crowded table. Jody said, "Jake's infidelity is not like anyone else's in the world. It doesn't feel like infidelity because the people are so nice". "That's crap" said Portia. "Well, maybe" continued Jody "but what's wrong with being in 2 or 3 committed relationships if you have the time? I don't think it's a stretch, look at how gay people were viewed 50 years ago as opposed to now. Maybe in time multi personal relations will be the norm". Coral asked Jody if she could navigate comfortably in the Yanick wall of women. "I can" said Jody. "I value Yanks as my dear friend and whether it's Adrienne or his B girl, I'll treat them like an extension of him, now if there were more than three, then I'd have a problem keeping the names straight". The group laughed at that comment. "Well, as an example, what do you guys talk about?" asked Coral. Jody retorted, "Everything. B was asking me about the whole process of artificial insemination.."
"She did?" Jake interrupted. "Yeah," Jody continued "and Adrienne who is much more reserved has great conversations with me and my spouse. So I guess that's why I don't think he's such a shit". Poppy stood up to make a toast, "To the guy who's my idol, that unfaithful piece of shit, Jake Yanick". The group stood, toasted and said, "Here, here". Jack Richards said, "Queenie Foxx must have written that one for

you" and the group laughed a bit more. Portia asked Jake if he had to choose between Woman A or Woman B, how would he handle that dilemma. "Now not to sound arrogant here" said Jake, "but I don't think that would ever happen." The group sat in silence waiting for the rest of his response, and then Coral broke the verbal logjam. "You bastard you, you'd find a Woman C wouldn't you?" Jake looked at the talk show host and said, "My God you are perceptive aren't you, wanna be my Woman C?" Jake grinned at her and did the gaze for her, focusing in on her face, gazing into her eyes as if they were the only two people in the room.

Coral said to the group, "I can take this fucker on, watch me". And the two locked into a staring match that lasted for what seemed like hours. Jake stared deeply into her eyes, looking away only to examine every inch and crevice of her face, saying nothing but saying everything. Finally, Coral said, "Shit, he's such a fucking bastard but it's impossible to be pissed at him. That's the worst type of man there is". Penelope and Jody nodded their heads in agreement.

The rest of the night was spent on telling radio stories, exchanging of account information and what the future would bring. Each person told their tale about how they got into radio, why they stayed so long and what they would do in the future. Jake said to the group, "You know it isn't going to matter in a hundred years who got this account, who had the best month or who got 100% of a bank's advertising budget. What's going to matter is how we treat our families and our true friends". All nodded in agreement. The group walked out to the parking lot and said goodnight to each other. Jake saw that Jack Richards made a point of giving everyone a hug before he got in his car to leave. He called Bernice up on his cell to ask her how the day went, then after a few minutes of conversation he headed home to Adrienne. Watching the lithe Coral Rock get into her Jeep, Jake wondered if he had time for three revolving relationships but quickly dismissed the idea. Pulling out of the parking lot and beeping to Coral, he said to himself, "Maybe 15 years ago when I was younger".

The illusion of what broadcasting meant to Jake was slowly fading away. Every day was an internal struggle of political machinations that made meeting with a difficult client a piece of cake. Jim Poppinaro was fond of saying that if one could get safely alive out of the building in the morning, the rest of the day was easy. For his part, there were days when Jake really loved his job. The ultimate people pleaser, Jake enjoyed working with clients to craft a message. He had the reputation of painting an image in the listener's mind and selling it. His client commercials ranged from dog food to massage parlors. Each radio spot was regarded highly for its creativity and innovation. That was the fun part. The downside was of course the constant pressure put on the sales reps for more billing to overcome the Fortress debt. More and more the strain was loading down Jake with stress and worry.

Bernice's solution to Jake's dilemma was to try to get him involved in the family business. Once when Jake visited his B girl in the rehab facility, they were joined by a relative of her family, Rocco Rambini. Jake learned that Rocco was a cousin and had a transportation service.

"So this is your guy, huh princess?" asked Rocco, a squat, bald man with a scar that began in the middle of his bald dome and cascaded to his left eye. "That's the guy" said Bernice proudly. "Jake is in marketing and sales, he works for Fortress broadcasting, you know "The Nifty 1050". "Oh geez, "The Nifty 1050", now that was a station. I grew up with those guys, I got through my teen years because of Little Johnny Walker, Tommy McMurtry, Double D, Dave Douglas, Timmy Brooks, Hank South, all of them. Those were the best days for guys our age, right"? he reminisced. "Yes they were" said Jake. "Even to this day, people buy "The Nifty 1050" for what it was, what it meant to them, not necessarily for what it is now". Bernice sat back and smiled admiring Jake's dexterity in blending in with just about anyone. "Jake" said Bernice, "Rocco is associated with my father's business. He's in transportation. You might want to talk to him about what he does because he can use a detail man like you". Jake was taken aback when he realized this was an impromptu job interview. At first he was annoyed but then flattered that the young beauty took an interest in his life. After all they had been through, Jake was still amazed at how much she cared for him. Jake smiled and asked Rocco to tell him about his business. "Well" said the man broadly smiling, "it's like this. I own three taxi cab services in our region. It's called the GDY Cab and Transport Company.

"That's you?" asked Jake who was familiar with the yellow taxis with the overhead external light that read "God Digs You". "Yep, that's my company" said Rocco, "and I can use a guy like you who can sweat the details. I need a guy who is serious but flexible and from what Bernice tells me here, that's the type of guy you seem to be". "Well, I pride myself on how hard I work but sometimes I get frustrated because the results aren't that gratifying," noted Jake. "I understand exactly what you're getting at, but the taxi business has many, many rewards. You get people to where they need to go. Then they pay you. We have to go through a series of Public Utility Commission regulations but that's not something that is hard to do. What is hard to do is keeping the cabs maintained. Now the first thing you want to do with a cab is have a clean, sanitary seating area. That's very important to the taxi. Out of 278 vehicles, 96 of them have leather seats. They need to be cleaned with a special compound mixing oils, a cleaning solution and a dash of polish that gives it a sheen. The other taxis have cloth seating. These 182 car seats are challenging because you need to vacuum them first, brush them for foreign matter and then use a less harsh cleaning compound that will fade the tone, not the colors. Out of the 96 leather seats, 90 of them are black leather with the other 6 being a burgundy hue. Now the cloth seating is very different. Out of the 182 seats, I have 28 that have horizontal stripes, 52 that have vertical stripes, these are pinstripes though and very thin, so thin they actually look like a solid but they aren't. I got a deal on 48 cabs that have a plain cloth base of blue colors. 13 of them are royal blue, 12 of them are navy and the other 23 are a pale panama blue, the latter being a very light color which I have to clean with a bleaching solution. You have to mix it just so because if you don't, well then it'll either fade or get too blotchy. One thing you don't want in a cab seat is a blemished seat. The worse part about it is that it looks unclean. Then it looks like you didn't clean it all. I mean I can go on and on about the seats in the cabs but there's more to it than that", said Rocco. Jake was relieved that Rocco got off the subject of taxi cab seats. Bernice sat filing her nails with a glazed look on her face. Rocco took a sip of Pepsi and then leaned toward Jake to get to what Jake hoped would be the meat of the topic. "Now the visors, oh brother those visors are precious. Many a cabbie has avoided the harsh sun because of a good visor. Now the way I figure it, I have to maintain 556 visors. All but 12 of them, that's counting 6 cars I had to get visors for from the junkyard. Now the visors have this steel catch, they hook onto the roof area, but there's a little lip that conceals it for appearances. If you didn't have that lip, the visor would look jagged, not smooth and you'd have a lot of pull and resistance, not the fluid motion you have when you lift it up and down. As you can well imagine, it is vitally important that the visor on the car lift easily because if it doesn't, well then my friend you can have a rough go of it. The visor won't work, you will not have your fluid motion but more importantly the more you try to pull it up and down, the harder that visor has to work and the next thing you know what should have been a visor that lasted the life of the vehicle, now has to be discarded and replaced. Now this might sound like a small matter but a thing like that builds up. If you don't pay attention to the little details, then things go to hell", concluded Rocco.

Bernice had fallen asleep and Jake's eyelids were getting heavy. He tried valiantly to stay focused on what the man was saying but found it very difficult. Jake tried to get up but there was no stopping Rocco who put a huge hand on the radio rep's shoulder and shoved him down. "Now let's talk about those ashtrays. Ashtrays used to be a very big thing long ago because most everyone smoked. Most of my cabs have ashtrays in the front, but only 22 in my fleet have ashtrays for customers in the back seat. When you sit there, you see the ashtrays that are anchored to the back of the front seat. Tells you something about consumer habits. No one smokes no more, so there's no need for a back seat ashtray. It is going to get to the point where if one of these ashtrays in the back seat corrode or some idiot pulls it off its settings, then I won't even replace it. I'll just patch a GDY logo on there or better yet an America flag to cover up where the opening was. There's no percentage in replacing it, taking a trip to the junkyard for something like that especially when few people are smoking these days. The front ashtrays are very durable mainly because they are set right in there. The only trouble we have is with the non smoking drivers who will put their cokes and coffees in the ashtray instead of the cup holder. I mean this is plain and simple just lazy. What do I have cup holders in the cars for, my good looks?!!!!????" screamed Rocco at Jake. Jake was desperate for a way to get out of this one sided dissertation on taxi minutia. Bernice, startled by Rocco's outburst awoke with a start and found that Rocco had been visiting for at least 90 minutes. Jake looked at his B girl for assistance and she did not let him down. "Maytag honey, don't forget you have to see Silvio about the bills for 4 Emerald, and you're way past your meeting, Rocco can we do this again sometime?" Bernice asked. Without

waiting for an answer, Jake got up, kissed
Bernice on the cheek and was headed out the
door and down the hallway. Rocco got up and
called after him, "Hey Jake, I'll buy you a coffee
and explain the rest of it to you sometime". Jake
nodded a perfunctory yes and kept galloping
toward the front entrance of the rehab facility.

Sitting in his car, away from Rocco
Rambini, Jake heard his pager go off and
returned a call from Adrienne. "Jake, I have a
proposition for you", she said sexily. "Really, tell
me more" replied Jake. "My friend's ex husband
Roy, you know the one with the funeral home, is
retiring. Turns out he has a heart condition but
wants to pass the business on to someone else.
Do you want to meet with him?" she asked.
"Sure, I can get a schedule together for him and
most likely get him a buyer, I'll do it in a very
dignified manner with maybe some baroque
music as a background, " said her husband
excited about the prospect of a new client. "No
Jake, no, no, he doesn't want to advertise, he
wants to talk to you about taking over the
business" said Adrienne. "The funeral parlor
game, the industry my mother refers to as the
"corpse houses", don't you have to go to school
for that?" Adrienne replied, "Well yes but we
have the money to send you and he'll stay on
until you get certified. Think about it, you make

your own hours, there are minor inconveniences when you do have a body, you are a great detail man and you'd get to wear a suit every day and drive a Cadillac." Jake blocked everything else out when she mentioned the suits and the car. Again, image trumped everything, even embalming fluid. "Okay, set up a meeting" added Jake.

Jake was both amused and grateful that the two women in his life wanted him to find something else to do with his career. He had loved radio for so long but it was becoming painfully clear radio, the way that he knew it in his life currently, did not love him back.

One afternoon, Jake met Roy Rotterdamn, the Funeral Director at a pizza place near the hospital. The two men sat, had a slice, got to know each other and then retreated to Roy's huge Cadillac Seville. Jake sat in the passenger seat that engulfed his large frame. Roy started the engine and drove to a side street and parked. Jake realized they were at the rear entrance to the hospital. Roy pulled out a huge cigar, lit it, lowered the windows and popped some Tom Jones on his CD player. "What are we here for?" asked Jake. "Just wait and see" said Roy puffing on his cigar. Both men sat listening to the music and saw nothing on the quiet street. A few more minutes passed and then the two saw three huge vans turn down the side street and pull up to the side of the loading dock. Three drivers exited and entered the hospital's side door. Roy pulled out of the glove compartment his pager and cell phone. Another 15 minutes went by until it happened. The three drivers exited the building and went to open the rear doors of the vans. One by one hospital workers pushed stretchers. On each gurney was a bluish gray bag. Today there were 9 souls in need of transport. As the men gingerly lifted the bodies into the vans, Roy sat silently, waiting. Jake and Roy watched as the vans started their engines. The silence was shattered by the sound of the pager. Roy jotted down the number. Another page, he repeated the process. The cell phone rang and Roy muttered "uh huh" into it before hanging up. The pager went off one more time. Roy smiled and looked at Jake saying simply, "Bingo, I got myself four bodies today!! Come on back to the ranch and we'll survey the merchandise, see what we have to do partner". Jake was bothered by the fact that Roy winked at him when he called him partner.

Jake followed Roy with his own vehicle. He met Roy at his funeral home. "You're going to have to lose that rag top if you want to be in this business. Gotta get something big and dignified like a Lincoln or a Crown Vic, never a ragtop or convertible though, it oozes playboy, Casanova," said Roy. Jake watched as the undertaker went up to one of the bags and unzipped it. Roy placed a hankie to his mouth area and said, "Whew this one's getting ripe, gotta get this fella on some ice quick". At that point, Jake excused himself, said he had just received a page and decided to head on back to the radio station.

Jake was sure that the taxicab and mortician options were great careers but not for him. Radio, for good or bad was in his blood. He popped the top on his car and drove toward the Fortress headquarters. On his way into the building, he encountered Thomas Patrick and Jack Richards. Patrick was in rare form railing because Bertha Black was horning in on one of his new accounts. Jack was momentarily amused by Patrick's rants. Jake, heeding Primo's advice, asked Jack how things were working out for him. Jack smiled, looked at Jake and simply said, "This is turning out to be one of the best times in my life Jake. And the reason is working side by side with a guy like you. Bernice is a lucky girl, our family is lucky to have you in our lives". Jake smiled and thanked him for the kind words. He was bothered though by this sudden out pouring of emotion from the normally placid man. Thomas Patrick was having none of this mutual admiration society or deep thinking and kept on fuming over his injustice. Jack rolled his eyes and Jake just laughed at the absurdity of the radio business. He concluded that it was indeed good to be home again, even the dysfunctional one called Fortress Broadcasting.

Fortress Broadcasting kept humming along despite the manager's efforts to derail it. Thanks to the 4 Emerald group's advertising, the veterans seemed to have been removed from Queenie Foxx's harsh microscope. For the first time since the take over, all the reps were given the chance to do their jobs. Poppy had predicted that this was simply the quiet before the storm but Jake was optimistic that things had gotten better. On the personal front, Jake's women were thriving. Adrienne was in full blown recovery giving speeches, writing articles on her experiences. She was taking one day at a time, though she needed rest after a particularly strenuous lecture tour. Bernice had full use of her legs and was dragging Jake to dancing lessons at the Jewish Community Center. Life seemed pretty good until one day Jake heard all the people employed at Fortress would be pulled off the street at 2pm. No one knew what to make of that but complied anyway.

All the reps were told to assemble in the meeting room and wait for GM Dash Drozdek to address the entire staff. Jake knew something was really up when the Programming staff joined the meeting. "We just got sold" said one of the traffic goddesses. "What the heck else could this be?" Drozdek walked in, took a chair, turned it around and straddled it so he was facing the group. Eyes downcast, he began very

308

deliberately and said, "We just got word today that Jack Richards shot himself". There was a collective gasp in the room as Drozdek surveyed the reaction. "We have no other news on this but we hear it doesn't look good, we'll keep you posted". The reps walked silently back to their desks and did paper work until there was a loud outburst from Bertha Black who bellowed, "Oh this is so depressing to me, it's making me so sad, why do things like this happen to me, oh woe is me, I'm going to need some counseling, oh me, oh my!!!!!". Tom Patrick left his desk and in disgust headed for the door. When Penelope asked him where he was going he said, "I'm gonna get Jack's gun and finish that one off" pointing to the sobbing sales rep. Jake called Bernice who hadn't heard the news. She was distraught but not surprised. "He had a tough life and you know I think some of us might have been nicer to him. I feel badly though" said his B girl. "I feel awful" replied Jake. "I was speaking with him yesterday and he seemed at peace, happy content. Told me this was the best time of his life, I just don't understand it". "Maytag honey, sometimes something like this can't be explained. Maybe he thought he'd never feel any better than this and just quit while he thought he was ahead", said Bernice. Jake was momentarily annoyed at what he perceived to be her peasant logic but stopped himself from saying something negative to her because he knew her intentions were pure. You coming to the funeral?" she continued. "Sure" said Jake, "but I'm going to be uneasy because your dad told me to look after him and obviously I failed miserably." Bernice reassured him, "Daddy is a reasonable man and from what I understood, you looked after him just fine. He was so proud about that order, he felt like a real success and you're the reason why. Daddy knows that, I know it but more importantly Jack knew it. He had other demons that you or I or even daddy couldn't beat. Got that straight?" Jake said he did and thanked her for the pep talk. "You still my Maytag?" she asked. "Always" answered Jake.

When Jake went home, he told Adrienne the news. Adrienne began to tell him how these things were very unpredictable, that the mind is a curious thing and that no one really will ever understand suicide. She confided to Jake that during her darkest brain injury days she contemplated ending it herself. "What stopped you?" asked Jake. "I'm not sure" said Adrienne, "I think a car backfired and scared me when I was leaning over the bridge". Jake, shocked said, "It was that close?" "Yup" answered his wife. Jake sat silently wondering what if that car had not appeared on the scene. Thinking about it, chills went down his spine.

The next day Bill Timmons called a sales meeting. Dash Drozdek came into the meeting and announced that Jack Richards had died at 3AM that morning. The staff bent their heads in sorrow.

Timmons then took command of the meeting. "Folks, we'll give you details on the upcoming services for Jack. But today I'd like you all to focus on Jack Richards. Remember his smiling face, that quiet sense of humor, the way he worked under my tutelage and great leadership. Today, I want each and every one of us to do what Jack might have done in this position, go out and sell. Bring back one order for Jack Richards. Sell it for him. See you back here at 4:30PM and let's see that tote board filled up today!!!" said Timmons. Jake's eyes met Penelope's in stunned disbelief. Walking back to their desks, Penelope asked Jake for a reality check, "A guy died this morning, right, what are they doing, turning it into a promotion? Jesus this is so wrong!" All Jake could do was stand in silent agreement with his fellow rep. It was at a time like this that Jake was thankful their friendship was repaired.

At Jack's funeral, people stood up and told the assembled multitude what they wanted to say about the recently departed man. The most gut wrenching testimony came from Jack's children who bade their fond goodbyes. After the services, Craig Storm took Jake aside and told him he was leaving and going back home to the Midwest. "I'll drive a truck if I have to" said Storm. Both Jake and he vowed to stay in touch with each other. They agreed that despite the hardships Fortress presented them, a good thing that came about was their friendship.

That night Jake had dinner at the Vitales. Primo II thanked Jake for his involvement with Jack, told him that Jake had always made his half brother's day and assured him the family held no ill will against him. Jake thanked him and the two men sat up until 1am talking about politics, sports and business, carefully avoiding any mention of Jack Richards. Bernice sat silent in a chair, legs folded, listening to the two men she most admired in the world talk until she drifted off to sleep. "Looks like we bored your dancer there Jake" said her father. "I guess so" said Jake silently taking his leave and driving home.

The day had left him thankful for his own existence fractured and scattered as it appeared to some. Not a man of deep prayer, Jake said out loud in a somber, emotional voice, "Thank you God for my life. Amen" and much to his surprise tears welled up in his eyes. He drove home and counted his blessings on the way.

The second installment of the 4 Emerald order was processed for another quarter of a million dollars. It was paid in cash. Fortress was doing a very good job for the consortium because orders for the disposal contraption were outpacing production. This should have been an uncomplicated happy relationship, but then again this was Fortress broadcasting.

Annoyed that the veteran reps had been out billing her new recruits, Queenie had a brainstorm that would send shock waves through the building. She announced a three day "lockdown" during where each rep would assess their accounts. After consulting with Queenie and Bill Timmons, the business would be either kept or reassigned. For many years Fortress had been cannibalizing its own rep's accounts. With 11 stations, a local business had 11 sales people to deal with. This caused annoyance, confusion but more obviously one local account couldn't feed 11 radio stations. Queenie had been told for many years that this was ineffective but stayed with the system because this is what corporate had always done. She resisted the change until the emergence of the 4 Emerald Group.

The three day lockdown resulted in the reassignment of accounts. One rep would represent one business for all stations. Queenie took all the 4 Emerald money and made Bertha Black the account manager. She also gave McDonalds, Chevrolet and

Wendy's to her uncouth protégé. The result was that Bertha Black, without breaking a sweat became the first million dollar rep in Fortress history. Other sales reps like Jake and Penelope had their account lists slashed to 3 paltry accounts. Even reps who got away relatively unscathed in this shocking reshuffling were appalled at the blatant power play. When Queenie gave Jake his list, with his income slashed, she told him as an experienced sales person he could make it up in good time. Bill Timmons hearing about Jake's sales list predicament put his arm around him and said, "We are going to rebuild your roster to its former glory, you can count on that" said the smiling aide of Queenie. "Suck my dick" was all Jake told him as he walked away.

Being the team player, Jake had to take Bertha Black to meet Frankie Panini and the 4 Emerald group. At the meeting, Bertha proposed a "Fire Drill" safety ad campaign in case there was an atomic attack some day. Both Primo and Frankie Panini looked incredulous when Bertha talked about building and safety evacuations along with "the bomb". Introducing new reps to mainstay clients did not just apply to Jake alone. Jim Poppinaro had to take Bertha to meet the fast food franchisees. People were polite at these meetings but calls started to come in to Fortress asking Queenie to give the business's back their old reps. One of Jake's health care accounts cancelled on the spot and Queenie accused Jake of asking the buyer to do so. Despite the protests, Queenie could not be budged. The sales staff by this time was in full revolt. When two of Queenie's minions went to lunch, Melanie Hazletten went into the conference room. She took the bible and lifeblood of any radio station, its dollar figures each account gave to the company. She then made copies and slipped the materials into large envelopes. In those reports was a line by line dollar amount of how much money an advertiser gave to Fortress. This was a highly guarded secret since it gave other stations the info on what the client they were pursuing was spending at another company. Portia Dion, upon finding these records had been taken from her safe by Foxx's careless flunkies quit on the spot. Hazleteen having carefully replaced the reports mailed the contents to Power 108 and the other to the competing radio group where Queenie Foxx had been previously employed.

Jake was summoned to a meeting with Primo and Frankie Panini. Gone was the glad handing from both men. Jake was told that 4 Emerald was unhappy with the buffoon who was representing them. They either wanted a change or their money back. Jake took out the terms and conditions of the contract from his briefcase and informed the men that since the advertising was paid in full, and there were signed contracts, Fortress could keep their money legally. There were two ways to get the money back, the first was to ask for a refund, if it was refused then the company was stuck. The only other way to get the money back was if Fortress broadcasting ceased to exist because of an unforeseen disaster. Jake suggested they call Queenie Foxx and try to get a refund of their monies. Frankie Panini placed the call and when he asked Queenie for the refund, the sales manager cackled into the phone and just hung up. Panini was stunned. No one hung up on Frankie Panini. Glaring at the men, he asked Primo to leave the premises and asked him to locate his son Danny. Without questioning him, Primo looked weakly at Jake and left. Panini and Jake sat in silence waiting for Danny.

A short time later, walking into the meeting, Danny nodded to Jake and sat down. "Daniel" said Panini, "we have a situation that requires your expertise and assistance. I need to solve a problem that has just exploded in my lap. Can I count on you?" Hearing the word exploded was all the encouragement Danny needed. Panini instructed Jake to bring him Bertha Black to a meeting to discuss her fire drill idea. Jake and Danny got separate instructions from Panini. The main objective was to get the investor's money back. Panini and Jake shared one common trait, they did not like major excitement in their respective lives. Both men picked easy over hard every time. Unfortunately, Queenie Foxx had decided to make this hard.

Panini met with Bertha and Jake promising the sales reps more money in the next quarter if he got what he wanted. Much to the delight of Bertha, Panini said he wanted commercials aired on fire and evacuation safety every day. But the caveat was that he wanted Fortress broadcasting to lead by example and conduct morning fire drills every day sharp at 9am. "Evacuate your building, broadcast it live, let the people see how committed you are against the atomic terror and fire!", said Panini. An excited Bertha said, "Oo oo, and maybe we can go out single file like we did in grade school." Panini recognizing his triumph milked it for all it was worth, "Yes my dear but you must make sure everyone is out of the building. No one is to remain, understood?" Bertha nodded in agreement. Panini reached behind his desk and pulled out a white and black fire captain's hat with a shiny beak. With great ceremony he handed it over to Bertha who placed it on her head. "I'll even have a man come down and serve you hot dogs when you have your first fire drill" added Panini. "Hotdogs!!!!!! Wow" exclaimed Bertha.

When Bertha and Jake returned from the meeting, they gave a report to Queenie Foxx. If any other sales person had come up with this idea, she would've thrown them out of her office. But because it was

Bertha, she loved it. Queenie even admonished Jake to "be more like Bertha in thinking outside the box".

The big day arrived for the first fire drill. Countless ads ran on the stations. The people at Power 108 thought it was a joke as did most of the other media people in the market. But all doubt was dispelled when Bertha appeared in her Fire Chief's hat. The day was bright, sunny and warm for an October Pennsylvania morning. Outside, in the perimeter of the parking lot, just like Panini promised was the hot dog man. Danny Vitale was dressed in a vendor's uniform drinking a coffee. Up since 3AM wiring the entire Fortress building he needed to be sharp to pull this off. Posing as a food vendor was going to be easy. However, Danny had to keep his mind on the fountain taps on his hot dog cart. The one marked cola dispensed soda, the one marked ginger ale was another matter. Danny watched as the smiling Bertha Black, decked out and resplendent in her fire hat led the Fortress staff outside the building.

Danny told Jake that if today was a "no go", he'd tip his hat to him. When the sales reps saw the free food, they stormed the hot dog cart. Danny was beside himself cooking hotdogs and dispensing drinks to the radio group staff. Unaccustomed to the converging mob of hungry radio folk clamoring for food, Danny tipped his hat to Jake. There was too much confusion to make this happen the right way. Much to his relief, Danny knew Panini was a patient man and the fireworks as well as the plan would be put off for one more day.

Amidst all this activity appeared a young woman who stopped by the station to pick up a prize pack of CDs she won from the urban format outlet. Jake immediately recognized her as the young waitress who had waited on Poppy and him a few months back. "Nancy, right?" said Jake. Thrilled to be remembered the young girl nodded vigorously in the affirmative. "I'm here to pick up some CDs I won but it looks kind of busy here. Shall I come back?" she asked. Jake looked at the young lady dressed in a short skirt, black thigh highs and matching vest and said, "No, no, the CDs are right at the front desk. I'll run up to the station and get them for you. I'll also leave you my business card in case you need anything else from us. Is that okay with you?" The bedazzled young girl answered, "It'll be more than okay!". As Jake trotted in to get the girl's prizes, a carnival atmosphere ensued outside the building. Running out of paper cups, Danny walked away from the hot dog cart for a split second to get more out of his van. Poppy moved behind the hot dog cart and said loudly, "I always wanted to be a soda jerk, step right up and have some suds. What's your pleasure ladies and gents, a little cola or a little ginger ale, hey, they got ginger ale here and didn't tell anyone". Picking up the fountain hose, Poppy tried to load his paper cup with ginger ale. Nothing was coming out. Danny turned and screamed,

"No!!!!!!!!!!!!!! Don't touch that!!!! No!!!!!" A few seconds later the Fortress Broadcasting building was leveled by a blast heard in three northeastern states.

After the explosion, Frankie Panini would get his refund, Danny escaped with the hot dog cart never being implicated in the blast, Queenie Foxx was fired, Fortress Broadcasting ceased to exist but "The Nifty 1050" lived on when it was bought by Primo Vitale as a birthday present for his daughter. Thomas Patrick's career as a life insurance agent also came to an abrupt end when Jake Yanick's beneficiaries got their very generous checks. The incident made CNN. Sitting in a bar in downtown Pittston watching TV were Power 108 deejays Billy Jefferson and Fontana. Hearing the tragic news accounts about their former co-worker Fontana and Jefferson raised their glasses to Jake Yanick and said in unison, "Anything for a chick!"

TWENTY THREE YEARS LATER

The hot political topic around the Governor's mansion was not the state budget or mandated funding but whether the chief executive of the state would be attending commencement exercises at Penn State. The press spokesmen were mum on what the Governor would do. Earlier in the storied political career the politician safely navigated around this personal issue.

In the meantime, Bernice and Crystal settled into their room at the Nittany Inn. "Ever regret you never got married?" asked Crystal. Bernice fixing her hair in the mirror said, "Sometimes I think I could have used help along the way but I think things turned out pretty well given the circumstances. God, I can't get used to having short hair". She reached for a necktie and began to informally arrange it against her blouse to match her suit. "Where did you get that?" asked her cousin. "Oh, just something I saved. As you know I save everything!" she said walking toward the door. Holding the door for her relative Crystal said, "I never saved nothing, except for that one time". Bernice looked at her and said fingering the navy blue cravat," "That's why I'm here today, all because you saved that one thing, one time in your life. And today, this is the end of that adventure".

The auditorium was packed and the two cousins were grateful for the VIP seating provided by the Governor. In amazement, Crystal looked at the stage. She was never this close to any major event. Waiting for the festivities to start, the front seats were also filled by Coral Rock, Portia Dion, and Crystal's husband. A few minutes before the ceremony, the Governor took the seat of power, acknowledging the crowd and her seatmates. As in any graduation, the names droned on until the commentator said, "And now the class valedictorian, Jake Yanick, Jr." The crowd stood and clapped in recognition. Adrienne stepped out of her role as governor and blew kisses at the young man. Crystal gave a rebel whoop and Bernice held back tears mouthing the words "thank you" to her boy. While the somber music played awaiting the address by the head of the class, Coral Rock used the opportunity to remark to the women what a wonderful man Jake Yanick, Jr. was going to be.

Booker, dressed in a suit for the first time since his wedding to Crystal, commented that the boy, while having a bright future was nonetheless gay. It was something all the people close to the engaging young man accepted. "But" Booker continued, "that means Jake Yanick Jr. would never fall in love with a girl or ever have the desire to feel a woman's touch or even have a curiosity about what made a woman tick". In unison, Adrienne, Bernice, Crystal, Coral and Portia exclaimed, "Good"!!!

EPILOGUE

Robin sat at the edge of the chair and looked at his partner. "Wow Jake, that is some story, these people seem so real to me. I wonder what they looked like" he said. Jake got up and went to his desk and pulled out a worn leather portfolio. Inside were 8 by 10 pictures he had kept since his mother presented them to him on Graduation Day. "Want to see the characters in this play?" he asked Robin. "Sure", answered Robin. The two looked at the photos. "This was before digital so be careful with them" warned Jake. "My God, your mother had so much hair" said Robin. "Yeah" said Jake, "she cut it right before I graduated from college. This was taken the night of the Super Bowl party with mom, this was Jake with Adrienne…. Robin stopped Jake, "Adrienne? She was a politician, right?" "Right, she was Governor of Pennsylvania for 7 years, then became Vice President for 8 years after that under two different Presidents, I think this was taken when they first started seeing each other" noted Jake. "Wow, this one here looks pretty familiar, is this an old lover of Jake's too?" Robin inquired. "No, but a very good friend. This is Jake with Coral Rock…." "Of course" Robin interrupted, "She was an anchor woman for CNN late in her life, right?" "Correct" added Jake, "she got killed when she helped wipe out a terrorist cell in Albania, whacked 45 of them until a sniper cut her down when she was walking to her plane". "Oh and here's your aunt Crystal, what the hell was she doing underneath that Christmas tree?" said Robin. "Not a clue" replied Jake. "So the common thread among all these women was Jake Yanick. Interesting, " observed Robin.

"How so?" asked Jake. "Well, all of these women had similarities, they all were beautiful, they all were smart and after Jake was gone they all achieved greatness in one way or another. The question is was it because of him or despite him?" said Robin. "I'd like to believe, shit I have to believe that it was because of him, I know my mom said she was a better person for having known him," said Jake.

Just then the phone rang. It was Jake's Attorney Ian Edwards calling about the estate. "Hey", Jake said into the phone, "I think I might want to keep that radio station, don't put that in any sales agreement. I'm going to hold on to it". Jake hung up and Robin smiled, "The Nifty 1050" lives on, huh?"

"As it should", replied Jake. The smile faded from Robin's face when he asked with concern, "Jake, what do we know about running an AM radio station?" Jake Yanick Junior stroked his chin thoughtfully and concluded, "The same thing they knew back then...absolutely nothing!!!"